"A writer of genius" – John Betjeman

"The missing writer of the Forties" – Clive James, *The New Review*, 1974

"Balchin writes about timeless things, the places in the heart" – Ruth Rendell, *Sunday Telegraph*, 1990

"...among the great masters of English fiction..." – Julian Fellowes, Foreword to *Separate Lies*, 2004

"Probably no other novelist of Mr. Balchin's value is so eminently and enjoyably *readable*" – Elizabeth Bowen, *Tatler*, 1949

"...his characters have only to open their mouths to reveal a personality" – L. P. Hartley, *Sketch*, 1945

"Mr. Balchin is a writer of real skill... He has established a firm monopoly on his peculiar but admirable territory" – Philip Toynbee, *New Statesman*, 1943

"To some good judges, Balchin, rather than C. P. Snow, was the novelist of men at work" –*The Guardian*, 1970

"I'd place him up there with Graham Greene..." – Philippa Gregory, BBC Radio 4, 2005

SEEN DIMLY BEFORE DAWN

NIGEL BALCHIN

First published by Collins, St James's Place, London, 1962

© Nigel Balchin 1962

Editorial content © Derek Collett 2021

This edition published in 2021 by Penhaligon Press.

ISBN 978 1 914076 19 0 (paperback)

ISBN 978 1 914076 20 6 (ebook)

Contents

Acknowledgements

I would like to express my gratitude to Nigel Balchin's son, Charles, for kindly granting me permission to republish this novel on behalf of the estate of his late father.

I am also exceedingly grateful to Andrew Chapman of Penhaligon Press, not only for scanning the book, typesetting it, preparing it for printing and designing the cover but also for his shrewd advice concerning the overall concept of the Nigel Balchin Collection.

Finally, heartfelt thanks to Paul Barnaby from the University of Edinburgh Library, who provided me with very helpful information about Sir Walter Scott's novel *The Talisman*.

Derek Collett

Inside Seen Dimly Before Dawn: The Story Behind the Story

It is respectfully suggested that, so as not to spoil your enjoyment of *Seen Dimly Before Dawn*, you should read it *before* reading this introduction.

Sources

In November 1959, Nigel Balchin's publisher, William Collins, wrote to his client, who was then living in a villa outside Florence. Collins concluded his letter by asking, somewhat plaintively, if Balchin was planning to write a new novel (his previous one, *The Fall of the Sparrow*, had been published more than four years earlier). In his reply to Collins, Balchin stated that there were two novels that he wanted to write. The book you are holding in your hands was one of them. Although Balchin began work on *Seen Dimly Before Dawn* less than eighteen months after receiving Collins' letter, the idea for the novel had germinated in his brain many years before.

Lengthy gestation periods were a feature of the books that Balchin wrote in the second half of his career as a novelist. Two other titles—*Sundry Creditors* (1953) and *In the Absence of Mrs Petersen* (1966)—also took a very long time to proceed from initial conception to final printed book. Speaking about this facet of his writing practice, Balchin once observed that the way in which the plot of a novel took shape in his mind resembled the way in which a chef prepares a stew:

> The basic ingredients of the story are shoved in a mental oven.
> I take the lid off now and then till I find it's cooked.

In the case of *Seen Dimly Before Dawn*, the ingredients of the story had simmered gently in Balchin's head for almost fifteen years before he put pen to paper because the two incidences of sheep worrying on the part of the Alsatian dog Remus, which supply the impetus for the novel's dramatic climax, are believed to have been inspired by real misdemeanours perpetrated by a dog owned by Balchin when he was living in Kent in the late 1940s.

Balchin also drew on memories of his time in The Garden of England to devise the principal setting for *Seen Dimly Before Dawn*. Two of the major characters, Patrick Parrish and his partner Leonie, inhabit a small fruit farm located 'about twenty minutes drive' from Canterbury. For about three years after World War Two, Balchin and his family lived in the village of Stelling Minnis, which is roughly the same distance away from Canterbury as the Parrishs' home. The house that the Balchins lived in was surrounded by about twenty-five acres of land, which the novelist converted into a fruit farm. Although Balchin's house was far grander than the 'pleasant little Queen Anne cottage' shared by Patrick and Leonie, it was situated, like Glebe Cottage, a few hundred yards from a main road in a quiet lane that did not lead anywhere else.

Several other elements of *Seen Dimly Before Dawn* have parallels with Balchin's own life. To begin with, the novel's juvenile hero, fifteen-year-old Walter Parrish, has much in common with Balchin at about the same age. With his love of cricket, poetry, classical music—especially the work of Mozart,

Bach and Handel—and long walks in the country, Walter is essentially a portrait of the author as a teenager, although it must be stressed that the young Balchin is not known to have had romantic designs on the partners of any of his three uncles.

Balchin's love of the English countryside, and particularly the pleasure that can be derived from walking in it, is a notable feature of *Seen Dimly Before Dawn*. In this respect, the book shares some common ground with *Simple Life*, the author's second novel, which was first published in 1935 and is scheduled for reissue in 2022 as part of the Nigel Balchin Collection. Both *Simple Life* and *Seen Dimly Before Dawn* are mostly set in the open air, in sparsely populated rural areas of southern England. Like Rufus Wade in *Simple Life*, who undertakes lengthy walks on the same Wiltshire chalk downs that Balchin had trodden as a boy, Walter in the later novel enjoys 'walking through the lovely Kentish country' that Balchin was surrounded by when he lived in Stelling Minnis in the 1940s.

On one level, *Seen Dimly Before Dawn* functions as a love letter to dogs, and especially Alsatians. But the book also contains an extended rumination on the nature of the very close relationship that can develop between a dog and its owner. During the course of Balchin's second marriage, he and his wife owned at least ten dogs of various breeds, several of them Alsatians. Being the sole female figure of any distinction in *Seen Dimly Before Dawn*, Leonie tends to dominate the scenes in which she appears but Remus, her hyper-intelligent yet 'extremely neurotic and over-sensitive' Alsatian, vies with his mistress and Walter as the novel's most engaging character.

Finally, evidence of the author's abiding passion for sport can be gleaned from the pages of *Seen Dimly Before Dawn*. Balchin was a very talented sportsman in his youth: in the mid-1920s, he captained his school at cricket and football and won colours for rugby and hockey; in 1930, shortly after going down from Cambridge, he played one game of Minor Counties cricket for Wiltshire. And yet this love of sport is only rarely reflected in his fiction. The cricket net session that Walter takes part in with Hawes, the bibulous curate who enlivens the middle chapters of *Seen Dimly Before Dawn*, is therefore almost a singular entity in the Balchin canon. Its only counterpart is to be found in 1955's *The Fall of the Sparrow*, where there are descriptions of Jason Pellew's prowess as a brilliant but eccentric exponent of the scrum-half's art on school rugby pitches.

Analysis

> Colonel Masters died last week. *The Times* obituary column records that he commanded a battalion of the North Gloucestershires in the First World War, and that he was something of a professional survivor, having served throughout the war on the Western Front and emerged unscratched. These things I knew. The obituary notice also says that he was awarded the D.S.O., and Bar and the M.C. This I did not know, but it does not surprise me. The Colonel certainly had plenty of courage of the medal-winning kind. It appears that he married, rather late in life, a woman considerably younger than himself, whom he survived. Again I am not surprised. He had a liking for young women, and surviving was his speciality.

The first paragraph of *Seen Dimly Before Dawn* is like a warm and welcoming handshake to the reader. But the novel's opening is cunning as well as welcoming as the narrator proceeds to tell us that the events he is about to describe happened more than thirty years earlier. It requires only the most elementary mathematics for the reader to deduce that the narrator must be aged at least forty-five, and therefore that the story that follows will have been written with the benefit of both experience and hindsight. The obituary notice deployed by Balchin is a clever technical device that permits him to write from the perspective of a gauche fifteen-year-old boy whilst also endowing his testament with the qualities of irony and world-weariness.

On the surface, *Seen Dimly Before Dawn* is a warm, nostalgic tale set in the Kent countryside in late summer about a schoolboy who falls in love, in a hopelessly romantic way, with his pretty young aunt. But, as so often with Balchin, there is more to the novel than at first meets the eye. It's also about a teenage boy, tiptoeing through that awkward netherworld between childhood and adulthood, who is made to learn the hard way that a child's view of an event rarely corresponds to that observed from an adult's perspective.

As the book unfolds, its contents become gradually darker. Some of the material is surprisingly graphic for Balchin and the reviewer who discussed *Seen Dimly Before Dawn* in the *Sunday Times* upon first publication, several years before the acknowledged beginning of the 'Swinging Sixties', was not too far wide of the mark when he labelled it 'disturbing'. Leaving aside the sexual content for a moment, this is, after all, a book in which a schoolboy attacks a clergyman, who is subsequently run over, and in which multiple deaths occur, both animal and human, some of them violent and others positively brutal.

Through the agency of Walter, Balchin places more emphasis on the physical than the romantic side of love than in any of his previous novels. Examples of this new candidness include Walter fondling Sally Greaves in the back of a car, the baseless, Potiphar's wife-like accusations of assault made against Walter by Veronica Simms and Walter's surreptitious observation of Leonie's naked form. And all of those events occur long before the climactic confrontation between Leonie and Colonel Masters that gives the book its title. Anthony Burgess wrote that the outcome of that encounter was obvious to anyone who had read the *Outline of Sexual Knowledge* (a book from the 1940s by B. N. Basu) but I haven't and, when I first read this novel, I found its denouement both completely unexpected and genuinely startling.

Seen Dimly Before Dawn is a book that triggers more questions in the mind of the reader than it attempts to answer. During my latest re-reading, just a few of those that occurred to me were:

- How did Leonie and Patrick first meet? Did she perhaps nurse him while he was recovering from having been gassed in World War One? She is just about old enough to have done so and displays nursing skills when she attends to Hawes at the roadside in Canterbury.
- Why does Leonie stay with Patrick if she is as bored and lonely as she makes out, and suffering from such obvious sexual frustration?
- What effect does Walter's eventful summer have on his later development, and especially his subsequent relationships with women?

Having read this gripping and mesmeric novel, perhaps you could try to think of some answers to those questions. But I suspect that you will be far too busy thinking of your own to bother with mine. *Seen Dimly Before Dawn* is that sort of book.

Press reaction

Understandably, after nearly seven years without a Balchin novel to review, it was a case of absence making the heart grow fonder when British book reviewers were at last given the opportunity to get their teeth into a new piece of Balchin fiction. But judged by any standards, the press reaction to the release of *Seen Dimly Before Dawn* was extremely positive.

The Times said that Balchin's novel was 'thoroughly readable and consistently entertaining', *The New Statesman* observed that 'the story pounds along eagerly with all senses alert' and *The Sunday Telegraph*'s reviewer put forward the astute opinion that Walter's 'callow, earnest, egocentric tone is brilliantly caught and sustained for the whole length of the narrative'. *The Guardian* said that Balchin had deployed 'all his usual lucidity, vigour, and devilish readability' and *The Sunday Times* remarked that, in his 'excellent new novel', Balchin had illuminated 'one of the oldest, most secretive areas of private experience'.

The sole negative review came from Anthony Burgess in *The Times Literary Supplement*. Although he had found *Seen Dimly Before Dawn* to be 'most readable', Burgess complained that Balchin's purpose appeared to be 'to titillate, in a popular novelist's manner, with an isolated hunk of over-simplified experience'.

UK publication history

First published in hardback 18 January 1962 by Collins.

First paperback edition published by Fontana in 1964.

Penhaligon Press paperback and ebook editions published in 2021.

Interesting fact

Seen Dimly Before Dawn topped the *Evening Standard* bestsellers' chart for two weeks at the beginning of 1962.

SEEN DIMLY BEFORE DAWN

Where are you now, you who ran over
the moonlit furrow and ruled it?
The thick light throbbing, and the
unheard trumpets calling
To what strange battle?

Low muttered words, and things seen
dimly before dawn
Informed you then, before the ice-glare of day
Came with its crude clarity.[1]

One

Colonel Masters died last week. *The Times* obituary column records that he commanded a battalion of the North Gloucestershires in the First World War, and that he was something of a professional survivor, having served throughout the war on the Western Front and emerged unscratched. These things I knew. The obituary notice also says that he was awarded the D.S.O.,[1] and Bar[2] and the M.C.[3] This I did not know, but it does not surprise me. The Colonel certainly had plenty of courage of the medal-winning kind. It appears that he married, rather late in life, a woman considerably younger than himself, whom he survived. Again I am not surprised. He had a liking for young women, and surviving was his speciality.

The only thing that *does* surprise me about this account of him, is that the Colonel's age is given as only seventy-five. After all, it is over thirty years ago that I took part in the plan to murder Masters, and he was a retired Colonel then. Everyone knows that retired Colonels are old. If I had ever thought about him at all in recent years, I think I must have assumed that he was dead long ago; dead, with Lord Birkenhead[4] and George Robey;[5] with 'Yes We Have No Bananas'[6] and the General Strike;[7] with Lawrence[8] and W. B. Yeats;[9] dead, in fact, with all that made up, for me, the later nineteen twenties;[10] and, above all, dead with my own childhood.

Perhaps the reason for my feelings about the Colonel's age lies in that last phrase. There are things in everybody's life which, because they were ludicrous, or shameful, or childish, he prefers to date as far back as possible.

Thus, I have been accustomed to think of the whole business of the Dog's Death as having taken place a vast time ago, when I was only a child, who could not be expected to know better; an innocent, deserving of everybody's sympathy—and particularly my own. I have been encouraged in this by the disappearance, long ago, of everyone else concerned in the story. My father and mother died within a year of one another, twelve years ago. Leonie, whom, barring accidents, I should have expected to live to be at least a hundred, drove her car at top speed into the back of a parked lorry on a dark night in 1935. My Uncle Patrick, who in 1928 seemed likely to die at any time, went on seemingly likely to die at any time for a long while; but even so he died in 1940. The dog Remus, of course, was dead before the last act of the ludicrous drama was even played.

So, for many years, I have been thinking of myself as the last survivor of the affair; yet now comes the confounded Colonel, popping up in the obituary column of *The Times*, only dead last week, and only seventy-five at that.

There is something curiously disconcerting about the thought that he has been about all these years; for it brings home to me that when the Dog Died, I was not really a child at all, but a hobbledehoy of fifteen, in the midst of all the messy complications of adolescence; that the messiness included being a monumental prig; and that, worst of all, I stood five feet ten, weighed eleven stone, was accounted old for my age, and was generally assumed, by new acquaintances, to be about seventeen or eighteen. Indisputably I should have known better. All that can be said in my defence is that I was an only child, and at a famous public school.

The motto of my very ancient and extremely expensive school was "Labor et Puritas";[11] and to these concepts it was firmly dedicated. "The proper translation of our motto," my friend Burke once remarked, "is Matriculation without Masturbation. Add something about games, and you have the place in a nutshell."

Burke often said things like that. He was seventeen, and the heir to a baronetcy and a large fortune. His father was a well-known racehorse owner and social figure. Burke himself was a sophisticated young man who looked on school life with a quiet, detached amusement. He was no trouble to the authorities. He conformed to the school rules with the same air of resigned, gentle contempt that a man may show towards inconvenient car-parking regulations.

I think Burke made me even more uneasy than he did most other people. As I have said, I was unusually well-developed for my age physically, and, in some respects, mentally. I had passed my School Certificate[12] Examination at fourteen, and at fifteen was in the sixth form. I was a good cricketer and already playing for my House. It seemed certain, if only by the passage of time, that I should end up in the Eleven, and probably a school prefect. At both work and games I was conscious that I could compete with anybody—even with Burke. But in every other respect he always made me feel desperately young and crude. I had none of his detachment or feeling of gentle patronage about school life. To me it was all intensely real and important; and, in the matter of Clynes, even passionate.

As the result of much chapel-going, good health, and a mildly romantic nature, I was at that time deeply religious, and deeply in love with Clynes. The existence of people like Clynes has always been one of the problems of systems of monastic purity.

Clynes was small but beautifully proportioned. He had curly dark hair, large dark brown eyes with long lashes, and an almost transparently fair skin, which, in summer, turned a beautiful even brown, showing off to great advantage very white, even teeth. His hair was always well brushed, his tie was always straight, his collar was always clean, and so were his nails.

In fact, there was nothing really effeminate about Clynes, either physically or mentally. He did not look like a girl—he merely looked like a miniature edition of a romantic film hero; and if he was a great deal more fastidious about his appearance than most boys of his age, he was also a fair footballer, an exceptionally good boxer, and in general, a tough and cheerful specimen. Later, during the war, he became a bomber pilot, and was shot down over the Ruhr, leaving a wife and two children.

Nevertheless, he was very beautiful, and I loved him with a love which was at once passionate and of snowy purity. I worried about Clynes all the time—about his progress and success in work and games, about his health, and about his happiness. When he boxed, I suffered all the agonies of a professional fighter's wife sitting at the ringside and watching her husband fight for a championship. Once, when he got into some obscure trouble and was given a sound and well-deserved caning by the head of the House, I was almost sick with horror at this terrible thing, and my utter powerlessness to prevent it.

I was, as I have already said, deeply religious at the time, and in one summer term I remembered that I prayed every night that Clynes should get through School Certificate. But the ways of God are inscrutable, and my prayers were not answered. To be frank, Clynes, like many other beautiful people, was neither very bright nor a very enthusiastic worker.

Like the school motto, however, I was interested in other things besides matriculation. I was afraid that Clynes might fall into bad hands and into bad ways—that some bigger boy, of less sterling principle than myself, might take him up. I used to talk to him occasionally about such things in a friendly, manly way which would have been very suitable in a fifty-year-old Chaplain to the Forces.

Not very surprisingly, my passion for Clynes was not returned. I think he thought that I was slightly mad, and a vast bore. But though he was only a couple of months younger than I, he was very much smaller, and much lower in the school in every respect. My attentions were flattering, and could sometimes be useful; so he tolerated me, and listened solemnly to my affectionate lectures, though I sometimes had a nasty feeling, when I saw him ragging about with other people, that Clynes was not altogether serious. I am deeply sorry that he was killed in the war, but at least his death removed one frightful possibility —that I might have met him again later in life, and that he might have remembered some of those lectures.

The affaire Clynes went on at its fullest intensity for over a year, and reached its climax at the end of the Spring Term with the performance of the school play. The play was *Twelfth Night*, and Clynes, looking as he did, and with a still unbroken voice, was natural casting for one of the female parts. Accordingly, he played Maria. I was not in the play, but I had some job as a sort of assistant stage manager, in charge of dressing and making-up some of the performers. I cannot remember whether I managed to arrange it, or whether it happened accidentally, but one of the characters for whom I was responsible was Maria, and this meant dressing and making-up Clynes.

I should perhaps say that though my feelings for Clynes were extremely—indeed almost painfully—pure, there were times when I fell disgracefully below my own standards. I never touched him except by accident, but if such an accident occurred, it was rather as though I had touched a high tension cable, and it was liable to produce some, at least, of the same results. In dreams, too, and in half-waking state at night or in the morning, ideas would come into my mind which needed to be trampled firmly underfoot. Trampling such feelings underfoot was, so to speak, part of the game. But here, in the dressing-rooms, was a situation where I could not only touch Clynes, but was obliged to do so. I had to put Maria's voluminous dress over his head and hook it up for him at the back. My hands shook so much in doing so that it took me about a quarter of an hour, by which time he was thoroughly out of patience with me.

The worst moment, however, was when he announced that he thought his pants were going to fall off. He was small for his age, and his mother had sensibly bought underpants which were, for the moment, rather too big for him. This did not matter as long as he had his shirt tucked inside them, but in Maria's costume, where there was nothing to tuck inside, it was obvious that the pants would fall down about his ankles as soon as he moved. I had to find a safety-pin, and, while he stood holding up the dress, to pin the pants more tightly round his waist. I do not think he noticed my agitation. He was not the sort of person who noticed things. He just stood there, holding up the dress, and occasionally shifting from one foot to the other, as I fumbled with the wretched pin.

Yet, though on that night of the school play I felt more excitement than I had ever felt before in my life, my feelings about Clynes were never after quite the same. Dressed as Maria, in a wig and a gown with a crossed laced front, the mere sight of him made my throat dry and my hands shaky. But to see him again afterwards as his own neat, pocket-sized-male-film-star self was somehow an anticlimax and a disappointment. In short, I found Clynes as Maria a great deal more exciting than Clynes as Clynes. Certainly, from that night onward, there was never any need to tread anything underfoot in connection with him; and this made the whole thing strangely dull and uninteresting.

I noticed this particularly during the holidays that followed almost immediately after the play. For the last year, I had regarded the holidays primarily as periods when I was separated from Clynes. My home was on the Wiltshire Downs, and I was in the habit of taking long walks over the Downs, particularly at night, declaiming verse to myself, and thinking about God, and how much I loved Clynes. But in these summer holidays, whilst I continued to take the walks, to declaim the verse and to think about God, the part of the ritual which involved thinking about Clynes was disappointing.

Having attended most of the rehearsals of *Twelfth Night*, I knew the play by heart, and had decided that Viola's unrevealed love for the Duke was really very similar to my own for Clynes. I continued to try to think so during these holidays. During one of my walks I was declaiming Viola's speech which contains the line "Halloo your name to the reverberate hills," and it occurred to me that the utterly deserted, moonlit Downs were an excellent place for such passionate hallooings. But Clynes's Christian name was Cyril, and Cyril is not an easy name to halloo satisfactorily. I made a couple of feeble attempts, but all that came out was a tentative bleat; and since I never called Clynes Cyril, or thought of him by that name, the whole business seemed rather silly and pointless, and completely lacking in excitement. It was a relief to give up thinking about Clynes, and to start declaiming "Go, lovely rose".[13] I did not realise it at the time, but at this point I fear that monastic purity had done its best for me and failed. It left something of a gap in my life. I walked home slowly that night, feeling rather depressed and empty.

Two

Luckily, this awkward gap in my life, which left me with nothing to feel convincingly and interestingly guilty about, was soon filled. My father was not a sociable man, and we had few friends. Since he did not care for holidays himself, he never felt it necessary to arrange any particular entertainment for me when I was home from school. I think his view was that as we lived in beautiful country and there were plenty of books about the place, I ought to be perfectly happy merely to be at home. Hence, presumably, the poetry and the ritual long walks.

For once, however, during these holidays we went to a party. I cannot remember much about it now, but I know that my father, who could never put up with any social event for more than a couple of hours, wanted to go home at about ten o'clock, when we were just about to play Charades. I was enjoying myself, but I should have gone home meekly enough if our host had not protested that I was necessary for the Charades. In the end, my father and mother went home, leaving me to be driven back later by our hosts.

The party consisted of a muddle of ages, varying from somebody's ten-year-old to somebody's grandfather. It was not a very big affair, and there were only about half a dozen people of anywhere near my own age. There were two Wykehamists[1] of fifteen and seventeen who had brought a sister and a cousin; there was the host's son, who was in his second year at Cambridge and who had brought his girl-of-the-moment; and there was Miss Sally Greaves, who did not seem to have been brought by anybody. She was a pretty girl of about eighteen, with pleasant dark red hair, a turned-up nose, and a rather big mouth.

Rather surprisingly, since I was an only child and very rarely met or had anything whatever to do with girls, I never found them alarming or embarrassing. I was merely quite uninterested in them, as people who, up to this point, had been nothing to do with my life. I quite liked Sally Greaves, who was a cheerful little soul with no affectations. Moreover, I liked looking at her because of the colour of her hair. Had I been in the habit of deciding whether girls were attractive or not, I should certainly have thought that she was.

At about half past eleven the party came to an end, and the question arose of how to get us all home. The son of the house volunteered to drive one party, which consisted of his girl-of-the-moment, the elder of the Wykehamists and his cousin, and Sally and me. The car was small, and I wondered for a moment how we were all going to get in. But the Cambridge man brushed this aside. He claimed that he had frequently carried ten people. All that was needed was what he called "a touch of the party spirit". He then placed his girl in the front seat beside him, put me and the Wykehamist in the back, and told the girls to sit on our knees.

It was an uncommonly tight fit, and if he ever had carried ten in the car, I think the other four must have sat on the bonnet. Moreover, the roof of the car was low, and prim perchings would have been quite impossible. The only way in which the girls could sit in any comfort was across our knees, leaning back against us, with everybody's arms around everybody else. I realised what the Cambridge man had meant by a "touch of the party spirit".

It was a strange drive. The accelerator of the car was placed, as accelerators quite often were in those days, between the clutch and the brake. The undergraduate was teaching his girl to drive. By getting as close to him as possible, and interlacing her feet with his, she could get her right foot on the central accelerator and her left on the clutch, with the gear lever in front of her. Meanwhile, he steered the car and controlled the brake. Progress was rather erratic since, whenever the girl's position became intolerably cramped, she heaved herself into a more comfortable one by pushing against the accelerator, the clutch, or both. Luckily, the roads over the Downs were quite empty.

I hardly noticed any of this, however, being preoccupied with the strange sensation of having Sally on my lap. I should perhaps say that though I had no experience of girls whatever, I had quite a fair theoretical knowledge of the whole business. After all, I was reasonably intelligent, and I had the run of a good library. Though vague about a detail here and there, I understood the anatomical and physiological mechanisms of sex quite well. I also knew a great deal about love as it appears in lyric poetry. It seemed, after all, to be very like my feelings about Clynes. But one side of my information was pure Anatomy and Physiology and the other was pure English Literature; and though I knew that they were connected, and that the physiology tended to produce the literature or vice versa, I had no idea quite why or how. I had accepted without much difficulty the text book accounts of the queer, rather clumsy, rather ugly-sounding process which leads on to pregnancy and childbirth; and Heaven knows I had accepted without any difficulty at all Sidney's feelings about Stella.[2] But between these extremes there had been a blank; and now, for the first time something was happening to me which fell in that uncharted country.

I had known, for example, that it was a standard part of love-making for the girl to sit on the man's knees. But it had never occurred to me that in doing so she would have any weight, and that that soft weight would be pressing down upon the man's thighs. I seem to have thought that when women sat on you they floated like balloons.

I was now discovering that when Sally Greaves sat on your lap, there was no floating about it. She was not a big girl or a fat one, but she was well and sensibly made to a proper female design, with nothing of the weightless nymph about her. In fact, after we had been travelling for a few minutes, I had to give a heave and a wriggle to shift her weight, because my left leg was going to sleep.

But the thing which most startled me was not that she was a ponderable object, but that she was warm. The soft weight pressing down on my thighs might be interesting, and in a stupid way, surprising. But the fact that it had a warmth of its own, which communicated itself to me, was exciting beyond measure. There was an intimacy about that warmth—almost a secrecy—which seemed to suggest that in some inexplicable way, this girl whom I had met for the first time that evening was sharing something with me that I had never before shared with any human being.

We must have travelled the first two miles of our six-mile journey before anybody in the back of the car spoke, though in front the driver was rattling out instructions, and his girl was giggling and occasionally letting out little squeaks.

Sally said, "Am I squashing you? I'm awfully heavy." I replied untruthfully that she was very light and wasn't squashing me at all, at the same time giving another slight heave and wriggle, because my right leg was now going to sleep.

There was silence for a few moments, and then the Wykehamist's cousin gave a slight moan, and pulling his face down to her own, began to kiss him vigorously. I was rather startled. She was, after all, his cousin. But he seemed neither worried nor surprised. He merely shifted his position so as to make her easier to get at, put his mouth to hers and kept it there.

Not wishing to be embarrassing, I stopped looking at them and turned back to Sally. Her face, with the turned-up nose and the big mouth, was within about six inches of mine, and she was looking at me with a pleasant, friendly grin. I knew that men kissed girls in the back of motor-cars, so I kissed her without hesitation and with pleasure, but in exactly the way that I should have kissed my mother, briefly and gently.

She held up her face to be kissed quite willingly, and indeed went on holding it up. I kissed her again. A glance at the Wykehamist and his cousin, however, showed me that they were still in exactly the same position as before, with their mouths still tightly pressed together. The girl was breathing heavily, and occasionally giving odd little shivers. As I watched the Wykehamist shifted his arm round her waist, and put his hand firmly on her breast.

That again was all right, and one of the things which I knew men did with girls. Accordingly, I put my mouth to Sally's and pressed my lips so hard against hers that my lips were almost bruised against my own teeth. At the same time, I tentatively shifted my hand, in imitation of the Wykehamist, to her breast. I thought she might object, as this seemed to me a much more intimate gesture than mere kissing; which, after all, was just a subject for jokes. She did indeed put her hand on mine as though to move it, but then apparently changing her mind, gave a little sigh, closed her eyes and pressed her hand hard on the top of mine so that I was holding the firm seventeen-year-old breast tightly. Again, I could feel that startling, unexpected, living warmth.

We remained in this position for some moments, in complete silence. Then the pressure of my lips became positively painful, and I pulled away and looked at Sally. Her eyes were closed, and she was no longer smiling. In the dim light of the back of the car her face looked serious, and, for the first time distinctly beautiful. The Wykehamist and his girl had managed to pull themselves away from us slightly, and they were now even more closely entwined. A good deal of heavy breathing was going on, and there was an occasional faint whisper.

I glanced down and caught the gleam of Sally's silk-clad knees. This was during one of the periods when skirts were very short. In the position in which she was sitting, Sally's skirt ended about two inches above her knees. They were very charming knees, perfectly rounded and plump in their silk stockings, and I was suddenly seized with an irresistible impulse to stroke them.

I gently stroked her knee-cap and a few inches down her shin. The feel of the warm silk was delightful. Sally opened her eyes and looked at me, I thought, a little questioningly. I paused in my exquisite stroking, and for a moment we looked at one another in silence. Then the mischievous grin flickered over her face and she closed her eyes again. As she did so the driver, without turning his head said, "Break away now, chaps, and comb your hair, girls. We're nearly there."

I was the first member of the party to be dropped, and I insisted that it was not worthwhile to drive down the lane in which our house stood. I wanted that two hundred yards' walk in which to think things over. It was a brilliant starlit night, but there was no moon, and the lane, with its overhanging trees, was very dark. I walked home in a state which was a curious mixture of exultation and puzzlement; exultation, at the recollection of the warm, intimate, secret pressure on my thighs; puzzlement, at my own behaviour. Of course one kissed girls, and kissing Sally had been pleasant enough, without being particularly exciting. Of course, when I came to think of it (though decidedly less of course) one put one's hand on their breasts; and the firm softness of Sally's breast beneath my hand, which fitted it exactly, had been delightful.

But the knee business left me utterly baffled. Nothing that I had ever heard of love-making included a wild desire to stroke the girl's knees. There was no mention of it that I could recall in

Shakespeare or Sidney, or any of the poets I knew, who, in most respects, seemed fairly outspoken. There were very few novels in my father's library, and I hardly ever went to the cinema. But in my limited knowledge of both novels and films, there was again nothing so very particular about knees. And yet to me stroking Sally's knees had been by far the most exciting part of the whole business; and, oddly enough, had given me most of that feeling of guilty delight which was my touchstone of real sensual pleasure. I remembered that Sally had opened her eyes when I first put my hand on her knee and looked at me in a rather curious, doubtful, questioning way. She had, of course, been surprised by such very odd behaviour. I decided ruefully that she probably thought that I was slightly mad, and wouldn't want to have any more to do with me.

Clearly, the only thing to do was to see Sally, apologise, and explain that it was just a way in which I was abnormal. After all, if she had been really offended or disgusted, she would presumably have said so.

In fact, I did not see Sally again for some time. I did not know her or her family, and I could hardly walk up to their house and demand to see their daughter because I wanted to apologise for stroking her knees. I thought of writing to her, but here again the letter was difficult to compose, and before I could get it properly worked out in my mind, it had been decided that I should go to stay with my uncle and aunt.

I do not remember that my home life at that time ever caused me positive unhappiness. It was the only home life I knew, and I was used to it. But looking back, I can see that it was at once rather peculiar and uncommonly dull. My father and mother had been married for twenty years, and they went on being married afterwards, doggedly, loyally, faithfully, and unhappily, for another twenty. In their own fashion they probably loved one another, but they also irritated one another in every possible way. The result was that they quarrelled regularly, monotonously and bitterly.

A part of the trouble, I imagine, was our way of life. My father and mother each had a small income, and in addition, my father made a small amount of money from reviewing and writing articles for literary magazines. His speciality was the lesser literary figures of the nineteenth century. If anyone wrote a book about Alfred Austin[3] or Lever,[4] it would be sent to my father for review, and if it contained the smallest error, my father would be on to it like a terrier on to a rat. He was not a kindly or magnanimous reviewer, and most of his notices seemed mainly concerned to prove that he knew more about the subject than the man who had written the book. "Mr. Parkinson," he would write, "informs us that Teale and Widgeon[5] left Norwich in the winter of 1863. It is surely common knowledge that the departure from Norwich took place just before Christmas 1862." His own articles were usually about neglected Victorian writers; and, for me at least, he usually managed to make the neglect very understandable.

In return for these efforts, my father probably earnt about three hundred pounds a year,[6] which, together with my mother's small income and his own, made it just possible for them to live and send me to school. But it left no margin for extravagances like holidays, expeditions to London, or a clothes allowance for my mother. We lived in the depth of the country in a small, rather ugly house which had been built at the turn of the century, and which my mother ran with the help of a charwoman.

All this suited my father quite well. He disliked holidays, and he disliked being with people. If he was not happy, he was, I think, no unhappier than he would have been elsewhere. But my mother, if she had been given the chance, might easily have been a rather sociable person, who liked female chatter, and new hats, and mild scandal. There was a deep black lake of bitterness underneath the thin cat-ice[7] of her everyday behaviour; and about once a week that ice broke.

My father and mother never quarrelled in front of me. When a row was approaching, an oppressive, sultry, thunderstorm atmosphere would gradually build up all day. About nine o'clock my mother, with a rather forced smile, would suggest that it was time I went to bed. Sometimes I would even suggest it myself when the tension in the air became too unbearable. I would then go to bed, and within five or ten minutes the storm would break.

The trouble, however, was that my parents never seemed to understand the acoustics of the house. The countryside was very quiet, and from my bedroom the sound of the row was perfectly audible, though one could only occasionally hear the actual words that were being used. This was oddly nerve-racking, and though I was not really interested in what they were saying, having heard it all many times before, I used to go out of my bedroom and sit at the top of the stairs (from which every word they said could be clearly heard), waiting for it all to be over, so that I could go back to my room, and read or go to sleep in peace.

My father was not a particularly quarrelsome man. There were few things that he felt strongly enough to wish to quarrel about them. But my mother was too skilful for him. When she was in that mood it was absolutely essential to her to make him lose his temper, and she knew from long experience and much practice exactly how to do it, jabbing the lance of her resentment into him like an expert picador.[8] Often, he held out for a long time. But there was always a time when he could stand it no longer and began to hit back—to talk loudly and angrily, and to answer accusation with accusation. Choosing her moment exquisitely, my mother would then change her tactics. With calm contempt, she would remind him that he was making an exhibition of himself, that he had no idea how ridiculous he looked with his eyes glaring like that, and that if he wanted to shout abuses at his wife he might at least remember that his only child was upstairs and would certainly hear him.

In the meantime, his only child, sitting on the stairs, would heave a sigh of relief, for this meant that the row was drawing to its end. Soon now my father would slam off to sleep on a divan in his study. The noise of the battle would die away, and I should be able to stand at my bedroom window and look out into the shadowed darkness, and feel that tremendous silence in which I could hear the beating of my own heart.

Two days after my curious experience with Sally a quarrel took place between my parents which did not follow the standard pattern. There had been the usual preliminaries, and from upstairs I heard my mother's voice giving out the first bars of the overture. But I wanted to think, and it was a very beautiful moonlit night, which always made me restless. I therefore deserted my usual post on the stairs and did the only other possible thing, which was to go for a walk. I knew that it would be at least half an hour before there was any danger that my mother and father would come upstairs.

When I returned, however, my father was not shouting, which he would usually have been doing by this time. In fact, they were both talking quietly. I sat down in my usual place at the top of the stairs to try to pick up the threads of what was going on.

My father said, "And what do you suggest should happen to your son during all this? Or have you just forgotten all about him?"

This told me a good deal. Whenever in these conversations I was referred to as "your son," or "my child," or as anything but just "Walter," it meant that one side or the other was using me as a weapon.

My mother said, "He can stay here with you. Perhaps you might even get to know one another."

"Don't be absurd," said my father irritably, "who's going to look after him?"

"Nobody looks after him much anyhow," said my mother bitterly.

My father said, "Listen, Elsie—if you are really so anxious to go off on this expedition and leave me to the tender mercies of a charwoman, I can't stop you, and don't even want to try. But I should have thought even you might have had some consideration for Walter. After all…"

"This sudden anxiety about Walter is amazing," said my mother sarcastically. "I wasn't at all sure that you even knew he was here. All right—if you don't want to be bothered with him while I'm away, send him to stay with Patrick."

There was a moment's pause. My father said, "You know perfectly well that he can't go to Patrick."

"Why not?"

"You know that too."

"Because of Leonie? Don't be ridiculous. This is the twentieth century."

"You know that I have always said…"

"All right, all right," said my mother impatiently. "You don't want him to stay here and you don't want him to go to Patrick. Now you suggest something you *do* want."

"The usual thing," said my father with weary bitterness. "You decide without a previous word to me that you are going to take a holiday, you make no sensible plans about it, and then you ask me what I am going to do about it."

"Well, what *are* you?" said my mother gently.

"What I am going to do," said my father, his voice rising, "is to *think*. It's a thing that *you* should try doing at times."

I heard the door open and close unnecessarily firmly behind him as he went out, and I went quietly back to my room.

～

My father's thinking did not seem to have been very productive, for the following morning I was told at breakfast that I was to go and stay with my Uncle Patrick and my Aunt Leonie. In accordance with my parents' principles, I was told it with a fine show of unanimity. It had been decided that my mother was in need of a rest and a change (which, Heaven knows, was probably true enough). She was therefore going to stay for a month with a friend in London. My father, who hated leaving home, would stay and be looked after by Mrs. Pratt from the village. I should go to my uncle and aunt.

My mother said, "It might be rather fun, Walter. They'll probably be picking some of the fruit by now."

I was rather pleased by this arrangement. There were five weeks more of the holidays, and it was uncommonly dull at home. I had only met my Uncle Patrick, my father's elder brother, on a couple of occasions, and remembered him as a silent man with a curious crooked smile, rather like my father in appearance, but with a gentler and more friendly manner. I knew that he had been badly gassed during the war, and had never altogether recovered, and that he had a small fruit farm somewhere in Kent. My Aunt Leonie I had never met, and knew nothing whatever about. I asked what she was like. There was a moment's pause during which my father vigorously scraped some butter on to a piece of toast.

"Oh, I think you'll like her," said my mother cheerfully. "She can be great fun. She's a good deal younger than Uncle Patrick, you know."

"Leonie's a clever girl in some ways," said my father. He crunched his toast for a few moments, as though trying to think of something more to say about my aunt. "Very fond of dogs," he added at last.

Three

My uncle's farm was a few miles from Canterbury, and one evening in August I arrived at Canterbury station, where my aunt and uncle were to meet me. It had been thought better that I should not go via London—presumably in case I should get lost between Paddington and Charing Cross.[1] As a result, the cross-country journey of not more than a hundred and twenty miles had taken five hours and a half, and involved three changes. I had in my pocket my return ticket, and thirty-two-and-sixpence[2] as pocket money. Considering how poor he was, my father was not at all mean about giving me money; but he always gave me some rather curious amount, which was the exact answer to a sum that he had worked out concerning what I should need.

I must have been an odd sight as I alighted at Canterbury. I had grown a great deal in the last six months and my suit, though not very old, had been intended for somebody at least two inches shorter in the legs and an inch shorter in the arms. I was wearing my school cap, simply because it was the only head covering that I had, and it had never occurred to either my mother or myself that I might have gone out bareheaded. Indeed, I even wore my cap on my country rambles in the dark.

There was nobody waiting for the train who was in the least like my Uncle Patrick, or who could very well have been my Aunt Leonie. I thought perhaps they had waited at the barrier, and gave up my ticket and went out. But though there were several cars outside, there was still no sign of my uncle or aunt.

This was disconcerting. I did not know their telephone number or even with any certainty the address of the farm or how far away it was. I thought of taking a taxi, but by that time there were no taxis. I was wondering what on earth to do, when an old bull-nosed Morris[3] four-seater came up the station approach at high speed and pulled up beside me with a squeal of brakes. A voice called, "Are you Walter? I'm Leonie," and a young woman in old blue trousers and a short-sleeved blouse scrambled out.

I was rather startled, as in those days a woman in trousers was a far less common sight than it is now. Moreover, though I had been told that my aunt was considerably younger than my Uncle Patrick, I had not expected her to be as young as this. Leonie looked about twenty-five; (as I was to learn later, she was, in fact, just about to be twenty-seven). She was a strikingly beautiful young woman in a slightly odd way. Her hair was cut in a short bob, very thick, and of a strange old-gold colour. She had black eyebrows and lashes, and large greenish-grey eyes that slanted up slightly at the outer corners. Her nose was small, and her mouth large and full-lipped, and when she smiled she showed very beautiful teeth.

We shook hands and my aunt said, "I'm sorry. Have you been waiting long? It's this damn business of there being two stations.[4] Did you know that there were two stations here? Of course I went to the wrong one. Heavens, you're tall! I thought you were only fifteen. You look about twenty—at least you would if you weren't wearing that ridiculous cap. Take it off and chuck it in the back. Patrick couldn't come. It's one of his bad days. Just this case? It can go in the back. No, you'd better let me do it because of Remus. All right, Remus. *Friend*, Remus. This is

Remus. Do you like dogs? Don't touch him but just put out your hand so that he can smell it. That's right. I can't stand these damn fools who will rush up to a dog and start patting it on the head without even introducing themselves. After all, how would *you* feel if some total stranger came and started patting *you* on the head?"

My aunt had said all this at top speed, without waiting for an answer to any of her questions. She spoke rapidly, jerkily, and rather breathlessly, and she had a habit of gazing at you very directly and seriously with the slanting green-grey eyes whilst she was speaking, and then breaking into a broad smile at the end of a sentence. She paused now as though, for once, she was waiting for a reply from me. I did not know what I should feel if a total stranger patted me on the head, so I just looked at the dog Remus and said that he was a beauty.

He was indeed a beauty. He was a big black-and-tan Alsatian, with a noble head which he cocked slightly on one side as he considered me. Very cautiously, he sniffed at my outstretched hand, and then put his head on one side again, and thought it over. Then he put his nose forward again and pushed my fingers very gently with it.

"Fine," said my aunt, with a nod of satisfaction. "That tells me a lot about you—most of it good. Remus isn't a dog really. He's a very intelligent person who just happens to look like a dog. All you have to remember is that being so intelligent, he's rather highly strung; that, and that he's very fond of me and very jealous. But I think he likes you. Come on—get in." It was about twenty minutes' drive to the farm—at least, with my Aunt Leonie driving. As soon as we were clear of Canterbury, she simply put the accelerator of the Morris flat on the floor of the car and kept it there, making no concession for anything short of a right-angled corner. In the meantime, she went on talking in the same rapid, rather breathless way, frequently asking me questions, and then going on before I had time to answer them. I noticed that she did not ask after my father and mother, and remembered that from what I had overheard they did not approve of her.

Personally I liked her, but I could see why they would not. My mother would not have approved of the trousers or of the "damns" and "bloodies." My father could never have liked anybody who talked as much as that. People who talked a lot always gave him a headache.

I managed at one point to get in a question about what was the matter with my Uncle Patrick. Aunt Leonie laughed gaily as she cut between a bus and a manure cart and said, "Oh, it's never any good asking what's wrong with your uncle. There about eight things that he gets, singly or in combinations, all the time. The best thing to do is to reckon that he's either fairly well, or rather ill, or very ill. The details are too complicated."

She did not say it unkindly, but all the same I was somewhat shocked. In our house people were ill very seldom, but when they were you talked about it in hushed voices and went about on tip-toe.

My uncle's farm stood at the end of a stretch of about two hundred yards, which was half-lane and half-drive, and which led through the orchards. The house itself was a pleasant little Queen Anne cottage, and in that setting on a sunny day it looked very charming. I said so. My aunt had been smiling happily, but the moment I said that the house was pretty, the smile left her face abruptly, and she stared round with an expression that seemed to mingle sadness and contempt.

"Oh yes," she said bitterly, "it's pretty enough. Particularly if you've never seen it before."

After that she fell silent, and remained so until we drew up beside the house. The change in her manner and expression was so marked that I wondered whether I had said something to offend her. Later, I was to become used to these sudden switches of mood, which were like the sun going in and out amongst heavy cloud.

As we alighted from the car I picked up my suitcase and reached for my cap.

My aunt said, "Never mind about the cap. Remus'll carry that for you."

She gave the cap to the Alsatian and said something to him in a low voice. He looked at her enquiringly for a moment, and then trotted away around the back of the house. I never saw the cap again.

The inside of Glebe Cottage, as it was called, was as charming as the outside, but even by my standards, which were not high, everything was rather rough and ready. The floors were made of big stone flags, so worn that one was in constant danger of spraining an ankle on them. The only floor covering was an occasional piece of ragged coconut matting. The furniture looked as if it had been bought at a local auction sale, and probably had. As I was to realise later, the fruit farm, pretty though it looked, was thoroughly badly planned and badly planted, and they did not own the land, but merely rented it. I doubt if it earnt my uncle five pounds a week,[5] and that and his pension were all they had to live on.

My aunt showed me my room, which was very small, with a delightful view over the orchards, and large damp patches on the ceiling. I shudder to think what it must have been like in winter, but in August it was pleasant enough. She also, to my great relief, showed me where the lavatory was. When I came down she at once thrust into my hand a large piece of home-made cake and a glass of milk and said, "Just wander around and make yourself at home. I want to go up and see how your uncle is."

I went outside. There was no real garden, but just a patch of grass which surrounded the house, and then merged into the orchards. The trees were big and old, and seemed to be carrying quite a heavy crop of apples, most of which were not yet ripe. Here and there a tree had fallen, or been cut down, and a young one had been planted in its place. Along the sides were plum trees, whilst over on the right were blackcurrants, raspberries, and strawberries. I was too late for the raspberries or strawberries, but there were some ripe plums.

I was wondering vaguely what the ethics of eating the crop on a fruit farm might be when Remus appeared. He stood about ten yards away and looked at me thoughtfully. I clicked my fingers, but he would come no nearer, and after a few moments he began to trot around me in a circle, reminding me of Saladin riding around the Crusader in *The Talisman.*[6] Nothing I could do would make him come to me. In the end I gave it up and sat down on a log, and still, for quite five minutes, he continued to circle me at his slow, beautifully graceful trot. As I watched him I could not help reflecting that whilst I liked both my aunt and Remus very much, they were rather odd people whom I did not as yet fully understand.

When I went back to the house my Uncle Patrick had appeared, and he sat and talked to me whilst my aunt was cooking the supper. My aunt had suggested that he was only slightly ill that day, but to look at him, I should have judged that he was very ill indeed. His face was a curious yellowish-grey colour and he coughed a good deal. When he coughed, his whole body seemed to jerk convulsively.

What was worse, it was obvious that talking cost him a tremendous effort. He was as I had remembered him—a quiet-voiced, gentle person with a strange crooked smile, and he went on doggedly for a long time asking me about my father and mother, about school and how I was doing there, and so on, and listening with the greatest courtesy to my replies. But I could see that it was tiring him, and as he tired his voice became more and more hoarse and strained. It was a great relief when my aunt brought in the supper.

We should have called the meal "dinner" at home, but it would certainly not have been half as good. My mother was a good, reliable cook but not a very imaginative one; whilst my Aunt Leonie's cooking was brilliant, if spasmodic. I remember particularly that evening an omelette with a cheese sauce and chives which was delicious.

My uncle sat with us, but did not eat, and as soon as we had finished Leonie went round to him and tenderly stroking his hair said, "Bed's the place for you, partner." He smiled up at her, and putting an arm round her hips, hugged her tightly to him for a moment. It was a very simple gesture, but I was surprised. In our house my mother and father never did things like that—at least, not in front of me.

After my uncle had gone to bed, apologising to me in his courteous way for being such poor company, my aunt and I cleared the table, and she went and settled down on an old sofa with her legs curled up under her and Remus lying on the floor beside her.

She said, "This is nice. You can't think how lovely it is for me to have somebody to talk to."

I suddenly realised how desperately lonely it must be for her, alone in the house with a sick man. I said something about it being nice for me too, and indeed it was. I should have been perfectly happy merely to sit and look at her as she lay coiled up there on the sofa, looking at me with the big slanting grey-green eyes, in the thin blouse and the tight old trousers. I found myself with a constant desire to swallow, and to hide my embarrassment, launched out into a highly embroidered account of a rag[7] that had taken place at school a couple of terms ago, which had involved letting off a fire extinguisher just as a master entered the classroom.

In fact, I had taken no part in the rag at all, being far too law-abiding a citizen. But there was something about my aunt which suggested that she preferred dashing blades to law-abiding citizens, and in this version of the story I became the ring-leader.

The story seemed to please Leonie and she laughed heartily and asked me a lot of questions. She had very little idea of what a Public School was like, and even seemed mildly surprised that it contained no girls.

She said, "What happens when they find out who did a thing like that?"

"They get tanned."

"You mean they get the cane?"

"Yes."

"Where?"

"Usually in Richardson's study," I said obtusely.

"No—I mean where on *them*? On their hands or their behinds?"

"On their behinds, of course," I said shortly, finding it irritating that my aunt should think that at my school we might be childishly caned on the hands like private school boys.

Leonie said, "Do *you* ever get tanned?"

"Not now," I said patiently. "I'm in the Sixth. But I used to sometimes."

"It must hurt like hell."

"It docs," I said briefly. For some reason I found the conversation embarrassing.

I asked some questions about the orchard, and she told me that most of the apples were not picked until the autumn. "Season of mists and mellow fruitfulness," I said, for no particular reason.

"What's that?" said Leonie.

"Keats' 'Ode to Autumn'."

My aunt sighed. "You'll have to realise," she said rather sadly, "that I am quite uneducated. I mean—I don't know anything about poetry, or things like that."

"Does anybody?" I said, in my best intellectual-conversation manner.

"It just doesn't mean anything to me," said my aunt with a puzzled frown. "I can't think why. I'm not really silly in most ways. But when people write poetry, I just don't see what they mean."

I said, "Try reading it aloud, and see if you like the sound of it, even if you don't know what some of it means."

"I can't read aloud."

"Of course you can. Everybody can. I shall make you read aloud to me sometimes."

"All right," said my aunt submissively.

We smiled at one another, and I found myself gulping hard. The thing was almost painfully pleasurable—the thought of making her—*making* her mark you—read verse to me—perhaps even instructing her in how to do it better. To have those big eyes looking at me respectfully, admiringly, and submissively…

I said, "Remus is a strange person." At the sound of his name, the Alsatian's head came up.

"Why is he strange?" said my aunt, putting down a hand and stroking one of his ears.

I told her about his trotting around me in the garden, not forgetting to put in that it had reminded me of Saladin riding around the Crusader.

I half-hoped that she would ask me who Saladin was, but she just said, "Oh, I can tell you why he did that. He wanted to take a good look while he was making up his mind about you. You see, he knows that you are not an enemy—or that at least, if you are, I don't know about it. But he's not sure yet that you're a friend."

The Alsatian knew that he was being talked about, and from time to time glanced from one of us to the other with his head slightly on one side.

"Remus's trouble," said Leonie, "is that he knows there is a secret, world-wide conspiracy against me, and that I don't realise it. I am surrounded by people who want to murder me, and only he can prevent it. There are all sorts of unexpected people in the plot—like the milkman, or the postman, or the man who brings the coal. They seem innocent enough to you and me, but Remus knows about their plot. So he has to be near me twenty-four hours of the day, so as to prevent them from killing me." My aunt shook her head pensively. "It's a difficult thing to get people to understand. You see *they* often don't realise they're in the plot themselves, and they tend to think that Remus is dangerous and a bit crazy. There was an awful business when I was working out in the orchard one day, and the postman came up behind me. Remus thought I hadn't seen him, and that the postman was sneaking up to put a knife in me, so he nearly tore the man's trousers off. I had a dreadful job to square it. The post office always make a terrific fuss if a dog goes for a postman."

I said, "You really think he believes that you're always in danger?"

"Oh yes. You'll notice that if I ever stand and talk to anybody, Remus will always stand beside me and just a little bit behind me, and he'll never take his eyes off the person I'm talking to. They've only got to make any sudden movement towards me and he'll nail them. Look—I'll show you."

Leonie uncoiled herself from the sofa and stood up. The Alsatian at once got up too and stood, as she had said, beside and slightly behind her.

Leonie said, "Now you get up too, and stand there in front of me, and we'll go on talking."

I got up and went and stood in front of her. Looking down at the beautiful, strange face, I realised for the first time that she was quite five inches shorter than I.

Leonie said, "We'll go on talking quite normally, and then when I say 'Now' put your hand on my shoulder, and watch what happens. Don't worry—I've got him. Go on—talk."

I could see the Alsatian's eyes staring at me unwaveringly. I said, "You mean he'll go for me?"

"Yes. And then I can tell him that he's got it all wrong, and that he must learn to trust you. After all," she added with a grin, "if you're going to be staying here you must be able to touch me if you want to, without having your throat torn out. *Now!*"

I raised my hand tentatively and put it on her shoulder. As I did so several things happened at once. The Alsatian came up like an arrow towards my face. Simultaneously, Leonie said "*Remus!*" sharply, and flung out a hand, and the dog seemed to curve in the air as he flung himself back from his spring. I had instinctively dropped my hand from Leonie's shoulder and jumped back.

Leonie turned to the dog and said quietly, "Now listen, Remus—this is something you must get into your head. Walter…" (pointing at me) "Walter—that's Walter there—is a friend. *Friend.* He's not part of your silly conspiracy, and he can do anything he likes to me, and it's all right. He can come near me, or touch me (Go on, Walter, put your hand back on my shoulder), or put his arm round me (Go on, do it) or anything else he likes, and it's nothing to do with you. See?"

I stood there with my arm still around her. The arm was quivering slightly, and I was afraid she might feel it. Leonie turned back from Remus and smiled up at me.

"There," she said, "we'll do that again to-morrow just to remind him, and after that you'll find he'll have got it."

I had a wild desire to say "and after that I can do anything to you… *anything*…" But I did not say it.

"Time for bed," said my aunt briskly. "You must be tired."

I was indeed tired, but even so it took me a long time to go to sleep that night. There could be no doubt about what was the matter with me, of course. I had been in love before, and knew the symptoms. But that was not all. For my new passion for my Aunt Leonie, like my former passion for Clynes, had in it that element of exquisite guilt which I always found highly stimulating. Here again, was a dark, secret, hopeless passion which must never be suspected by anybody—particularly the beloved; and which must be converted by prayer and agony into a pure and holy love.

But the prayer and agony could come later. It was enough for that night to recall in lingering detail how my aunt had looked as she sat on the sofa; how I had said that I would make her read aloud, and she had submitted; how she had stood looking up at me, and how it had felt when I put my hand on her shoulder—put my arm round her—during the demonstration for Remus.

I also worked out exactly how I would behave when, as she had promised, we carried out the demonstration again to fix it in Remus's mind. Emboldened by sleepiness, I even speculated on whether, when I put my arm round her, I might shift it so that my hand was on her breast, as I had done with Sally. But this was going too far, and I sternly reminded myself that Leonie was my aunt. The reminder seemed to help quite disgracefully little.

Four

I cannot really remember the details of my first few days at Glebe Cottage. My Uncle Patrick reappeared, and seemed better, and I think all three of us went in the car to Canterbury on one occasion. I know that we all picked plums, because I have a very vivid recollection of Leonie going up a ladder. Indeed, such recollections as I have are all mere excuses for remembering moments when Leonie was more than usually agonisingly attractive.

I remember, for example, the evening when she first changed the old blue trousers for a skirt, and put on stockings. In my defence, it was a very short skirt, and Leonie had very beautiful legs of which, I fancy, she was proud. When she was sitting on the sofa in her usual position, talking to me, I found it quite impossible to keep my eyes off those legs. I tried looking round the room, I tried staring straight into her eyes, and I tried looking at my own fingernails. But within a few moments I would catch myself again staring, as though half-hypnotised, at those long, beautifully-shaped silken legs.

It was even worse when my Uncle Patrick was with us. He was a nice man, and he was very kind to me, and yet there was I, his nephew, constantly glancing with uncontrollable lust at the legs of his wife. Uncle Patrick must have thought that I was either very shy, or very stupid, for on these occasions, I was constantly reduced to mumblings, stutterings, and blushings. It was no help to remind myself that he could not possibly have dreamed of what was going on inside me. *I* knew, and that was enough to reduce me to an agony of guilty embarrassment.

I cannot say that Leonie herself really helped me much in my battle to tread these thoughts underfoot. She was a cheerfully frank young woman, and except on certain occasions when it amused her to treat me as though I was ten years old, she treated me as an adult and an equal. In fact, sometimes when she spoke with her innocent bluntness, I saw my uncle shoot a glance at her which seemed half-surprised and half-reproving. She always kissed me good night, and kissed me again when we said good morning, so that the day both began and ended for me with that peculiar sensation which I always likened to touching a live electric wire. It was my standard nightmare that one day she would guess, in some strange way, how I felt as my lips touched her cheek, and turn from me in sick disgust for ever.

It must have been about a week after my arrival that a letter came for my uncle while we were at breakfast. Leonie had gone to the door when the postman knocked, and I saw her glance at the envelope and make a slightly wry face before she handed it to him.

My uncle opened the letter and read it, and then handed it silently across the table to her. I thought his face looked, if possible, even greyer and more haggard than usual as he stared at her while she read.

Leonie replaced the letter carefully in its envelope and said bitterly, "Well, that's exactly what we needed at the moment, isn't it?"

There was a pause. Then my uncle said, without conviction, "I could go to Masters. He always…"

"You could," said Leonie with decision, "but you certainly won't."

Uncle Patrick gave a helpless little shrug.

Leonie suddenly smiled at him brightly and said, "Don't worry about it, darling. I'll cope. He's coming at three?"

"Yes."

"All right then—you go to bed and I'll tell him that you're not well, and… and deal with it."

"*No*," said my uncle, with unusual emphasis and decision. "I don't want you to have anything to do with that man. This is a thing that I must handle myself."

"But how, darling?"

"I don't know yet, but I'll think of something. After all, he knows he'll only have to wait another fortnight."

Leonie began, "I'd much rather you let me…" but he cut her short, saying quietly, "The best thing for you to do is to go and get on with your job, picking those plums, and leave me to do mine."

I knew, of course, that this was all something to do with money. I lived in a household in which there were frequent financial crises, and knew the peculiar, harried expression which comes over people's faces on these occasions. I was in the first flush of my love for Leonie, and I wished desperately that I could have laid my thirty-two-and-sixpence at her feet to help. But I also knew that financial crises were not usually matters of thirty-two-and-sixpence. We finished breakfast in gloomy silence, though once Leonie caught my eye and gave me a gallant and reassuring smile.

My uncle and aunt went away together after breakfast and I heard them arguing; but Uncle Patrick must have carried his point, because soon after luncheon Leonie said, "Come on, Walter—let's go and get on with the plums." We went out, leaving my uncle alone. As she passed him, Leonie kissed him lightly on the top of the head.

Leonie was unusually silent as we worked, and her eyes kept going to the gate. After about half an hour a car stopped outside, and a man came down the path to the house. My uncle came to the door and they went inside together.

I said, "Who's that?"

"That," said Leonie carefully, "is Mr. Philip Edwards. He's an estate agent." She paused for a moment and then added viciously, "He's also a first-class twerp." She turned and started to pull plums off the tree with vicious jerks, of the sort she had taught me never to use when picking fruit.

We went on picking for about a quarter of an hour and then Leonie suddenly turned and glanced towards the house and said, "Look—I think your uncle probably needs reinforcements. He isn't very good at this sort of thing." She started to walk quickly back towards the house. Remus, of course, followed, and so did I.

My uncle and Edwards were in the living-room. They looked up as we entered and I saw that my uncle's face was pale, and that the corner of his mouth was twitching slightly. Edwards was frowning, but at the sight of Leonie he broke into a peculiar, rather sheepish grin, and gave a little sighing grunt, which might have been one of resignation.

Leonie smiled at him and said, "Hello, Philip." And he said, "Hello, Leonie. How's tricks?" He made no attempt to get up.

Leonie went across to the sofa and flopped down on it, showing even more leg than usual, and said, "Did you go to the Horse Show?"

"Yes."

"What was it like?"

"Fine," said Edwards briefly. He was an unpleasant-looking man of about thirty, with a large, dark-skinned, greasy-looking face, and small brown eyes which had a curious opacity about them, as though they were made of some sort of polished stone.

He was wearing a rose in his buttonhole, and a handkerchief projected from his breastpocket.

Leonie gave him an arch smile and said, "I nearly rang you up to see if you'd take me."

"Did you now?" said Edwards dryly. But he grinned back at her and I saw the stony little eyes looking her over appreciatively.

I had remained standing near the door. Nobody had offered to introduce me to Edwards. Leonie smoothed back her hair and said, "Well now, Walter dear—this is all going to be very dull business, so perhaps you'd like to go and get on with the plums, and I'll be back with you in a few minutes." I went out, and as I passed the open window of the living-room, I heard Edwards say sullenly, "…nothing to do with me, Leonie. I've got my instructions…"

About half an hour later, Edwards and Leonie came out of the house and walked up the path towards his car. As they did so, he gave her a familiar slap on the behind, and laughed about something. They stood beside his car talking and laughing for a few moments and then Edwards leant close to her and said something into her ear. Leonie giggled, and giving him a slight push, turned back to the gate. Edwards got into the car and drove away.

As Leonie reached the house, my uncle appeared at the door. His whole body seemed curiously slack, as though there was not a bone in it, and he had one hand on the doorpost, to support himself. He looked at Leonie as she came down the path, and his face was puckered and drawn as though with pain. He said something to her with a crooked little grin of infinite bitterness. She took his head between her hands and drew it down to her and kissed him, and spoke to him for a few moments in a low voice, looking up at him with her brightest smile. Then he turned away and went into the house, and Leonie came on down to where I was still picking plums. The smile had gone now, and I noticed for the first time little lines at the corners of her mouth and eyes, such as I had seen in my mother, and other older women.

She heaved a sigh and said, "Well, that's that," and started to pick. After a moment she said, "It's extraordinary what you can do when you have to. My word, Walter—you have picked a lot."

I did not know exactly what she had done, but I knew that it had cost her a lot, and I loved her more than ever.

During this period I suffered only one major disappointment. The demonstration with Remus was never repeated, as had been promised. I rehearsed the scene a dozen times when alone, and the more I rehearsed it the more colourful and daring it became. But, in fact, it never happened.

This was probably because it was quite unnecessary. Within twenty-four hours of my arrival at Glebe Cottage, Remus had accepted that I was not an active part of the world conspiracy to murder my aunt, and he would even lie looking on calmly (and, I sometimes fancied, a trifle cynically), whilst I gave her a good morning or good night kiss. We even became close friends, insofar as Remus, in his capacity as bodyguard, could be friendly with anybody. He would never come for a walk with me, unless my aunt came too, because that would have left the milkman, the postman, and the coalman an open field for their murderous designs. But as long as Leonie was in the house, he would come and play with me in the orchard for hours together, occasionally trotting back to the house with a slightly worried expression, just to make sure that she was still there and still alive.

My aunt had claimed that Remus was not a dog at all, but just a very intelligent person who happened to look like a dog. This was the usual irritating exaggeration common to many dog owners, in the best tradition of he-understands-every-word-you-say. Remus was no transmogrified Auden and Isherwood character,[1] but nevertheless he was certainly a very remarkable dog. Even for an Alsatian he was quite exceptionally intelligent. He had a passion for learning things, however useless, only equalled, in my experience, by certain science students whom I met later at Cambridge. He learnt remarkably quickly; and moreover, it was easy to teach him things that involved *going away* from me. Most intelligent dogs can easily be taught to retrieve, to sit, lie, or walk at heel; anything, in fact, of which oneself is the obvious centre. But Remus could learn very quickly to do things by himself, in which one was not immediately concerned.

Thus, one morning, I taught him, in ten minutes, to go to a certain tree, pick up a piece of wood which I had put there, carry this piece of wood to another tree fifty yards farther away, put it down there, pick up another piece of wood that he would find under the second tree, and bring that back to the first tree. I showed him what I wanted him to do, and then told him to go and do it again. He got it wrong the first time, half-right the second time, and completely right the third time, and never thereafter forgot it.

One could hardly call some of these things play, for he would carry them out with all the concentration, the alertness, and the quivering excitement of a man solving a difficult and vital problem. As he worked he would shoot an occasional sharp glance at me. If I nodded, he knew that he was on the right track. If I shook my head, he knew that something was going wrong. And when he eventually got it right he would do a sort of war dance of triumph, consisting of a series of tremendous leaps vertically into the air.

There was no doubt that by canine standards Remus was in the genius class. But like many other geniuses, he was extremely neurotic and over-sensitive. He was not only easily downcast, but very difficult to cheer up once he became depressed. If my aunt spoke sharply to him he would mourn for days, lying and gazing at her sadly and abjectly, long after the offence had been not only forgiven but forgotten. I remember once saying to my aunt, "What's the matter with Remus? He seems very sad," and getting the reply, "Oh, I called him an ass last Tuesday, and it hurt his feelings. There's nothing you can do about it once his feelings are hurt. He'll get over it in a few days."

I was not really sorry that Remus would not come for walks with me. All my life, I have preferred to go for walks by myself, with no one to talk to, and not even a dog to distract my thoughts. This would not have applied to Leonie of course; like Remus, I would gladly have been with her for twenty-four hours of the day. But often when she was busy about the house I felt that I was in the way; and then I would go off by myself perhaps for several hours, walking through the lovely Kentish country, and repeating to myself my favourite verses about hopeless love. This was in the day-time. Since I had been at Glebe Cottage, I had not yet ventured on one of my night walks with their full ritual.

It was during one of these rambles that I came on the parish church. It was in an unexpected place, standing quite alone in a fold of the hills, with no other building of any kind in sight. It was small and very early—I should judge that it was at least partly Saxon. It was surrounded by a beautifully kept graveyard with some notably fine standard rose trees. Around the graveyard was an iron fence, and from its gate a footpath led away over the hills. That was all, except for the bare sweep of the hills, shimmering in the heat. It was an immensely peaceful place.

I had been thinking a good deal about God in the previous few days, since I could hardly expect him to approve of my feelings about Aunt Leonie. True, when I went to bed at night I had tried to explain matters. But when I was at school and having similar difficulties in the matter of Clynes, I had always found prayers in Chapel much more satisfying and reassuring than those said elsewhere. Besides, the idea of prayer in this lovely, deserted place exactly chimed with my mood at the moment. I think the standard roses had a good deal to do with it.

Accordingly, I went into the church and was at once confronted by the Table of Kindred and Affinity,[2] painted in antique gold lettering on a blackboard and attached to a wall facing the door. I looked at it with a bitter little smile. It was quite unnecessary to remind me that a man may not marry his father's brother's wife. I knew it only too well.

I wandered round for a short while, trying to capture the proper mood for my prayers. But the inside of the church was disappointing and slightly unsympathetic. There were two or three old brasses, and the choir stalls were interestingly carved. There was also the tomb of a knight and his lady who lay side by side on top of it in attitudes of rigid piety. But the stained glass was modern and bad, and the pews were covered with an unpleasant shiny varnish. I wished that I had stayed outside among the rose trees and the grey-lichened tombstones. But I remembered one of my school chaplain's favourite exhortations —"A church isn't a concert hall or a museum. You don't go there to listen to the music or admire the stained glass, but to talk to God and to listen to him." I knelt down in a pew at the rear of the church.

It was not my habit, on such occasions, to make a full and detailed confession of my sins, as a priest would have made me do. I knew from experience that if I did so there was a danger that my mind would wander off into a pleasant, warm process of recollection, with very little of repentance in it. I therefore usually made a blanket apology for all my sins and a general, if rather vague, appeal that I might be absolved and strengthened for the future. It was only after this that I came to what was usually the most satisfying and heart-warming part of my prayers, which was to ask God's help for the immediate subject of my affections.

Here, however, I quickly ran into difficulties. It had been easy to pray for Clynes. I knew what he wanted, what would be good for him, and what were the difficulties and dangers that beset him. But I realised, with something of a shock, that I knew none of these things about my Aunt Leonie. She did not desperately want to get into the House Second Fifteen, and it was not necessary for her to get through School Certificate. Nor, as far as I knew, was there a constant danger that she would be taken up by the wrong people and led into bad ways.

In fact, after a good deal of thought, the only things that I could remember which seemed positively wrong with my Aunt Leonie's life were that she swore, sometimes struck me as being lonely, and did not really like poetry. I asked that she might be forgiven for the first, and helped and made happy over the other two. But this seemed a feeble and colourless way of expressing my passionate love for her. I could not help wishing that there was something bigger and more tangible wrong with my Aunt Leonie's life—something which I could pray hard about, and do something about, preferably at great risk and hardship to myself. Remus at least thought that there was a world conspiracy against her, and had the satisfaction of devoting his life to foiling it, even if it was all just his imagination. But I did nothing for her, except make her read verse. I just crudely, selfishly, voraciously, and warmly loved Leonie, with a deplorable absence of real spirituality. I ended my prayers rather dispiritedly, with an appeal that she might be happy, that she might like me more and more every day, and that she might never guess that my love for her was an impure thing.

As I came out of the church, I saw a man sitting on one of the stone benches at the side of the porch. He was wearing a grey clerical suit with a dog collar[3] and stock,[4] but he had removed his jacket and rolled up his sleeves, and he had a handkerchief bound round his forehead to act as a sweatband. A small mower stood on the grass of the graveyard outside. The clergyman was sitting with his eyes closed, but as I came out he opened them, peered at me through his glasses and said, "Ah—hello. Now let's see, who are you?"

I said, "My name's Walter Parrish."

"Of *this* parish?" he said with a giggle.

"No. I'm staying with my uncle and aunt."

He said, "Ah yes—the beautiful Mrs. Parrish," and giggled again.

He took off his spectacles, took the handkerchief from his head, polished the spectacles, and putting them on again, stared at me for a few moments in silence.

"It's hot work that," he said, jerking his head towards the mower. "The grass always grows very thick in graveyards. Well manured. Do you like our church?"

"It's very nice," I said politely.

"I think it's terrible," he said promptly. "But what can you expect with a vicar who's senile, and a parish of five hundred barbarians?"

I was rather startled, since I had assumed that he *was* the vicar. He guessed what was in my mind and said, "You see, I'm just the curate. Which means that he gets the stipend[5] and I do the work. That's the Church of England for you. What were you doing in the church?"

"Just… just looking at it."

"If *I* were staying with that lovely lady of yours, *I* wouldn't waste my time looking at an awful place like that. I'd spend it looking at her." He giggled for some moments.

"Do you mean Mrs. Parrish?" I said coldly.

"You can put it like that if you like. Isn't she lovely?" He leant forward and lowered his voice. "Now come on—confess. *Isn't* she lovely?"

He went off again into his almost silent giggling. I felt slightly sick. I said as stiffly as I could, "My aunt certainly is very beautiful," and tried to pass.

He put out a hand to stop me and said, "Don't go. My

name's Hawes. I'm the curate here. Has it ever struck you as strange that so few people know about Pusey?"

I said, "About *what*?"

"Pusey.[6] Dr. Pusey. There you are," he added triumphantly, "you've never heard of him. Newman—yes. Keble—yes. But Pusey seems to have been forgotten. And yet so much the greatest of the three. Do you play cricket?"

"Yes."

"Bat or bowl?"

"Bat chiefly. I bowl a bit too."

"I bowl. Left arm quickies. Does your uncle make any money out of that fruit farm?"

"I don't know."

"I shouldn't think he does. But why should he want money anyhow? He's got something far better than money. Don't you think so?"

I said, "I must go now."

"All right," he said, rising. "I suppose I must get on with this sweaty job."

He walked beside me towards his mower. I realised that he was very tall and extremely thin, and he walked with a curious gait, seeming to drag his legs after him as though they were heavy.

He fumbled with the handkerchief, trying to tie it in position again round his forehead, and said, "My name's Hawes. I'm the curate here. If you want the job you can have it. And I'll have yours." He giggled, and nudged me with his bony elbow. "Staying up at Glebe Cottage. All among the fruit trees."

He suddenly paused and stood glaring at me angrily through his spectacles. "Do you realise that that's church land?" he said, in a voice which seemed to quiver with anger. "*Church land.* That's why it's called Glebe Cottage.[7] If I had my way, I'd report the whole thing to the Ecclesiastical Commissioners, and have them out of there in very short order."

"What do you mean?" I said, startled by his sudden change of tone. "Report what?"

He was silent for a moment. Then the angry glare vanished and his thin, bloodless lips broke into a smile. "Nothing," he said. "I was just joking. The trouble about a parish like this is that you can never make a joke. People don't see it. Barbarians. I make jokes all the time and nobody ever sees them. I suppose I shan't see you at church?"

"I don't know. I…"

He shook his head. "Oh no, I shan't," he said with quiet finality. "Not from Glebe Cottage."

He turned his back on me and started to push his mower away, seeming to trail after it with his long thin legs dragging. It was with great relief that I closed the gate of the churchyard behind me. The man was obviously mad and to be pitied. But pity was not what I was feeling, and somehow the Saxon church and the green graveyard and the roses made it all much worse.

When I told my aunt that I had met Mr. Hawes, and that he seemed very strange, she answered promptly with the single word "Drunk."

This threw a new light on the matter. I said, "Do you think he can have been? I thought he was mad."

"Oh no," said my aunt. "He'll just have been drunk. He usually is. What was he doing?"

"Mowing the churchyard."

"That's right. He goes down there and mows the churchyard, and takes a few bottles of beer with him, and by the time he's been going for an hour he's as tight as a lord. It's always happening. One day some of the villagers went past and found him lying on somebody's grave, flat out. They had to carry him home."

"But why doesn't he lose his job if he's always getting drunk? I mean…?"

My aunt shrugged. "I suppose nobody cares. Nobody goes to that church anyhow. If they want to go to church, they go over to Petcrham." She shot a quick glance at me. "What did he say to you?"

"Oh, nothing much," I said awkwardly. "He talked about cricket… and a man named Pusey, whom I'd never heard of."

"Did he know you were staying here?"

"Yes."

"Did he say anything about that?"

I hesitated. "He said you were very beautiful."

"That was damn nice of him," said my aunt bitterly. "Anything else?"

"Something about this being church land. Is it?"

"Yes. We lease it from the Ecclesiastical Commissioners. What had the Reverend Mr. Hawes got to say about that?" Then, as I hesitated, "It's all right—I get the general drift of it."

I said, "Well *I* don't. I didn't see what he was talking about."

My aunt, who had been stacking some plates away in a cupboard, with her back half-turned to me, turned quickly and looked me full in the face. "Didn't you?" she said quietly.

"No," I said truthfully, surprised by her tone. "I was never sure whether he was trying to make a joke or trying to be unpleasant, or what."

"Well well," said Leonie, turning back to her dishes. "Heaven knows it doesn't matter what Hawes says. He's a nasty little tick, and everybody knows it. You'll probably see him again to-morrow night. We're going to Masters for a drink, and I expect he'll be there."

"Who's Masters?"

"Man who has a farm just down there. Retired Colonel."

"Nice?"

"God no. As bad as Hawes, though in a different way."

"Then why do you go to have a drink with him?"

Leonie sighed. "In this place," she said sombrely, "you go to have a drink with anybody who asks you. Particularly if you're us." She was silent for a moment and then added, "Masters doesn't like me, and what's worse, he doesn't like Remus."

"Why not?"

"Absolutely no reason at all," said Leonie, turning quickly and speaking almost angrily. "He's got nothing against him. *Nothing.* He… he's just taken against Remus. That's all. Are you going to make me read this evening?"

"Yes. Of course."

These verse-reading sessions with my aunt took place almost every evening, and I think she enjoyed them nearly as much as I did. But the convention remained that it was a thing that I "made" her do. There were very few books in the house, but there was a copy of the Oxford Book of English Verse, and a complete Shakespeare. Her reading was better than I had expected, although she was shy about it, and liable to swallow her words, as though she was afraid somebody might hear them. But she always steadily insisted that she had no idea what she was reading about, and at the end of each poem I had to explain "what he meant".

This was excellent practice for me, and after a while, it made me careful in my choice of verses for her to read; for I found, rather disconcertingly, that in many poems which I knew well, or could even repeat by heart, there were moments when I myself was not altogether sure about "what he meant". I remember coming a notable cropper over Wyatt's "They flee from me that sometime did me seek,"[8] and feeling Leonie's big, slanting greenish eyes fixed on me with the odd and slightly derisive expression which meant she knew that I was out of my depth.

On the whole, however, she was delightfully humble and admiring, asking me beautifully easy questions, and receiving the answers most reverently and respectfully, as I might have received an answer from Coleridge[9] or T. S. Eliot.[10]

The result was that by the end of one of these sessions my ego had always been blown up to a vast size. At such moments I felt at least a decade older than Leonie, and infinitely stronger and more knowledgeable. Indeed, in thinking about it afterwards, I was always surprised that I had not taken advantage of the occasion to possess her—to put my arm round her and to put my hand on her breast, to kiss her as much as I wanted to, and even to stroke her knees, doing all these things calmly, masterfully, and as a matter of right. But somehow, I was always so busy explaining what "bare ruined choirs"[11] meant, that the appropriate moment for these decisive masculine gestures never arrived, and all too soon Leonie would say "time for bed" and uncoil herself from the sofa, and the moment of magic opportunity would have passed.

We never read if my uncle was present. It was necessary for him to get as much rest as possible, and usually he went to bed almost immediately after supper. It was after this that our poetry readings took place. Occasionally he would stay up and play the piano, and these evenings were largely, but not entirely, a waste for me. My great desire was to be alone with Leonie; and as I have said, I always felt a certain degree of guilty awkwardness when I was with both of them. Nevertheless, I enjoyed hearing my Uncle Patrick play. His tastes were very like my own—no Chopin, little Beethoven or Brahms, and a great deal of Mozart, Bach and Handel. But apart from the music, it gave me a chance to show off before Leonie. There was something of the same sense of power and superiority which came out of poetry reading about being able to ask my uncle to play Number Two of Book Two of the Forty-eight Preludes and Fugues,[12] and to hum the fugal subject before he did so.

I do not think this particular method of spreading my tail feathers was any great success with Leonie. She was not interested in music, and if my uncle and I discussed it she was liable to become jealous. She would sit and knit sulkily without speaking to anybody, occasionally giving little sighs of impatience. But even this could be turned to my advantage; for whilst my uncle was playing, with his back to us, and Leonie was sulkily knitting with lowered head, I could look at her as much as I wanted to, frankly and openly, and without feeling embarrassed every time that my eyes were drawn to those lovely legs.

Five

On the evening when we were going to Colonel Masters my aunt called me into her bedroom shortly before we were due to leave. A hook at the back of her dress had come undone, and could not be done up again without help. I, who had been so excited about putting a safety-pin in Clynes's pants, was too surprised by her appearance to be excited now. I had never seen her before in anything but her blue trousers or an old cotton frock, and now that she was dressed to go out the effect was startling. The dress itself I cannot remember, except that it was of a sort of sea-coloured silk which set off her curious, dark gold hair, and her greenish eyes perfectly; and that it had a tight bodice (hence the trouble with the hook). But I know that the general effect was very dashing, and, what was more, intentionally so. It is curious that however much female fashions change, there is something quite unmistakable about any female garment which is intended to be unusually enterprising. My aunt's dress was one of the unmistakable ones.

Yet it was her face that surprised me most. When at the farm she wore practically no make-up, but now she was wearing a great deal. In these days, when young girls are sometimes to be seen wearing green eye-shadow and mascara on a sunny morning, the effect would probably have been less striking. But to me my Aunt Leonie, with eye-shadow, mascara, eyebrow pencil, lipstick, and so on, made a very striking figure indeed.

I disliked the effect intensely. The face that I had gazed at with rapture for so many hours was now not exactly a mask, but an over-coloured portrait of itself. It was still beautiful, but to me its beauty was of a different kind, and one which I did not like as well. I think I was probably quite right. I doubt if Leonie was really very good at making up her face. She had too little practice.

She must have seen my face in the mirror as I did up her dress, for she said quietly, "Well—will I do?"

"You look absolutely beautiful," I said politely.

"Sure," said my aunt ironically. "Well, they asked for it, and now they can damn well have it."

"Who asked for what?"

"I never knew a person like you for wanting everything *explained*," said Leonie irritably. "You always want to know exactly what everybody means, even when very often they don't mean anything. I suppose it's all this dam' poetry. Your hair's sticking up at the back. Go and put some water on it or something."

We were invited, I gathered, for seven o'clock, and by five minutes to seven we were ready. But when my uncle mildly suggested that we should go, Leonie replied irritably that we should be far too early, and could not possibly start for another quarter of an hour.

During most of this quarter of an hour we sat in silence, my aunt occasionally fidgeting with the contents of her handbag, or putting a hand to her hair. Several times she took the hand mirror out of her bag, looked at herself, made some tiny adjustment, and put the mirror back again. Occasionally she would give a sharp tug to pull her dress down over her knees. She seemed to be in a very bad temper. My uncle must have thought so too, because once he put out his hand and patted hers soothingly. She looked at him, and for a moment I thought she was going to smile. Then she looked away again grimly and withdrew her hand.

My uncle said quietly, "We'll only stay for a few minutes, darling."

"Why?" said Leonie loudly, "why should we only stay a few minutes? Let's stay all night and get drunk."

It was only about a mile to Colonel Masters's house; which was as well, for it was along a narrow winding road, and my aunt drove the Morris even more furiously than usual. Then, when we were about three hundred yards from the house, she suddenly stopped, announced that we were still far too early and had better sit in the car for a while, changed her mind, and drove on at top speed. My uncle caught my eye and gave me his odd, crooked smile. I knew he was really explaining to me why my aunt was behaving oddly, and I smiled back knowingly. But in truth I was puzzled as to why she should be so angry with everybody.

Colonel Masters's house was a very much bigger and smarter affair than Glebe Cottage, though of about the same age. One reached it through large iron gates hung on big stone pillars, and in front of it there was a well-kept garden. We were met at the door by a manservant, who told us that the party was outside, and conducted us round the side of the house to a large, beautiful balustraded terrace overlooking a rose garden, where about thirty people were standing or sitting, and making that remarkable noise that people do make at such affairs.

The chatter went on as we stood for a moment unnoticed at the side of the terrace. Then our host saw us and came towards us; and as he did so the noise suddenly died away to little more than a mutter, as every head seemed to turn in our direction.

My first impression of Colonel Masters was that he was a very big man. In fact he was not much more than six feet in height, but there was an immense solidity about his shoulders and chest, and about his thick, powerful neck. His hair was cropped short, and speckled with grey, and his rugged face was both red and sun-tanned, so that his complexion reminded me of the skin of a blood orange. Twenty years before, he must have been a handsome man, and even now, for a retired Colonel, he looked to me in uncommonly good condition. I felt then, as I was to feel again several times later, that nothing short of an axe wielded by a powerful man would have made much physical impression on Colonel Masters.

He greeted my Uncle Patrick cordially, in the rather surprisingly high voice that big, heavy men often have, asked after my uncle's health, and told him that he must take care of himself. Then, still with his head turned towards my uncle as he finished what he was saying, he put out a hand in the direction of my aunt. My aunt took it, but the Colonel had not finished his sentence, and there was what seemed to me an awkward moment while the Colonel stood in the attitude of shaking hands with Leonie, whilst still talking to my uncle.

At last he turned to her and said, "Well, Leonie—how are you? My word, you have got yourself up. This is Peterham, not Piccadilly."

My aunt flushed and released his hand, and from that moment I hated Colonel Masters—partly because of the half-contemptuous way in which he said it, partly because of the rather unpleasant grin that accompanied the words, but mainly because the words themselves were obviously justified. From the moment we had come in sight of the group on the terrace I had realised that Leonie was wearing the wrong clothes. I have no idea now, and indeed probably had no idea then, what the other women were wearing. I only know that they were unnoticeable clothes—clothes in which one would never have given them a second glance if one had met them in the street; whereas no one could have failed to notice my Aunt Leonie in that dress. Besides, they were all wearing hats, whilst she was not. I felt the same wave of agonised embarrassment, both for her and for myself, that I had felt on one occasion when my father had visited some school function wearing new brown shoes which were altogether too bright in colour.

My uncle was saying, "This is my nephew, Walter Parrish."

Colonel Masters took my hand in his huge fist and said, "How d'you do. First time you've been here?"

I said that it was. The Colonel stared at me for a moment in silence, and I saw that his eyes were of a strange, washed-out light blue colour and very slightly bloodshot. Then he said, "Humph! Well—come and get yourself a drink, Parrish," and taking my uncle by the arm led him away, whilst Leonie and I followed behind. It was noticeable that when Masters spoke to my uncle, he did so in a tone which, while slightly patronising, had genuine affection—a tone quite different from the half-sneer with which he had spoken to Leonie.

The table where the drinks were being served was at the opposite end of the terrace. To get to it, we had to pass through the middle of the company, and I could not help noticing that whereas several people greeted my uncle, nobody said a word to Leonie. A couple of youngish men nodded to her rather shyly, but the rest just looked away or started a conversation as Leonie and I approached them. People drew aside to let us pass with a courtesy that was definitely not of the right kind. I did not know much about social behaviour but I knew plenty about people being cut;[1] and there was no doubt that my Aunt Leonie was being pointedly cut. I glanced at her to see how she was taking it. Her face was slightly flushed, and she was walking with her head held high, looking straight in front of her. There was something very moving about the poise of her head, and quite instinctively I slipped my hand through her arm. She looked up at me and smiled an unhappy little smile. Then suddenly she said in a clear penetrating voice, "Golly, Walter—what a bunch of stinkers! Let's get ourselves a drink, for God's sake."

My uncle and Colonel Masters were already standing at the improvised bar, and a manservant was handing them their drinks. The Colonel turned his head as we approached, glanced at us for a moment, turned back to the manservant and said, "One pink gin and…" turned to me and said, "What do they let you drink? Sherry?" and then, before I could reply, to the manservant, "and a sherry."

Leonie said, "I think I'd rather have sherry too, please."

The Colonel was just taking the pink gin from the waiter. He said, "Take this and don't argue," and pushed it into her hand.

He handed me a glass of dark brown sherry and turned back to my Uncle Patrick. The whole thing was done in a way which might have been taken for rudeness, or for friendly teasing by an old acquaintance. For a moment Leonie hesitated, and I thought she was either going to hand the pink gin back to the waiter, or throw it at the Colonel. Then I saw her catch my Uncle Patrick's eye. He gave her his quick crooked smile, and she relaxed with something like a sigh.

More or less over his shoulder, Masters said, "And how's that lovely dog of yours?"

"He's very well, thank you," said Leonie coldly.

"Good," said Masters with a grim smile. "And as long as he stays at home, he'll probably go on being very well."

Leonie turned away and said, almost to herself, "I suppose pink gin *is* the right thing to drink at a show like this. It's got such a filthy taste that it takes your mind off the people. Ever tried it?"

"No."

"Then have a sip of this and you'll see what I mean."

I took a sip of the pink gin. It was indeed a very nasty taste. At this moment, there was a giggle behind me, and a voice said, "Ah—the beautiful lady. And how are *you* this evening?"

I turned and saw that Mr. Hawes, the curate, was standing beside us, gazing down at Leonie with his thin-lipped grin. He had a large tumbler of whisky and soda in his hand. Leonie glanced at him for a moment, and then looked away without speaking.

"Teaching the young the euphoric joys of alcohol?" said

Hawes, pointing to the glass in my hand. "Well well—that was to be expected. Don't bother to introduce me to this young man. We have already met. His name's Parrish. *Really* Parrish. We talked about you. Did he tell you what I said about you?"

Leonie said, "I don't want to hear…"

Hawes bent forward from his great height. "I told him," he said in a half-whisper, "that you were more beautiful than the dawn, but as dangerous as deadly nightshade. I said…"

"I tell you I don't want to hear it," said Leonie with weary irritation. "Come on, Walter.'

She turned as though to move away, but Hawes laid a hand on her arm. The silly grin had vanished, and he was looking at her with wide-staring, angry eyes. He said, "Just a minute. I'd like you to know, beautiful lady, that I have this day drafted a letter to the Ecclesiastical Commissioners…"

"Oh God!" said Leonie with weary contempt. "Patrick— d'you mind getting rid of this person? He's being a nuisance."

My uncle, who was still talking to Masters, looked up sharply. But before he could do anything, the Colonel turned quickly and said, "Nuisance? Who…? Oh—Hawes."

He put out a large hand and taking the curate by the arm turned him round so that they were facing one another. "Listen, Hawes," he said quietly, "you've had too much to drink. Put that whisky and soda down and go home."

Hawes said, "I was merely telling this lovely lady…"

"I said, 'Go home'," said Masters, still quietly, but in the tone of a man who is not used to having his orders queried.

The curate hesitated and glanced from him to Leonie and back again. Then he drew himself to his full lanky height. "Very well," he said with dignity, "the hospitality of Peterham… Barbarians…"

He turned and walked away unsteadily, still carrying his drink. After he had gone a few yards he stopped, gulped down the drink, put the glass on the base of a marble bust which stood on the terrace, and disappeared round the comer of the house.

Leonie said to Masters, "Why on earth do you ask that poisonous drunk here?"

The Colonel looked at her with the same half-contemptuous, half-mocking smile that I had noticed before. He said, "I like to have all sorts at my parties—the godly and the ungodly. Besides, he's an ardent admirer of yours. I thought it would be nice for you."

"Thanks," said Leonie bitterly. "But there are some sorts of admiration that I can do without."

"Then you're a very unusual woman." He looked her up and down in the cool, appraising manner which I found so intolerable. "Anyhow, he's only a village curate. He's not used to seeing visions like you."

Leonie glanced at her watch and said, "Patrick—it's nearly quarter to eight. We ought to be going."

"Going?" said Masters, with apparent indignation. "Damn it, I give a party mainly for your benefit, and invite all your special friends, and then you want to go away after about ten minutes. Don't be silly." He turned to the waiter. "Harry—two more whiskies and sodas and another pink gin."

Leonie said quietly, "I don't want another drink." She was looking, not at Masters, but at my Uncle Patrick, who had stood silently throughout the conversation. I knew that she was asking him to rescue her—to take her away. And I also knew, and knew that she knew, that he would not.

He returned her glance for a moment, and then looked away and said uncomfortably, "Just a quick one, Leonie," and took the drink which the waiter was offering him.

I heard my aunt give a sort of little groan. She almost snatched the pink gin from the Colonel's hand, and then, staring him steadily in the eyes, drank it at a single gulp.

"That's more like it," said Masters.

We drove home in silence, more slowly than we had come, but if anything even more dangerously, since Leonie steered by a series of sharp, angry, careless yanks at the wheel. I glanced at her from time to time, and once her lips were quivering, and I thought she was going to cry. But she bit her lips, and threw her head back, and narrowed her eyes, and I knew then that she was not going to cry, but merely to be furiously angry. I saw my uncle look at her uneasily also, as a man might look at an approaching thundercloud. I was not at all surprised that, when we reached home, he said he felt tired and thought that he would go straight to bed.

In fact, going to bed did not save him, for Leonie, brushing aside Remus who, as usual, was going into ecstasies about her return, immediately followed him upstairs, and I was left alone for the moment.

I was glad to be alone, for I had found Colonel Masters's party both puzzling and upsetting. It was not merely the general attitude of cold disapproval of Leonie which I had noticed in the other guests; after all, she was younger, prettier, and differently dressed, and obviously liked them no better than they liked her. Nor was it Hawes who had upset me, though he had given me the same feeling of sick distaste that I had felt when I met him in the churchyard. It was obvious that, as Leonie had said, the man was a drunk and perhaps even slightly mad. The thing that had really stuck in my throat was Colonel Masters himself, and the strange half-sneering, half-bullying manner in which he treated Leonie.

I also had to admit to myself that, though I liked him, my Uncle Patrick had not come out of the matter very well. I could not have said how, with any very great clarity, but I had an uneasy feeling that my aunt had been deserted in hostile surroundings when she needed help; help which I would willingly have given her had I known how.

I heard Leonie's voice upstairs, and she seemed to be speaking angrily. It reminded me of home, and suddenly I remembered that my father had objected to my coming to stay with my aunt and uncle "because of Leonie". There had been that same note of cold disapproval in his voice then that I had noticed this evening at Colonel Masters's party. It all added up. But the trouble was that it did not add up to any clear answer.

I looked at Remus, who was lying with his ears cocked and his head up, listening intently to the occasional sound of my aunt's voice from upstairs, and reflected that it almost seemed as though there was something in his conviction of a world conspiracy against his mistress. I remembered that proudly upflung head as we walked through the guests, and suddenly found my eyes full of tears of pity and anger. I rubbed Remus's head between his ears and said, "It's all right, Remus. She's got us."

After about half an hour my aunt came downstairs and started to prepare the supper. She had changed into one of her old cotton frocks, and had taken off most of her make-up, which I found a relief. She was much quieter than usual, and though she was quite pleasant to me, I fancied that it was an effort to her.

During supper and while we cleared it away and washed up, she did not mention the party. When we were in our usual after-supper positions, with Leonie curled up on the sofa, I asked her if she would like to read, but she merely shook her head, and for some while went on staring thoughtfully before her in silence.

Then suddenly, without turning her head, she said, "Well—did you like the lovely party?"

I said, "No. I thought it was beastly."

"It must have been very dull for you," said Leonie with a bitter little smile.

"It wasn't that it was dull. I just didn't like anybody much."

"Why not?" said Leonie ironically. "They're all perfectly charming if you get to know them. Or so they tell me."

"I think the curate's awful."

"Just drunk, as usual."

58

"And I didn't like Colonel Masters. I think he's a stinker."

"Yes," said Leonie briefly. She hesitated for a moment and then shrugged her shoulders. "I suppose he got so used to ordering people about during the war that he can't stop now," she added.

There was a long silence. I wanted to ask her the answer to the problem which was puzzling me, but it is difficult to ask a person why nobody seems to like them.

I began, "Aunt Leonie…" and then paused, groping for how to put it.

She frowned slightly and said, "What?" And then before I could answer, "Anyhow, for God's sake stop calling me Aunt Leonie."

"Why?" I said, puzzled.

"Because I'm not your aunt of course, idiot. Nor anybody else's."

"Not my aunt?"

"No."

"But you're married to my Uncle Patrick, so surely…"

"I'm *not* married to your Uncle Patrick, darling," said Leonie with weary patience. "That's the point." Then, as she saw my startled face, she added irritably, "Oh, come on, Walter, surely you've heard before now of a man and a woman living together without being married?"

I had, of course, heard of unmarried lovers, and I knew that the woman was then the man's mistress. All my favourite poets seemed to have had mistresses, to whom they were constantly writing verses. But I had not visualised these ladies as living in the same house with the poets, and certainly it had never occurred to me that if a man had a mistress she would do the cooking and the washing up. Mistresses, to me, had always been purely decorative.

"Well, what are you looking like that about?" said Leonie, irritated by my silence. "Don't tell me you're shocked. After all…"

"Of course, I'm not shocked," I said hurriedly. "It's just that I don't quite see *why*?"

"Why what?"

"Well… why you're not married? After all, you live here and —and so on…"

"Why should we be if we don't want to?" said Leonie defensively.

"But… *why* don't you want to?"

"Mind your own business," said Leonie shortly. "I've only told you this because I thought you might be puzzled about those bastards this evening. Anyhow, somebody would be sure to tell you sooner or later, so you might as well have it from me. I'm amazed that your father didn't tell you. You must be the only acquaintance of ours that he hasn't told the moment he got the chance."

She brushed back her hair with an impatient gesture, and then suddenly grinned at me with a curious, almost cheeky grin. "So there you are," she said. "Now you know the awful truth. My name's Leonie Sloane, I'm not your aunt, I'm not married to your Uncle Patrick, and I'm not related to your damned family in any way, thank God. And that's why those old… old *walruses* treat me as though I'd got leprosy. That's why Masters treats me as though I was somebody off the streets that his old pal Patrick has got mixed up with. In fact, that's why a hell of a lot of things."

"How about Hawes? Why does he…?"

"Oh, he'd like to sleep with me," said Leonie calmly. "And because he can't it makes him angry, and he talks about writing to the Ecclesiastical Commissioners. This is their land, you see, and Edwards manages it. What Hawes is threatening to do is to tell them that their holy land, for which we pay them a whacking rent by the way, is being occupied by two people who are living in sin. He may have told them for all I know. Or care."

She stood up and stretched herself luxuriously and said, "I think it's time I went to bed. I've had enough of to-day. Usually we don't go to things about here, of course, but to-night I knew that Patrick wanted to go. He rather likes Masters, because they knew one another in the war. Anyway, I couldn't really believe that people could go on being as filthy as that. And then when we came back I chewed him up for not coming away when I wanted to. And…" with a shrug, "anyhow—it hasn't been a good day."

I stood up too. She looked up at me, again with that strange, attractive, almost impudent grin which was new to me, and said, "Kiss your ex-aunty good night."

I put my arms around her, and kissed her gently on the cheek as I always did. She said, "Dear Walter. *You* aren't a walrus anyhow. You don't *mind* about this, do you?"

"No," I said, "I don't mind. Why should I?"

Six

I sat by my bedroom window for a long time that night, staring out into the darkness, and tingling with excitement. Two things above all, in what Leonie had told me, had suddenly changed my life. The first was that she was not my aunt, for thereby the whole Table of Kindred and Affinity was thrown into the wastepaper basket. Mrs. Parrish, my father's brother's wife, had disappeared, and there remained Leonie Sloane—*Miss* Leonie Sloane. With that, my love for her at a blow ceased to be a hopeless and incestuous passion, and became something with a new detail and reality, like a distant scene viewed for the first time through a telescope.

But the second, and if possible even more exciting thing, was the realisation that Leonie was a sinner—that she, like myself, must know the flower-scented agonies of temptation and remorse. The fact that Leonie, instead of being dully and decently married, was living a life of sin with my uncle—the fact that she was positively a mistress—drove me nearly mad with a mixture of pain and love. When I had been in the church, I had found it difficult to pray for her, not knowing what she needed. But now I could, and must, pray that God would forgive Leonie's sins, secure in the knowledge that there was something which urgently needed to be forgiven, and that there might be other things to forgive in the future. I think that hour of realisation that Leonie was neither my aunt nor virtuous was one of the most exquisite of my life.

Yet for the next couple of days I was somewhat disappointed by how little change there was in our relationship. On that night when she made her revelations, I had foreseen a new world, starting as from breakfast the following morning. In practice, nothing of the kind happened. Leonie had never treated me, after all, as though she was my aunt or virtuous. She still treated me as an equal, kissed me good night and good morning, showed off her legs rather shamelessly, and occasionally said things which were too frank to be lady-like. In my imagination I did all the exciting things with her that I had done with Sally. But in her actual presence I was as shy of her as I had ever been. In fact, for this short while, the only sign of the new Heaven and new earth was that Leonie, in talking to me, would sometimes refer to herself, with a grin, as "aunty", which seemed to me irritating and in bad taste. I think I had secretly hoped that, since I now knew her guilty secret, Leonie's behaviour towards me would have had in it a little more of the penitent Magdalen.[1] But she remained her cheerful self to a point which seemed to me almost brazen in the circumstances. I could not help feeling, as I had sometimes felt in the past about Clynes, that Leonie was not entirely serious.

During these days came the only really wet spell of the summer. The rain came down in torrents, and there were soon pools of water standing in the orchards, which, amongst their many other deficiencies, were very badly drained. Nothing could be done outside, and one morning, when it was still raining heavily, I was listening to my uncle playing the piano while Leonie knitted when Remus suddenly set up an excited barking and rushed out into the garden. Leonie glanced out of the window and said, "Oh God! A visitation. I'm out." She gathered up her knitting and went quickly upstairs.

I looked out of the window and saw that Colonel Masters was just entering at the garden gate. He was wearing an oilskin hat and coat and gum-boots,[2] which made him look burlier than ever. With his big red face he looked like a lifeboat coxswain, or one of those advertisements for sardines. Remus was standing just inside the gate barking furiously, with his ears quite flat, and a ridge of hair sticking up along his spine. I had never seen Remus in a really vicious mood before, and I must say he was a frightening sight. I thought that at any moment he would make that arrowlike leap for the Colonel's throat, as he had once done for mine.

Masters took no notice whatever. He simply walked straight on down the path towards the house, with Remus backing away before him, snarling and barking. I saw him say something to the dog, but I could not hear what it was, and waited breathlessly for the leap to come. But it never did. Instead, Remus backed away, and then suddenly circled round the Colonel so as to get behind him. Masters did not even turn his head. He just walked on, splashing through the puddles, until he arrived at the door with Remus still snarling at his heels. I did not like Colonel Masters, but I realised then that he was not a man who was easily frightened, or deflected from any path along which he might decide to walk.

My uncle had gone to the door to meet him, and to shout at Remus, who stopped barking but continued to snarl in a sort of undertone. Masters removed his oilskins, but he came into the living-room still wearing his gum-boots, which were very muddy.

He shook hands briefly with me and said, "Hallo, young fella." He then sat down, without being invited to do so, in the chair which my uncle usually occupied, and taking out his pipe, began to load it. He might have been a Commanding Officer in his battalion's Mess. My uncle, meanwhile, had produced a bottle of gin. He poured out half a tumbler-full, and handed it to the Colonel, who took it with a little grunt of thanks.

My uncle said, "Well—how does the weather suit you?"

Masters shrugged his heavy shoulders and said, "All right for me, as long as it doesn't go on too long. This place of yours is like a swimming-pool. Why don't you drain it? Never do any good until you do."

"Can't afford it."

"You can get a subsidy. Or make the holy fathers do it. It's their land, isn't it?" The Colonel took a sip of his gin and said, "Where's Leonie? Got a bone to pick with her."

"What about?" said Uncle Patrick uneasily.

"The dog," said Masters, jerking his head towards Remus, who by this time had stopped snarling and was merely sitting tensely, his eyes never leaving the Colonel.

"Oh God!" said my uncle unhappily. "I think Leonie's upstairs." He started towards the stairs.

I said, "I think she's gone out," but my uncle took no notice and went on up the stairs.

Masters took another sip of his gin and turned his blood-orange face towards Remus. "Look at him sitting there," he said with a peculiar little smile. "You'd love to have *my* throat out, wouldn't you, my pretty, if you dared."

I said, "I thought he was going for you, sir, when you came in the gate."

"He knows better," said Masters calmly. "Where d'you go to school?"

I told him. He nodded, but without interest, and after that we sat in silence until Leonie and my uncle came downstairs.

I thought Leonie's face looked set, and rather defensive. Masters did not get up as she came into the room. He just took his pipe out of his mouth and said, "Hallo, Leonie. Sorry if my muddy boots are spoiling your carpets." The only carpets in the living-room were some battered old fragments of coconut matting, and the way he said it made them seem even more battered than they were. Leonie said, "There's not much to spoil, is there? Patrick says you want to talk to me?"

"That's right," said Masters. He was staring at her with the strange, long-focus, light-blue eyes, and, still staring at her, he took a sip of gin. I had the idea that he was enjoying himself and did not want the interview to be over too quickly.

"What about?" said Leonie curtly.

"What d'you think?"

"I've no idea," said Leonie coldly, sitting down opposite him in an attitude of polite attention. I noticed that, for once, she pulled her skirt down carefully over her knees.

"It's Remus," said my Uncle Patrick unhappily.

Leonie sighed. "Dear God," she said wearily, "surely we're not going to have that song and dance all over again?"

The Colonel smiled unpleasantly. "I've just heard," he said gently, "that your dog has been up in Top Field running my sheep. Again."

"For the last twenty-four hours," said Leonie evenly, "my dog has never been off this place."

"He was with you all the time, eh?"

"Yes. As he always is."

"Then it's a remarkable thing, isn't it, that two of my men should have seen him chasing sheep in Top Field?"

"They may have seen a dog chasing sheep, but it certainly wasn't Remus." Leonie brushed back her hair impatiently. "We've been into all this before, and I tell you—Remus doesn't go off chasing sheep."

"Then how is it my men see him doing it?"

"I've told you that before too. If your men see an Alsatian chasing sheep, then it must be another Alsatian. It certainly isn't Remus."

Colonel Masters put his glass down rather unnecessarily hard. "Oh, come off it, Leonie," he said roughly. "You know as well as I do that there isn't another Alsatian like Remus in the district. The men know him well."

"In the dark?"

"This wasn't in the dark. It was at first light this morning."

"At first light this morning," said Leonie, "Remus was lying outside the door of my room, as he always is."

"How can you be sure of that?"

"Because I saw him, of course."

"You get up uncommonly early, don't you?" said the Colonel with his unpleasant grin.

Leonie said quietly, "Are you suggesting that I'm a liar, Colonel Masters? Because if you are…" Her eyes had gone to my Uncle Patrick. He gave a little grunt and made a slight deprecatory movement with his hands.

Masters said, "I'm suggesting that you're very fond of your dog." He finished his gin, knocked out his pipe and rose, so that with his height and bulk he seemed to tower over her. He said, "I'm also telling you something. The next time he's caught at it, I shall put a bullet in him. Understand?"

Leonie rose slowly to her feet and stood looking at him. I had never seen her look like that before. The slant eyes were narrowed and her mouth had suddenly become very small. She said very quietly, "If you ever dared put a bullet in Remus, I'd put one in you. I mean that."

Masters stared back at her with a slight smile. Once again it was obvious that he was enjoying himself. He said, "If you ever find me in your orchards, breaking down your trees, you'll be perfectly justified in putting a bullet in me. Good-bye, my dear." He turned and, with a curt nod to my uncle, went out.

We heard the rustle of his oilskins as he put them on, and his tread as he went out into the rain, closing the door behind him. Remus snarled, but Leonie held up a finger to him and he stopped at once. After that there was complete silence in the room, until we heard the sound of the Colonel's car driving away. Only then did Leonie's body relax, and she sat down suddenly on the sofa, as though her legs had given way under her.

My uncle started to say, "You know I think we ought…" but she interrupted him and said fiercely, "Why did you come upstairs? Why did you let him know I was here? I told you to say I was out."

"Don't be silly, Leonie," said my uncle in what was, for him, an unusual tone of irritation. "If the man comes to complain, you've got to listen to him. It's no good just pretending to be out."

"I don't want to hear his complaints. I've heard them all before, and I've proof that there's nothing in them. Just because he doesn't like Remus…"

"It isn't that," said my uncle. "You must try to be reasonable about it, Leonie. If his men come and tell him that they've seen Remus chasing the sheep, of course he'll come and complain. You would, in his place."

"I see," said Leonie viciously. "So Masters is to be allowed to come here and call me a liar as often as he likes, and all you're going to do is to tell me to be reasonable?"

"He didn't call you a liar," said my Uncle Patrick uncomfortably.

Leonie said, "Well, it sounded to me as though he did. Didn't it to you, Walter?"

I was rather embarrassed at being brought into the discussion. I said, "I thought he was rude, but I don't think he *exactly* called you a liar. I think what he was saying was that you were fond of Remus, and wouldn't believe that he could do a thing like that."

"Well, there must be something wrong with my hearing then," said Leonie, obviously angry at the qualified nature of my support. "It seemed to me that I told him that I'd seen Remus outside my door, at the time when he was supposed to be a mile away from the house, and that he just said that he didn't believe me."

"What he *said*…" I began, but Leonie broke in angrily, "Oh, to hell with it—I know what he said, and what he meant and so do both of you. But as usual nobody's got the guts to back me up. But anyhow, I meant just what *I* said. If that big bully ever shoots my Remus, I'll shoot him."

"But he only said he'd shoot Remus if he caught him sheep chasing," said my uncle gently. "And as Remus never does go sheep chasing, he won't get shot, will he?"

There was something very reminiscent of home in the reasonableness of this remark, and I suddenly remembered that Uncle Patrick was, after all, my father's brother.

Leonie said, "Oh, my God, Patrick—there are times when you are enough to drive anybody crazy."

With that she turned and went out to the kitchen and proceeded to do something which involved several tin bowls or saucepans and a lot of energy.

My uncle looked at me with his crooked smile and said quietly, "One thing you should remember, Walter—never try to be reasonable with an angry woman. It only makes her angrier."

He hesitated, as though he was going to say more; and then, changing his mind, went out. A few moments later I heard him sawing wood in an out-house.

Leonie was very sulky for the rest of the day, and it was clear that she had not forgiven my uncle for his lack of support against the Colonel. I was worried because I thought she might not have forgiven me either, and profoundly regretted that I had not been more positive in supporting her when she appealed to me. But the truth of the matter was that, whilst I disliked Colonel Masters intensely, and adored both Leonie and Remus, I could not quite see why Leonie should be so anxious to believe that Masters had called her a liar, or why she should be so angry with my uncle for wanting to listen to what was, after all, a perfectly reasonable complaint. To us, who knew that Remus was always outside Leonie's door all night, the idea that he would go off chasing sheep was, of course, absurd. But I could not altogether get away from the logic of my uncle's comment that since Remus did not chase sheep, there was no danger of his being shot, and therefore nothing to worry about.

Nevertheless, I had a nasty sense of having let Leonie down, and it was a great relief to find, after my uncle had gone to bed, that her eyes were no longer angrily narrowed, and that her mouth was its normal size again.

The rain had stopped, and a high wind had sprung up and was whistling among the trees in the orchard and moaning about the cottage. I have always found windy nights extremely exciting, and had I been at home, I should certainly have gone for a walk. I happened to say so to Leonie, and to my surprise she replied, "Why don't you go for one here?"

"I don't know," I said lamely. "I've just never thought of it." It was difficult to explain to her that my night walks were not just ordinary walks, and that they involved certain rituals which could only be carried out properly in certain places which I knew, and which knew me.

Leonie suddenly said, "Let's *go* for a walk. After all, we've been indoors all day, and it does sound as though it might be rather fun outside. Remus can come and look after us." We wrapped ourselves up and went out into the tumble and gallop of the night. It was a big, soft southerly wind, blowing half a gale, yet so warm that it felt almost like tepid water against the face and hands. Heavy black clouds were still driving across a half-moon. We walked arm in arm, with the wind at our backs so strong that we could lean upon it, whilst occasionally an extra-strong gust would send us staggering forward in a half-run.

Leonie said, "This is fun, but rather frightening. You feel that there may be all sorts of things flying about. Witches on brooms and so forth."

I said,

"The North wind blew so strongly
and the North wind blew so loud
That never a corpse in the churchyard
had a certain hold of its shroud."

Leonie gave a slight squeak and said, "Don't say things like that, for Heaven's sake. I hate churchyards, even in day-time."

"This is about witches in a churchyard."

"Who wrote it?"

"I did."

"I didn't know you ever *wrote* poetry, Walter."

"I don't much—except in the autumn. It's the wind that always makes me feel like that."

"Say some more of it."

"I can't remember it all, but it starts

"The North wind blew so strongly
and the North wind blew so loud
That never a corpse in a churchyard
had a certain hold of its shroud.
And even the black-clad Upright Man
could hardly say it nay
For we thought we saw him shiver
and his piping died away."

"What's an Upright Man?" said Leonie with a slight giggle.

"The… the sort of Master of Ceremonies at a witches' sabbat."[3]

"Why is he called that?"

"I'm not really quite sure."

"One can think of reasons," said Leonie.

I was about to ask her what these reasons were, since the business about the Upright Man had always puzzled me; but at this moment I realised that we had come to a steep grassy downslope, and I decided to try at least one part of the ritual of a proper walk upon Leonie.

Letting go of her arm I took her hand and said, "Look, here's a nice thing to do. When you're going down a hill with the wind behind you, you can do the most tremendous hops, first on one foot and then on the other. When I say hop, hop. *Hop!*"

We hopped. I had never done it before hand in hand with another person, and I must say that it was a tremendous improvement on the same game played alone. There were times when we seemed to be covering twenty yards at a single hop— times when it seemed that the wind would carry us away altogether, and that we should not touch the ground at all. Remus joined in and bounced vast distances in the air beside us, barking. But both his barks, and Leonie's little squeaks of excitement and fright were snatched by the wind and hurled away before us, as we went bounding, feather-light, over the close-cropped, rabbity grass.

We paused at the bottom for breath. Leonie was panting and laughing rather hysterically, and suddenly her arms were round my neck, and her lips pressed hard against mine. I was startled, and for a moment I tried to pull away from her. But she clung to me and pressed her mouth even harder against mine, and then suddenly I felt an urgent thrust parting my closed lips and felt the strange, inexpressible blandness of her tongue against mine. It was only for a moment, and then as suddenly she broke away from me, leaving me still startled and confused by the quickness and unexpectedness of that strange bland touch.

She said, "I just want to be sure that Remus is still all right with you, even when he's excited. Good boy, Remus." And then, before I could say anything, even if I had had anything to say, "What shall we do now?"

The exultation of bounding down the hill in the wind, which had almost left me for a moment as she kissed me, came flooding back, and I said, "We'll go to the churchyard and hold a sabbat. It's only just over there."

"What d'you *do* at a sabbat?"

"Well," I said rather hesitantly, "you dance and sing, and have feasts, and things like that. There really ought to be more of us. A proper coven was nine."

"Was it at a coven that you had an Upright Man?"

"At a sabbat. Yes."

"All right, all right. Then you can be the Upright Man, and Remus and I will be nine witches, and dance."

She suddenly let go of my arm, to which she had been clinging tightly, and taking the skirts of her coat and frock in her hands, pirouetted away in the moonlight, singing loudly what sounded very like a modified version of 'Yes We Have No Bananas'. Remus went bounding after her, leaping high in the air and barking, the following wind blowing his ruff up to a surprising size.

I followed, laughing, and was just about to say, "Careful, or you'll break your neck," when she caught her foot in an anthill, and fell sprawling. I rushed to pick her up, but she said quickly and sharply, "No—don't touch me!" and scrambled to her feet. "Sorry," she said, "but you must never touch me when I'm on the ground. That's the one thing that drives Remus crazy."

I said, "Did you hurt yourself?"

"No," said Leonie, brushing the front of her coat. "But I'm bloody muddy. Never mind—it's an old coat. Come on—let's go to the coven."

"The sabbat," I said instinctively.

The little Saxon church stood squat and silent in the fitful moonlight. One could sense, rather than see, the red of the roses, bordering the green of the shaven grass and the grey of the tombstones. Occasionally marble gleamed almost phosphorescently white in the thick light. We paused instinctively at the gate. The wind seemed suddenly to have dropped, and the whole place had about it an indescribable air of silent, serene menace.

Leonie was holding my arm tightly. She said, almost in a

whisper, "I don't know that I'm going to like this. It's rather terrifying."

"Sabbats always were," I said. "That's why people went to them." I felt her hand tremble a little on my arm, and realised exultantly that Leonie was frightened. For that matter, I was frightened myself, but it was the sort of fright that I was used to —the sort of fright that was a natural, and indeed necessary, part of a proper night walk.

I had started to push open the gate, and was about to lead her through it, when suddenly Remus started to bark violently, and simultaneously a figure, which seemed in the uncertain light to be of enormous height, arose in our path. I felt that ice-cold chill of sudden fear that one only feels once or twice in a lifetime, and instinctively pulled back, shutting the gate behind me as I did so. It was just as well, for Remus, less startled or less timid than I, was hurling himself against the gate in a frenzy. And then suddenly the figure called, in a high, slurred voice, "What d'you want? Glass of beer? Who are you anyhow?"

Leonie gave a loud snort, half of relief and half of laughter, and said, "My God, it's Hawes! Come on, let's bolt," and we turned and ran hand in hand, as hard as we could, by the way we had come.

We ran until we were over the brow of the rise, and hidden from the church, and then paused for breath, giggling. Leonie said, "God, that frightened me!"

"And me. What on earth's he doing there at this time of night?"

"It's only about half past nine. He's always about there anyhow. He holds queer services that nobody ever goes to, by himself, at all sorts of odd times."

"But where did he spring from? He seemed to get up right from under our feet."

"Sitting on a tombstone or lying on a grave or something. It's a good job he didn't turn up like that when we'd started our what-d'you-call-it. I was thinking of dancing naked round a tomb. *That* would have given him something to write to the Ecclesiastical Commissioners about. Hell, look at the front of this coat. And the mud here sticks like glue."

We walked home soberly and silently. The wind had dropped, and taken with it its drunken magic, and I think we were both feeling slightly foolish. Leonie was worrying about her coat, the front of which was plastered with greyish-white mud from her fall. For myself, I was feeling a sense of melancholy and deflation that usually came at the end of my own night walks; and moreover I was conscious, as I so often was when I had been alone with Leonie, of a sense of frustration and lost opportunity.

When we reached the house Leonie went off to sponge her coat, and when she came back said that she was going to bed. I gave her the usual chaste good night kiss, and then, with my arms still round her said, "Why did you kiss me like that?"

"When? Like what?"

"Out there—when you were seeing that Remus would be all right. With your tongue."

Leonie said, "Oh… that was a mistake." She suddenly looked up at me with the cheeky grin, and said, "Why? Didn't you like it?"

"I'm not quite sure," I said frankly. "It was a rather odd feeling. But why did you do it, anyhow? You never have before."

"I don't know," said Leonie. "It must have been force of habit. I was forgetting who you were."

"You mean you often do that when you kiss people?"

Leonie closed her eyes and put a hand to her forehead. "Oh God, Walter… how, when, why, where…? I never knew anyone like you. Surely you know that people who… who are fond of one another *do* kiss like that? Or perhaps you don't. I keep forgetting that…"

"Of course I know," I said quickly and, surprising as it may seem, quite untruthfully. "I only wondered…"

"Then stop wondering and go to bed," said Leonie briskly. She gave me a sharp jab on the solar plexus and went upstairs.

As I lay in bed, I reflected glumly that it was always the same with Leonie. Strange, exciting things would suddenly dance into sight, and then as quickly vanish before one's slow hands could grasp them. She had asked me if I liked being kissed like that. I had said I did not know, and it had been true at the time. But it was not true now. I lay and thought of that strange, bland, secret contact which had made me start back in surprise; and now I groaned and writhed with my longing for it. She had said that she had meant to dance naked in the churchyard, and groping back to that ineffable moment when we bounded down the hill in the wind, there seemed nothing surprising nor improbable in the idea. Yet I had let that moment escape me, and now Leonie in her old skimpy cotton frock seemed as completely clothed—as utterly inaccessible—as though she had been wearing a suit of armour.

I drifted off at last into a dream in which Leonie and I were floating hand in hand in a wind which buffeted us like a rough sea, and I was trying to call "Cyril, Cyril!" but could not, because the wind blew my cries away before I could hear them.

Seven

Apart from the tradesmen, very few people ever seemed to come to Glebe Cottage. The main road was only a couple of hundred yards away, but it was hidden from us, and the lane which led to the cottage led nowhere else. It was possible to stay there for days together without seeing anyone but my uncle, Leonie, the old man who came and worked silently in the orchard, the postman, the milkman and the baker. The fact that nobody ever came to call, or for a drink or a meal, was presumably the result of Leonie's unorthodox social position, but this never occurred to me at the time. After all, my mother and father were as respectably married as two people could well be, yet nobody ever came to call on us either. To me, social isolation was the natural state.

When Leonie went to Canterbury, however, which she did at least twice or three times a week, she occasionally met an acquaintance, particularly in the coffee shop where we used to go when we had finished shopping. Thus, one day one of the youngish men who had nodded to her at Colonel Masters's party paused at our table and chatted quite amiably and a trifle roguishly with Leonie.

Then there was Mrs. Simms, who, on a couple of occasions,

positively came and sat at our table and had coffee with us. I did not care much for Mrs. Simms, who was a big, strapping woman of about forty, with artificially blonde hair and too much make-up. She called me by my Christian name at our first meeting, referred to me in conversation with Leonie as "my lord here", and ate cream buns with a knife and fork, all of which were things of which I disapproved.

But the worst thing about Mrs. Simms was her archness, and her apparent feeling that I must, and should, have an insatiable interest in girls; and that, during the holidays at least, I must naturally spend all my time taking them to dances or to the pictures. This I found both boring and embarrassing. Luckily, Leonie and Mrs. Simms were usually too busy talking about clothes, and the virtues and vices of their respective dressmakers, to worry much about me. I fancy that Leonie exaggerated a good deal on these occasions, for as far as I know she never went to a dressmaker during the period that I was at Glebe Cottage; nor, with the exception of the frock in which she had gone to Colonel Masters's party, did she ever wear anything but trousers or cheap old cotton frocks.

My general feeling was that Mrs. Simms was not a worthy friend for Leonie, and tended to bring out the worst in her. I was therefore not very pleased when, returning one day from a walk, I found that Mrs. Simms had come to tea. Worse, she had brought her daughter, a thin dark girl of about seventeen with a bad skin and a discontented expression, whose name was Veronica.

I was introduced, and Veronica said "Hallo" in a sort of grunt, gave my hand the briefest of shakes, and then let go of it with a jerk as if she was trying to throw it away. She turned to her mother and said, "What did you say his name was?"

"Walter Parrish," said her mother. "Mr. and Mrs. Parrish's nephew."

Veronica shot a sardonic sidelong glance first at her mother and then at Leonie, and grinned rather unpleasantly. I realised at once that she knew that Leonie was not married to my Uncle Patrick, that Leonie was therefore not Mrs. Parrish, and that I therefore was not her nephew. I decided that I disliked Veronica intensely.

"You're about the same age," said Mrs. Simms, as though that was to form a bond between us. "And what a wonderful age to be!"

"How old is he then?" said Veronica.

I said, "I'm fifteen."

"Well, I'm seventeen, so we *aren't* the same age, are we?" said Veronica sarcastically to her mother, ignoring me.

"I said you were *about* the same age, darling."

"Well, seventeen and fifteen *aren't* about the same age, so it's just a silly thing to say," said Veronica contemptuously.

"Yes, darling, mother was being silly as usual," said Mrs. Simms lovingly. "Anyhow, Walter's old for his age, aren't you, Walter?" She contrived to get into the phrase an unbelievable amount of roguish insinuation. Veronica gave a slight snort of contempt.

Tea was a miserable affair. My uncle was out, and instead of sitting at the dining-table as we usually did, eating sensible chunks of bread and butter and jam, and one of Leonie's excellent home-made cakes, we sat round a low table which was really too small for the purpose and ate thinly cut sandwiches and little cakes which had been bought in Canterbury. Mrs. Simms and Leonie talked about their dressmakers, and Leonie told her usual tall stories about clothes that she was having made. Veronica occasionally contradicted her mother brusquely and contemptuously, and for the rest of the time ate largely, occasionally taking a piece of sandwich or bun away from her mouth and looking at it with a frown as though she had found a beetle in it. She never looked at or spoke to me, and for my own part I simply kept quiet.

Even Veronica had at last finished eating, and I was reflecting with relief that they must go soon, when to my horror

Mrs. Simms suddenly said, "Why don't you take Veronica and show her around the orchards, Walter? She's never been here before."

I instinctively glanced at Leonie, hoping for aid in this ghastly crisis. But she only smiled at me and said, "Yes—go on, Walter. And there are still some decent plums down in Half Acre, if Veronica likes plums."

I was left with no alternative. I said to Veronica, "Would you care to come and look at the orchards?"

Veronica looked angrily at her mother and said, "Oh *mother*…!" threw down her napkin and stalked out into the garden, leaving me to follow her.

As we walked away together I said, "There's no need to go round the orchards really, if you don't want to," and with difficulty restrained myself from adding, "*I* certainly don't want to go round them with you."

Veronica shrugged and said, "What else is there to do?"

I said, "We can just go and sit on a big log that's down the bottom there. It's rather a nice place."

"*Oh* no, *oh* no!" said Veronica with an emphasis that startled me. "We'll just keep walking, *thank* you."

I was puzzled by her tone, but accordingly I took her down through the orchards, airily, if inaccurately, naming the species of the fruit. Yet to my surprise when we reached the bottom of the first orchard Veronica suddenly said, "Is that your log over there?" I said it was, whereupon she said, "All right—then let's go and sit on it if you want to." She said it with the air of one who is yielding to extreme pressure—an air of slightly contemptuous resignation.

We went over to the log and Veronica promptly sat down astride it, so that her frock pulled up and displayed her thighs and the bottom of the legs of her knickers. She looked at me with her eyes half-closed and a slight, rather sardonic smile, and said, "So you're old for your age, eh?"

I said, "In some ways, but not in others."

"And which are the ones you're old in?" said Veronica, still looking at me through her lashes, which, combined with the smile, her bad skin, and the display of knicker, produced a combined effect of almost indescribable horror. I looked hastily away and said coldly, "Physically, I am rather highly developed. Mentally, I vary from…"

"Never mind about that," said Veronica. "If you've got the necessary, you'll do." She straddled her way a few inches nearer to me on the log and leant forward, at the same time saying in a half-whisper, "You're not bad looking. I don't mind telling you that it's not every kid that could get me to come and sit down like this with him, just for the asking."

I realised with cold, sick horror that Veronica now expected me to do things to her—to touch her—put my arm round her—perhaps even kiss her. I remembered for an instant the touch of Leonie's tongue against mine, and wondered if this awful person expected to be kissed "like that".

I think Veronica must have seen something of my feelings in my face, for she drew back a trifle and said irritably, "Well, come on—what did we come here for anyway? To talk about the weather?"

I said as icily as I could, "We came out because your mother suggested it. We came here because you seemed to want to."

She drew back further and said, "I'll bet you never kissed a girl in your life. Or…"

I said, "I don't kiss people unless I want to."

Veronica said, "You bastard!" and suddenly, bursting into tears, scrambled off the log and ran at full speed towards the house.

I instinctively got up to follow her; but then I realised that somehow I could not face any more of Veronica and Mrs. Simms until I had got rid of an overwhelming desire to be sick. I therefore sat down again on the log and waited to see if I was really going to be sick or not. At the end of about ten minutes I knew that I was not, but by that time it was difficult to see what to do. Veronica would have gone back to the house and given some explanation of why I had not come back too, and I did not know what she would have said, or how I should now be expected to behave. On the whole it seemed wisest to stay where I was and await developments.

A quarter of an hour later Leonie came down the orchard. I got up, but Leonie just said, "It's all right. They've gone," and sat down on the log, smiling at me rather wryly. I sat down too. Leonie said, "Look, Walter—what happened with Veronica?"

"What did *she* say happened?" I said cautiously, unwilling to sneak, even on Veronica.

"Well, she came back terribly fussed, and said that you… you had tried to mess about with her."

This was too much. I said, "That *I'd* tried to? Why…"

"Did you?"

"Of course not. I think she's awful. She makes me feel sick."

"I thought it didn't seem very like you. You didn't even kiss her or anything?"

"Of course I didn't. She kept edging up close to me and… and so on. Then she said she'd bet that I'd never kissed a girl, and I said I only kissed people when I wanted to."

Leonie looked at me for a moment in silence, and I suddenly realised, with a shock of surprise, that she was making up her mind whether I was telling the truth.

She said, "Well, whatever happened, it doesn't matter. Mildred Simms was very sensible about it, and just told her not to make such a fuss, and took her away. I should think this sort of thing has happened before. You must always remember, Walter, that some girls—and women too, for that matter—like to try to get men to make passes at them, and then to kick up a tremendous fuss about it. Let's just forget the whole thing."

I found this extremely irritating. To me, "let's forget the whole thing" meant that one was being graciously pardoned for some misdeed; and I was in no mood to be pardoned about Veronica.

I said, "But don't you understand—I didn't do anything to her—not anything at all. I never even touched her."

"Of course you didn't," said Leonie soothingly. "But the point is that if you had it wouldn't have been anything to feel guilty about or…"

"I'm *not* feeling guilty," I almost shouted. "I didn't do anything to her or say anything to her like that, and if she says I did, she's a dirty little liar."

Leonie looked at me for a moment in silence and this time I could see that she believed me. Oddly enough, there was a trace of disappointment in her face as she said quietly, "All right then, Walter. Tell me exactly what *did* happen."

I told her. She listened carefully, asking me, I thought, an almost unnecessary number of questions about exactly how Veronica sat on the log and exactly what words she had used. I found this unpleasant. At the end Leonie said, "And you never even *wanted* to touch her or—or anything? I mean—she can't have *thought* you wanted to?"

"I've told you I didn't want to. I thought she was awful. If she believed I wanted anything to do with her she must be mad."

"I don't know," said Leonie, "plenty of other boys seem to have made passes at her, according to her mother. That's why I thought at first possibly you had." She gave me a quick smile and added, "Boys of your age aren't always as nice as you, Walter."

We were sitting close together on the log, and her face was close to mine, and smiling at me. I suddenly had a wild desire that she should be sitting straddling the log, with her thighs and underclothes showing, and her head and body thrust forward towards me, and her voice speaking in a half-whisper.

I swallowed hard and said, "I don't know that I'm as nice as all that. If it had been somebody I liked, it would have been different. But she looks as though she doesn't wash."

Leonie laughed and said, "I see exactly what you mean."

She put a hand on mine and gave it a squeeze and then got up quickly. As we were walking back to the house she said, "Look, I think I'd better tell your uncle about this, in case it gets back to him through Mildred Simms. There's no need to worry. He'll understand. He's good at understanding things."

Except for the silent old man, who did not seem to come every day, my Uncle Patrick and Leonie looked after the orchards themselves. I believe they usually sold the fruit on the trees instead of picking it, but even so there was a good deal of work to be done—more, perhaps, than my uncle should have attempted.

Often I used to go and help him. It was a pathetic business. If we ever did anything which involved strength, like sawing a branch off a tree, he would always insist on trying to do it himself, and in ten minutes he would be panting and bathed in sweat, and would have to sit down to recover his breath, whilst I went on with the job under his directions. It was the following day after our tea party, when we had cut off a branch and I was sawing it into logs, that I heard the last of the Veronica affair.

Uncle Patrick suddenly said, "I hear you had a sort of Potiphar's wife business[1] yesterday with the Simms girl."

It took me a moment to remember who Potiphar's wife was. Then I said "Yes" briefly. Once I knew that Leonie had believed me, I was anxious to forget Veronica.

My uncle said, "I knew a man once, years ago, who was always terrified that something like that would happen to him. He used to warn me never to travel in a railway train alone with a woman passenger, in case she should suddenly pull the communication cord and complain to the guard that I'd tried to rape her."

"Why should she?" I said, puzzled.

"Why indeed? But then why should Veronica Simms have done that to you yesterday?"

"I think she was hairy[2] because I wouldn't kiss her, and just wanted to get me into a row."

"Hell hath no fury like a woman scorned,"[3] said my uncle with a smile. I was fond of my Uncle Patrick in a way, and forgave him the misquotation without difficulty.

My uncle took a pinch of the special snuff that was supposed to be good for him and said, "My father never talked to us about any of these things—about women or sex or anything like that. Does your father to you?"

"No."

"I don't suppose he knows quite what to say," said my uncle with a shake of the head. "I know I shouldn't, if I had any children."

There seemed to me to be a faint note of apology in his voice. I said gruffly, "You can always read about it in books, anyhow."

"That's right," said Uncle Patrick with some relief. "Only I think Leonie rather wanted me to talk to you about this business of the Simms girl. She was afraid you'd be upset. But you're not, are you?"

"Not at all," I said. I certainly had no desire for a hesitant and probably inaccurate lecture on the facts of life from my Uncle Patrick. But inwardly I was irritated that Leonie should have thought it necessary. After all, I was not twelve; and you don't kiss people like that, or say you'll dance naked round tombstones with them, if you think they don't know these things.

But though a talk from Uncle Patrick about the facts of life may not have been what I needed, it became sadly obvious that I needed *something*. Whether because of the impact of Miss Simms or not, I do not know, but during the next few days my passion for Leonie increased until it became an all-pervading, throbbing ache which no medicine would calm. I walked until I could hardly drag my heavy legs after me. I worked in the orchard until my hands were blistered and my shirt wet through with sweat. I wrote a large amount of verse. For me, writing verse was purely a thing for autumn, when the winds and the falling leaves always brought into my mind suitably melancholy reflections. Now it was still high summer, and strictly speaking, the verse season was not yet open. Nevertheless, I wrote verse in my best Elizabethan pastiche style; and naturally I added to my poem about the witches a verse describing how a very beautiful young witch had danced naked. None of these things cured the intolerable ache, and some of them merely increased it.

Almost as bad as the ache itself was my realisation of its entirely earthy quality. I was used to being an occasional battleground between Good and Evil. I had been one in the matter of Clynes, and had rather enjoyed it, secure in the certainty that my real feelings were pure and exalted. In my first few days at Glebe Cottage, when thinking about Leonie, I had allowed myself a short daily period during which my imagination could run wild, like a dog taken for a scamper in Regent's Park. But having had its scamper, my imagination should, in theory, have been put on the lead of righteousness again, so that for the remainder of the twenty-four hours I was Leonie's very perfect gentle knight. Yet now, alas, what I had suspected when I prayed for her in the church was confirmed. There was no battle here between Good and Evil, since Good simply had no troops in the field. Even to a practised and widely experienced self-deceiver like myself, the very-perfect-gentle-knight business would no longer bear examination. The dog of my imagination had run away and was rushing wildly round the park, and I was quite unable to catch it.

The obsession (for it was nothing less than an obsession) took many strange and varied forms, but the nub of it was perfectly simple. I wanted to see Leonie naked. There was no need for her to dance round tombstones—in fact any quick movement would have been deplorable. All I wanted was for her to be standing naked, quite still, so that I could look at her, and perhaps walk round her and look at her from different angles, as one might at a statue.

I thought of various ingenious schemes by which I might get this thing which had become so necessary to me. I thought of announcing that I was passionately fond of sketching, and then, after a couple of days to establish my right to be regarded as an artist, casually asking Leonie if she would sit for me in the nude. Again, I might take her for a walk, and having found a quiet stream, make some poetic statement about the need for close communion with nature, cast off my clothes, and leap into the water in the hope that she would follow. I knew that Leonie was inclined to take me seriously as some sort of poet or artist; and both these schemes—posing in the nude or poetic bathing—she might accept as mere expressions of the artistic temperament.

In the end, however, there was no need to bring art into it, for the bathroom at Glebe Cottage was on the ground floor. Once I had remembered this, the rest was comparatively easy. The bathroom curtains, like everything else at the cottage, were old and skimpy, and would only cover the window properly if drawn with great care and pinned together. Leonie was not by nature a taker of great care or a pinner together of curtains; and anyhow the window only looked on a hedge of nut bushes. The whole arrangement might have been designed for my purpose.

One night Leonie, as she had often done before, broke off our evening talk rather early, and announced that she was going to have a bath. She said, "Are you going to read, Walter, or are you going to bed?"

I yawned carefully and said I thought I would go to bed. I could feel my legs trembling with excitement as I gave her the usual good night kiss.

Leonie went out, and a few moments later I heard the water running in the bathroom and the distant clanking of the automatic pump, which always sprang into furious action when one turned on a tap. I gave it ten minutes by my watch, and then put out the lights in the living-room and went out into the garden.

There was still a light in my uncle's bedroom, and I guessed that he was reading. In order to get to the bathroom window it was necessary to go right round the house, and there was a gravel path which scrunched horribly under my feet. I made a long hopping jump, and landed safely on the more silent grass.

Everything was as I had hoped and expected. Leonie had pulled the curtains, but there was still a gap of at least three inches, through which a shaft of light from the bathroom fell on the nut bushes. To my dismay, however, I found that the nut bushes were some six feet from the window, and that the window was rather high, so that from the cover of the bushes all I could see was a strip of the wall opposite the window. There was nothing for it but to leave cover and move closer, being careful to be quite silent and not to get in the ray of light from the window. This I did with great care, urged on by occasional faint sounds of splashing from the bathroom. Then I cautiously raised my head and, with every limb trembling, looked into the room.

About eight feet away from me Leonie was sitting in her bath. She had her hair bound up in a green silk handkerchief, and at that moment she was, I think, washing her feet. The side of the bath hid most of her body from me, but her bare shoulders and breasts were gloriously visible. They alone were enough to give me a curious, giddy sensation, so that for a moment I had to close my eyes. But even as I opened them again Leonie gave a final splash and rose to her feet. Stooping, she flicked over the waste tap of the bath, picked up a towel, rubbed it vaguely across her shoulders and back for a few moments and then, stepping out of the bath, stood directly facing me, towelling herself vigorously and giving odd little puffs which made her lips pout as she did so.

I had never seen a living naked woman before, but I had seen plenty of marble ones, and there was nothing startling or new to me in the mere facts of female anatomy. I am not quite sure whether I knew that living women, as opposed to marble ones, had pubic hair. If I did not, the discovery certainly did not surprise me. Indeed, nothing about Leonie's body surprised me except perhaps the extreme fairness of her skin, and if I remember her now as having been exceptionally beautifully made, it was not because of anything I noticed on this occasion.

For the truth is that the moment Leonie stepped from her bath and stood there drying herself and making little puffing noises, and innocently showing herself to me, the hot, throbbing, purely sensual ache which had plagued me for days was replaced, or perhaps supplemented, by something quite different. It was not that I was disappointed or uninterested; or that I found myself considering Leonie in terms of sheer beauty of line and plane. When she lifted her hands to untie the scarf about her hair, and the movement raised her breasts —when she bent slightly to toss the towel carelessly away, so that thigh and buttock, which had been contiguous but different curves, moved smoothly into one for a moment— when she turned to the mirror so that she was standing sideways to me, and I could see the wonderful balance of head, breasts and hips, running down to those long, beautifully-modelled legs which had caused me so much pain —I was almost beside myself with purely sensual pleasure. But over and above this there was a feeling which, if possible, was even stronger—a feeling of a close intimacy, and of sharing, even though uninvited, in something essentially personal and secret.

Leonie had stopped making her curious little puffing noises now, and was examining herself with great care in the mirror. Suddenly she smiled at her reflection, and her lips moved as though she was speaking. Then the smile vanished, and she stood with her head slightly on one side as though listening carefully. Meanwhile, an expression of some surprise and concern spread over her face. She appeared to ask a question, and the answer must have been amusing, for she threw back her head and laughed, at the same time passing a hand over her hair in one of her favourite gestures.

Suddenly she stopped laughing, and moving so that her face was close to the mirror, minutely examined a place on her upper lip. Apparently satisfied, she moved back again and seemed to speak again, this time curtly and apparently angrily, for her eyes narrowed and her mouth seemed to grow smaller, as I had seen it do when she was in a bad temper.

This quarrel which she was having with somebody went on for perhaps a minute. Then she suddenly seemed to grow tired of it and picked up a hairbrush. She turned back to the mirror and for a few seconds stood with her hands, one of them still holding the hairbrush, extended imploringly towards it, with her head thrown back, her lips parted, and her whole face full of passionate longing. Then she raised her eyebrows, gave a little shrug, and began to brush her thick hair vigorously, whistling between her teeth in time to the strokes of the brush.

All these strange little posturings and rehearsals gave me exquisite pleasure in their intimacy, their privacy, and their utter unconsciousness of being observed. It was as though I was being allowed to see Leonie, not only physically naked, but mentally naked as well. Years later, during the war, I had an office in London which was on the ground floor, next to the street. My window was half-concealed by sandbags and barbed wire and I sat close to it, so that the people passing on the pavement outside were often within three or four feet of me, though they felt themselves to be completely alone and unobserved. I remember that it was difficult to get any work done, because of the fascination of those faces, seen at close range, unconscious of the watcher, and strangely defenceless.

I think it was this same defencelessness which deeply affected me as I watched Leonie. Like many women, she looked much smaller without her clothes and without shoes to give her additional height; and somehow the fair skin, and the soft curves of the breasts and thighs gave an impression of frailty—of being something desperately easy to damage—which sent through me a great shudder, not of lust, but of protectiveness. I knew that if I stayed any longer I should burst into tears, and I turned and stole silently away from the window into the darkness of the garden, a Peeping Tom[4] experiencing many of the emotions of a Sir Galahad.[5]

Eight

The following morning I had a letter from my mother from London. She seemed to be having an excellent time, full of theatre-going and parties. It was characteristic of her that though she had little time to think about me when we were at home, where she had her own problems and frustrations to occupy her, now that she was away and happy she should begin to worry about whether I was enjoying myself. She even suggested that I might come to London for a day or two.

I had, however, only one desire, and that was to be with Leonie. Already the time left to me at Glebe Cottage before term began to seem heartbreakingly short, and I had no desire to shorten it further, even for the golden prospect of going to London.

I think my Uncle Patrick and Leonie were touched and flattered when I said that I would prefer to stay on at Glebe Cottage. My uncle, in particular, was worried about whether it was dull for me—which, in other circumstances, it certainly would have been. It was probably because of this that he suggested that Leonie and I should go to the fair at Peterham.[1]

Peterham is too big for a village and too small for a town, and charmingly built round a large village green. It is on the

green that the annual fair was, and probably still is, held towards
the end of August.

I have a lifelong dislike of fairs, which I find at once
fascinating and frightening. I am told that I was taken to one
when I was only about three years old by somebody who, with
the kindest intentions, took me on the roundabouts and the
switchback, and in a swingboat, so that I had to be taken home
almost hysterical with fright. Nowadays nobody is likely to make
me go on a switchback or in a swingboat against my will; but
nevertheless to this day I have only to hear the sound of a steam-
organ, or any of the characteristic noises of an old-fashioned
fair, to be seized by a ridiculous feeling that I am now going to
be forced, or at least expected, to do something frightening.

Obviously I could not tell Leonie how I felt about fairs,
partly because it was childish, and partly because if I had done
so she might have said that we would not go, and I should have
lost the chance of an expedition alone with her. I expressed great
delight at the idea of going to the fair, and at about seven o'clock
in the evening Leonie and I set off, leaving Remus, obviously
hurt and indignant, with my uncle.

As we approached Peterham, and could hear the sound of
the steam-organs, I experienced the usual sinking feeling in my
stomach, and I was surprised and relieved when, instead of
driving straight to the green, Leonie stopped the Morris at a
small hotel and said, "The one thing you must always do when
you're going to a fair is to have a drink first. Anyhow, we'd better
leave the car here. There'll be a hell of a jam farther down."

We went into the pleasant little bar of the hotel. It contained
about twenty men, but only a couple of women. The estate
agent, Edwards, was standing at the bar, and he greeted Leonie
with his usual rather unpleasant gallantry. We passed him by and
went and sat in a corner by ourselves. I still had practically all of
my original thirty-two-and-sixpence, and it gave me rare
pleasure to ask Leonie casually what she would like to drink. To
my surprise she chose a pink gin.

I said, "I thought you didn't like pink gin."

Leonie said, "I don't. Nobody could. But I dislike it less than most drinks."

"You made a fuss when Colonel Masters made you drink one."

"I don't like anything that Masters gives me. I don't like being bullied."

I said, "I hate that man. I hate the way he talks to you."

"Do you?" said Leonie, turning and looking at me with a pleased little smile. "Do you really hate him, Walter?"

"Yes."

"How absolutely splendid!" said Leonie. "I'm so glad. Because he's a brute, that man. You only have to look at his face to see what he is. And I hate him because of this business about Remus." She gave a worried little frown and added, "I do hope Patrick remembers to keep Remus in. I forgot to remind him."

I said, "But Remus never *does* go off by himself, does he?"

"Of course not," said Leonie quickly. "But I just don't want to take any chances."

Edwards passed on his way to the door. He waved a hand at Leonie and said, "See you on the roundabouts."

Leonie said, "Now that's another nasty bit of work, but in a different way. If you ever had any trouble with *him*, you could just slap his face and he'd burst into tears. But Masters is such a great ox."

We sipped our drinks—Leonie her pink gin and I my sherry —and Leonie said with a giggle, "I wonder what your mother would say if she could see you sitting in a pub drinking with me?"

"I don't know," I said, though in fact I had a very fair idea.

"She doesn't approve of me, does she?" Leonie shrugged. "Well—I suppose she hardly would. Not many people do, if it comes to that."

I said, "*I* approve of you."

"Do you?" said Leonie, suddenly turning to me and speaking very seriously.

I said, "Yes, I think you're the loveliest person I've ever seen —and the nicest." I had never said anything like that to Leonie before, but now it came entirely easily.

Leonie gave me a quick smile and a quick pat on the hand and said, "Darling Walter. We'd hold hands if we weren't in a pub." She finished her drink and said, "Now I'll have one more drink, for which I will pay, and then we'll go to the fair. You'd better not have another, had you?"

"Why ever not?" I said offhandedly, and ordered two more drinks. Leonie looked a trifle doubtful, but said nothing.

The sherry was dark, sweet, heavy stuff, and it was served in glasses of generous size. By the time I had finished my second one I was finding it a great deal easier than usual to talk to Leonie. I remember that I drew a parallel between the appearance and taste of the sherry and somebody's poetry—I cannot now remember whose. The parallel seemed extremely clever at the time, and Leonie was duly impressed.

I also confided to Leonie my real feelings about fairs, and was much relieved to find that she, too, hated swingboats and switchbacks, though she confessed to a weakness for roundabouts.

"But anyhow," she said, "you're in charge, Walter, and I'll just go on the things you take me on. That's what must be so nice about being a man."

I said,

> *"And to conclude, I know myself a man,*
> *Which is a proud and yet a wretched thing,"*[2]

and then had to explain who wrote that, and what he meant. Leonie waited a few moments after I had finished explaining, to make it clear that I had not been boring her, and then said,

"Come on—let's go to the fair." As we rose I realised that my head was swimming slightly.

Peterham Fair is well-known, and it was probably fairly big; but that evening it seemed to me to be about the size of Coney Island.[3] As a concession to my dislike of "going on things" we wandered round for a while looking at the sideshows. I knocked down a coconut with my very first ball and we made the man break it open, but the flesh tasted dry and slightly rancid, so we threw it away. Leonie won a china ornament at Hoop-la, but we put that down somewhere and lost it. We fired rifles at ping-pong balls dancing on jets of water, and I was surprised and faintly annoyed to find that Leonie was a better shot than I. Once she turned to me as she was about to fire and said, "Practising for shooting Masters."

I said, "But he isn't a bit like a ping-pong ball," and we both laughed a great deal.

In fact we laughed a great deal throughout the evening, the climax coming when we arrived outside the fat lady's tent and heard a big man wearing a bowler hat shouting through a megaphone, "Over thirty stone of her. Nine inches above the knee guaranteed, and no vulgarity." He pronounced it "vulgaritee" and for some reason the phrase convulsed us with laughter. Indeed, from that time on, throughout my acquaintance with Leonie, if we were in a certain mood one of us was sure to say "nine inches above the knee guaranteed and no vulgaritee", and we would both fall into helpless giggles.

After about an hour of this Leonie announced that she was hungry and that we must have something to eat, and we went and bought some fish and chips and ate it with our fingers out of newspaper. I have never understood why some smart and expensive restaurant has not made a speciality out of fish and chips wrapped in newspaper. It has one of the most characteristic and delicious tastes in the world. I explained solemnly to Leonie that this flavour came from the printer's ink, and that really skilled fish-and-chip eaters could detect the difference between *The Times* flavour and the *Daily Express* flavour.

As we were finishing our fish and chips we came on a spiral slide[4] down which people were sliding on mats, with much squeaking and display of legs from the girls. I tried hard to get Leonie to go on the slide, but she absolutely refused, saying she was too old for that sort of thing.

I said, "But think how nice it would be for me. You mustn't be *selfish*," and smiled at her suggestively. Sir Galahad was off duty that evening. It must have been the effects of the sherry.

I was rather damped when Leonie replied, "Walter, darling, don't *leer* at me when you say things like that. It reminds me of Edwards. Look, I want to go on the roundabouts. You needn't come if you don't want to."

I said stiffly, "Of course I shall come." I was hurt at being compared with Edwards.

The roundabouts were not frightening, but the combination of noise, the up and down movement, and the circling was not what I really needed after the sherry and the fish and chips. Leonie obviously enjoyed herself immensely, and even carried on a certain amount of giggling chatter with two men on the horses immediately behind her. When, after three full "goes" Leonie rather reluctantly agreed to get off, I was in a bad temper.

I said, "If you're going to make such a fuss about anybody seeing your legs, you oughtn't to go on roundabouts."

To my surprise she said, "I'm sorry" meekly, and taking my arm looked up at me penitently, so that I was completely melted. Then she suddenly giggled and said, "Nine inches above the knee guaranteed, and no vulgaritee. Come on—let's try over the other side."

By this time I was beginning to feel tired, and moreover there were indications that the sherry and fish and chips and the roundabouts were forming some sort of an alliance against me. I think Leonie sensed this, because, quite suddenly, she looked at me keenly and said, "I'm getting rather tired. Don't you think we'd better go home soon, Walter?"

I said, "Just as you like. Stay if you'd like to."

But she shook her head and said firmly, "No—I think I've had enough. Let's go home," and to my great relief led me out of the fairground and towards where we had left the car.

She squeezed my arm gently and smiled up at me and said, "You must always take girls home when they start feeling tired. They get tired quicker than you do."

I knew perfectly well that she could have gone on at the fair for hours.

It had seemed a good idea to leave the car at the hotel, but in the event it was not. The bar was just closing, and half a dozen young men, with Edwards amongst them, were standing on the steps talking loudly. I think they were all a little drunk, and Leonie's appearance was hailed with loud cries of welcome.

Edwards entreated her to come in and have a last drink, and when she curtly refused, they said they would come down and see us safely out of the gates.

I noticed that they stood round the back of the car, and when Leonie started the engine they called loud good nights. But when she let the clutch in the car did not move, though the engine raced furiously.

Leonie knew at once what was happening.

She said out of the corner of her mouth, "Silly bastards. They're lifting the back wheels."

Meanwhile, there were roars of laughter, and shouted questions as to what we were waiting for. Edwards came up beside us and said with a grin, "I think you've burnt your clutch out, Leonie. You'd better let me take you home."

Leonie took no notice and tried again, but they were too quick for her, and again the four at the back of the car lifted its back wheels slightly, so that we could not move. Again there were roars of laughter, and suggestions that Leonie should let one of them drive her home.

It seemed as though the joke would go on indefinitely, and I was just deciding desperately that the only thing to do was to get out of the car and hit one of them when Leonie leant out of the window and called, "Come here, all of you—I've got something funny to tell you—something that happened to me this evening."

The simple drunks immediately left their places at the back of the car and clustered round the driver's window, whereupon Leonie let in the clutch with such suddenness that we nearly rammed the gate posts, and turned into the main road pursued by cries of disappointment.

Leonie said, "Sorry, Walter. I might have known that bunch would be there."

I said "Yes" vaguely; for in truth I hardly heard what she said, finding myself confronted by a major problem. I was very tired, I had a headache, and I felt slightly sick. The one thing in the world I wanted was to be in bed. Yet I realised that here again was one of those opportunities which one should not miss. I was not, perhaps, exactly taking Leonie home. But at least we were going home together in a car in the dark, and despite my headache I felt much more in charge of the situation than usual.

The air blowing through the draughty old car helped my headache, and just before we reached the turning into our own lane I managed to pluck up the courage to say, "Don't let's go home yet, Leonie. Stop for a moment."

She said, "What for? D'you want to go to the loo or something? Because we shall be home in a couple of minutes." But at the same time she slowed down to a walking-pace.

I said, "I just want to stop for a moment."

Leonie seemed to hesitate and then she said, "Oh—all right," and pulled into the side of the road and stopped.

I saw the almost ghostly glimmer of her face as she turned to me and said, "What do you want to stop for?"

I put my arm round her shoulders and said, "I want to kiss you."

She hesitated and then said, "It's a long time since I was kissed in a car…" She turned and kissed me quickly, exactly as she used to kiss me night and morning.

But I said, "No—not like that. Like this," and pulling her face tight against mine kissed her hard on the mouth, and forced my tongue between her lips. I think she was surprised, but she did not resist, and let my tongue have its way. Then as I paused for breath, she said dryly, but entirely kindly, "Well—will that do?"

I wanted desperately to say that it would *not* do—that I had hardly begun. I wanted to press home to the full what was obviously a strong tactical situation. But unfortunately at that moment I realised that I was going to be sick. I had just time to tear open the door of the car and almost fall out into the ditch when it happened. It was all very quick, painless and comprehensive, and then I was standing panting and wiping my lips with my handkerchief, and Leonie was beside me saying, "Poor Walter—you're the first man who has actually thrown up because he kissed me."

I panted out some apology, but she just smoothed my hair back from my forehead, and said, "That better? Sit down on the bank for a moment. It's that damned sherry. I knew I oughtn't to let you have the second one. I don't look after you properly. In fact I don't look after you at all—in any way. I just don't remember about you."

She said it with a curious note of bitter sincerity, and I realised that she was not apologising for having let me drink the second sherry, but for having let me kiss her. This was almost more than I could bear, and I started to stammer out something —about having wanted to kiss her for days—about the fact that I loved her—about how much that kiss had meant to me. But she cut me short and said firmly, "Come on—home. You've had enough for one evening," and there was nothing to do but to climb miserably into the car and let myself be driven home, like a small boy who has been sick after eating too much at a tea party. I felt as Melas must have felt after Marengo.[5] The hard-won cup of victory had been capriciously dashed from my lips, leaving nothing but disaster, and the bitter taste of vomit in my mouth.

Nine

We went to bed as soon as we reached home. As was usual with me, the mere act of being sick had relieved me of all my symptoms, and my headache had gone. But I was too tired even to worry about the disappointing end to the evening, and I went to sleep at once.

I do not know how long I slept, but it cannot have been for very long; and then suddenly I found myself broad awake again, and listening intently for some sound that had wakened me. I listened for some moments in the almost palpable silence of the house, and then I heard the sound. It was a curious whistle of two alternating notes, and it seemed to be coming from the orchard. I thought at first that it was some night bird. But the sound was strangely familiar; and then I remembered that it was a whistle that I had heard Leonie use to call Remus.

I went to the window and looked out. The moon was only just rising, and amongst the trees in the orchard it was very dark. I could see nothing unusual, but as I stood at the window I heard the whistle again, this time farther away. I suddenly half-understood quite a number of things which had previously puzzled me, and hustling on my clothes I went downstairs and out into the garden.

I paused and listened, but the whistling had stopped, so I went quickly and as quietly as I could towards the bottom of the orchard, from which it had seemed to come. I say "as quietly as I could" because in that utter silence the very sound of my breathing seemed loud, and once when I trod on a dry twig it snapped with a noise that seemed almost an explosion.

I reached the bottom of the orchard having heard nothing and seen nothing but the black shapes of the trees against the sky and the glimmer of the leaves where, in places, the light of the rising moon touched them. At the end of the orchard two gates led out, one to the left and the other to the right, into the flanking orchards; whilst immediately ahead was the high barbed-wire fence which separated our land from one of Colonel Masters's fields.

I hesitated, uncertain whether to go to the right or left. As I did so I heard the characteristic whistle again, now almost startlingly close at hand to my right; and then I realised that Leonie was standing some twenty yards away from me, close to the wire, her figure silhouetted against the brightening sky, but otherwise almost invisible in the moonlight in an old khaki coloured mackintosh. She had her back half-turned to me, and she seemed to be staring out intently through the wire.

I called "Leonie!" in a low voice and went towards her. She whipped round sharply, and I saw for a moment that her face was frightened and strangely guilty, as though I had caught her in some crime.

I went closer and said, "Leonie—what is it? What's happening?"

She stared at me almost wildly for a moment, and then suddenly she buried her face in her hands and her whole body seemed to shake with a terrible dry sobbing.

I put my arm round her and said again, "What is it? Is it Remus?" She nodded silently, without raising her face from her hands. "Has he gone off somewhere?"

Her voice was muffled and incoherent. She said, "That

damn fool Patrick. He left a window open downstairs. Of course Remus can get out of any window. It's my fault—going off and leaving him like that. That's when it always happens. He can't bear it when I go away and leave him, and then…" She trailed away into silence.

I said comfortingly, "Never mind—he'll come back."

"Come back?" said Leonie bitterly. "Of course he'll come back—if he gets the chance. But… but… he *won't* get the chance. They're out there, Walter. You heard what Masters said. They're out there every night, waiting for him…" She began to sob again.

I said, "You think he's after the sheep?"

"Of course he is, you bloody fool!" said Leonie violently. Suddenly she stiffened and said in a half-whisper "Listen… here they come now."

I listened. In the distance there was a curious sound—a sort of half-tap, half-thudding noise. It was coming nearer, and as it did so there was another sound also—a rustle of laboured breathing.

We moved closer to the wire and stood tensely, staring out into the faint moonlight, and as we did so it suddenly seemed as though the ground in front of us began to move. Then I realised that the moving ground was a flock of sheep as they swept by me, their feet drumming on the hard ground and the air alive with their agonised panting.

"Now—now!" said Leonie in a low excited voice. "Now's the time to get him…" She started to whistle the curious two-note whistle.

I said, "Why not call him?"

"No no!" said Leonie in terror. "If you call him they'll hear, and then they'll know it's Remus and…"

She started to whistle again repeatedly. The whole flock had passed us now, and just for one moment I fancied I saw the shadowy figure of their pursuer as he loped past thirty or forty yards away. It may have been my fancy, and in a moment it was gone, and so were the sheep and the sound of their hooves and the sound of their panting, and there was complete silence again.

Leonie stopped whistling and stood leaning against the wire fence with her head resting on her arm, in a position of complete despair.

Trying to be comforting I said, "I think I saw him. He didn't seem to be chasing them very hard."

She laughed bitterly and said, "He *doesn't* chase them hard. That's part of the game. He just follows them and keeps them running until they drop from exhaustion. Then he starts to nip them, because he wants them to run some more. And then he draws blood on one and after that…" She gave a sort of despairing shrug. Then she tensed and said quickly, "There you are, you see—he's turned them."

The thudding and panting were growing louder again, and we heard the flock pass us, though they were now on the other side of the field and we could not see them.

I said, "Shall I go in and see if I can catch him?"

"It's no good," said Leonie drearily. "You'd never get him. He won't even come to me, or take any notice of me, when he's up to this game. You just have to… wait for him to come back."

We waited for another quarter of an hour or so, and Leonie whistled occasionally, but everything was absolutely silent, and even by putting my ear to the ground I could hear no sound of the ghostly flock. It was a warm night, but I saw that Leonie was shivering and said gently, "If you don't think he'll come back until he wants to, wouldn't it be better to go back to the house and wait?"

Leonie hesitated and then with a little shrug set off towards the house without a word. When we reached it Leonie said, "You'd better go to bed."

I said, "Are you going to sit up and wait for him?"

"Of course," said Leonie impatiently.

She went out into the kitchen and put a kettle of water on to boil. I thought that perhaps she was going to make some tea, but then I saw that she was getting out soap, a stiff brush, cloths, and a large bowl.

I said, "What's all that for?"

"Oh, for God's sake, shut up!" said Leonie with a sudden burst of nervous irritation. Then she turned quickly and put a hand on my arm and said, "I'm sorry, Walter. Don't take any notice of me. The point is that when he does come back—*if* he comes back, that is—he'll probably be in a hell of a mess, and we shall have to get him cleaned up before Masters can get here."

She fussed about for a few minutes arranging the washing materials and rearranging them, and then went and dropped wearily into a chair, still in her mackintosh, and said, "Now— what's the story to be?"

"The story?" I said stupidly. I was beginning to realise that I was very tired.

"The story for Masters about where he's been this evening," said Leonie with weary patience. "We must be able to prove that he was here all night."

I considered and said, "Does Uncle Patrick know he's gone off?"

"Lord no. He's fast asleep and snoring," said Leonie bitterly. "He will have thought that Remus couldn't get out— and of course he couldn't have, if the window hadn't been left open."

I said, "All right then—we just say that he was here when we came back from the fair, and that he stayed outside your room all night, as he always does."

"But how do we *know* that he can't have got out in the night? That's what Masters will ask. We had it last time, and you remember that I told Masters that I happened to get up at first light and saw that he was there. He as good as called me a liar then."

I said, "Supposing I'd asked you when we came in if he

could come and sleep in my bedroom for a night, and you'd let him? Then he couldn't have got out."

"Remus wouldn't sleep in your room."

"But Masters isn't to know. And it would be better for me to prove that he was here than you because…" I hesitated. I had been about to say "because Masters knows you tell lies about it anyhow," but I changed my mind and said, "because after all, he isn't *my* dog, and so…"

Leonie said, "That's not a bad idea…" She turned quickly and said, "Would you do that for me, Walter?" as though she had some doubts about it.

I smiled and said, "You know I'd always do anything for you."

"All right then," said Leonie briskly. "Then we came home about ten-thirty, the house was shut up and Remus was here. You asked me if you could have him in your bedroom and I said you could. After that Remus was in your room with the door shut until you woke up this morning. Masters won't believe it of course, but it doesn't really matter whether he believes it as long as he can't prove it isn't true."

We must have waited for at least four hours. During that time Leonie told me the whole history of Remus's expeditions. They had been going on, it seemed, for over two years—that is to say, ever since he was about nine months old. They happened almost always on some occasion when Leonie had gone out without him. He was very clever at getting out of the house, and had once even managed to get out of an upstairs window and had presumably jumped from it on to the porch and then to the ground. He had never been caught red-handed, and it was only recently that Masters had begun to claim positively that he knew that Remus was a sheep worrier. Uncle Patrick knew nothing about it, though Leonie felt that he was beginning to be suspicious. It was vital that he should not know as, though he was fond of Remus, he would certainly never have kept a dog which damaged other people's stock.

"Your Uncle Patrick is like that," said Leonie rather bitterly. "If you get into a row with anybody he always sees their point of view. I've told him dozens of times that if there's a row the only point of view to see is your own. But he won't have it."

From time to time the water in the kettle boiled away and Leonie went out to refill it. Once while she was doing so I must have dozed off, for when I woke, she was not in the kitchen but outside, and I could hear her speaking in a half-whisper. A moment later she came in, hauling Remus after her by the scruff of the neck. We had left the door open, but he had not come in. Leonie had heard a sound, and had found him lying outside.

He was a terrifying sight. His jaws and lips were covered with blood, and in some places where the blood had dried little tufts of white wool were sticking to it. There was blood on his ruff, and on his paws. But apart from this, any jury would have convicted Remus on sight from his manner, which was one of half-cringing guilt, of a kind quite different from his ordinary worried consciousness of sin. He was a magnificent dog, but at that moment there was nothing magnificent about him.

"Come on," said Leonie urgently. "Get him into the kitchen. Mind he doesn't touch anything."

We hauled him into the kitchen. Remus seemed half-dazed, and had to be pushed and pulled when we wanted him to stand up or lie down. But once we got him into a position, he stayed in it completely meekly whilst Leonie and I soaped and scrubbed and sponged him. Leonie had drawn the curtains and locked the outer door, and closed the door of the kitchen. We worked quickly and in almost complete silence. It was a very difficult job, for where the blood had dried and matted his coat it did not come off at all easily, and Leonie insisted that every trace must be removed. I remember that it was particularly difficult to get rid of it from between his toes.

The dawn was breaking before Leonie finally straightened up and said, "There—I think that's all right. Now all we've got to do is to clear this place up. I'll bet Masters will be here by breakfast time. Go up to bed, Walter, and try to get a bit of sleep."

It must have been five o'clock before I went to bed, but even so I woke at my usual time and went downstairs to breakfast. It was a curious and rather uneasy meal. Leonie looked tired, and she spoke to my Uncle Patrick with the sharp-tongued irritability which I had grown to know meant that she was tense and nervous.

Remus was lying on the floor of the living-room asleep, and when I came into the room he did not even raise his head, which was most unusual for him. In fact he seemed so listless and exhausted that Uncle Patrick remarked on it. I was on the point of saying "No wonder he's tired after all that" when I remembered that my uncle knew nothing about the adventure of the night before.

We were just finishing breakfast when there was the sound of a car outside. Leonie's eyes met mine for a moment, and then, very deliberately she took a piece of toast and began to butter it carefully. I saw that her hands were shaking.

We heard the garden gate open. Usually this would have been enough to send Remus into a frenzy of excitement, but this morning he just raised his head slightly for a moment, then lowered it again on to his paws and lay staring at the door.

My uncle said, "Hallo—who's this?" and went to the door. I put out a hand and squeezed Leonie's, and she gave me a pathetic little smile of gratitude.

We heard Uncle Patrick say, "Hallo—you're early this morning," and that unexpectedly high voice of Masters saying, "Where's that nice dog of yours, Parrish?"

Then they were in the room and Masters, looking, if possible, even bigger than usual, was towering over Leonie and me as we sat at the table.

Leonie said quietly, "Good morning, Colonel. Come to breakfast?"

The Colonel's eyes had gone to Remus. I thought I saw a tiny flicker of disappointment on his face, and I guessed that when Remus had not rushed out when he arrived, Masters had thought and hoped that he was still out. At the same time I realised that Leonie and I were going to get no help from the suspect himself in establishing our alibi; for instead of going through his usual performance of registering dislike and suspicion of Masters, Remus continued to lie with his nose on his paws and to stare at the Colonel in a way which, to my eyes at least, was almost a confession of guilt.

Masters nodded towards him and said curtly, "Quieter than usual."

"Yes," said my Uncle Patrick innocently. "He's very subdued this morning. I think he's tired or something."

"I'm not surprised at that," said Masters grimly. He turned to Leonie and said, "I should like to have a look at that dog. Any objection?"

"Of course not," said Leonie with a little frown which was a masterpiece of puzzled surprise. "But I wouldn't touch him if I were you. He doesn't care for it."

Masters said, "I'll take my chance on that. D'you mind telling him to get up?"

Leonie said quietly, "Get up, Remus. Colonel Masters wants to look at you."

The dog rose slowly and, it seemed, unwillingly, and stood quite still. His ears were back, and his tail was drooping. Masters went quickly across to him and started to examine him carefully, particularly about his lips and jaws, and then about his chest and ruff. Leonie's eyes met mine, and I knew we were both praying that we had missed no spot of blood and no tell-tale fragment of wool. Finally Masters turned his attention to Remus's feet, and I became a little happier; for I had been personally responsible for Remus's feet, and knew that all that awkward cleaning between the toes and scrubbing of the pads had been thoroughly done.

Remus meekly submitted to the whole of the examination without even a growl, but with the general expression of a traveller having his luggage searched by the Customs authorities, who knows full well that he has six undeclared bottles of brandy in his suitcase.

Meanwhile, Uncle Patrick was watching with a puzzled frown. Once he shot a questioning glance at Leonie, but she merely shrugged her shoulders and spread out her hands to indicate that she was as puzzled as he. Masters had gone back to Remus's chest now, and was carefully parting the hair on it so as to see the skin beneath.

Uncle Patrick said, "What are you looking for, Colonel?"

Masters straightened up and said, "I'm looking to see if this dog has been killing my sheep." His face was dark, and I knew at once that he had found no incriminating traces on Remus.

Leonie sighed and said, wearily, "Oh, not *again*!"

Masters said, "Look—I don't want to beat about the bush. Last night I had four prize sheep killed, and a dozen others savaged. They were down in a field at the bottom of your orchard. I know your dog chases sheep, though you always deny it. I was looking to see whether he had any blood or wool on him."

"And has he?" said Leonie gently.

Masters turned and stared at her with his angry pale-blue eyes. "No," he said. "He's beautifully clean. In fact he's still damp in places."

"What d'you mean by that?" said Leonie dangerously. I realised that the note of indignation in her voice was not just a piece of acting. She genuinely resented the insinuation behind the Colonel's words. The fact that the insinuation happened to be true was neither here nor there. I remembered her anger on a previous occasion when Masters had seemed to doubt her word, when, in fact, she had been lying like a trooper.

"Where was the dog last night and early this morning?" said Masters. He said it rather wearily, and I fancied that he realised that he had lost.

"He was here, of course," said Leonie.

"And naturally you got up every half-hour during the night and saw him?" said Masters sarcastically.

Leonie shook her head. "No," she said gently. "In fact I didn't see him all night."

"Then how can you be sure he was here?" said Masters sharply, blundering into the trap. I thought the moment had come to go into the witness box.

I said, "You see, Colonel Masters, he was in my bedroom."

Masters whipped round and turned the long-focussed blue eyes squarely on me. I had been prepared for that, and gazed back at him with what I hope was transparent innocence. I was disconcerted, however, to realise that Uncle Patrick was also staring at me with a slightly puzzled frown. He was, of course, surprised to hear that Remus would have slept anywhere but in his usual place across the threshold of Leonie's bedroom.

I said, "We went to the fair, and when we came back I asked if Remus could sleep in my room. We thought he probably wouldn't stay there, and he was a bit restless for a bit. But he soon settled down."

There was a moment's pause. Masters gave a tiny shrug of his heavy shoulders, and I knew that for the moment we had won.

I decided that a little embroidery would do no harm and said, "He couldn't possibly have got out; and anyhow I know he didn't, because I woke up once in the night and saw him. It gave me rather a fright, because I'd forgotten that he was in the room." This had seemed a convincing touch when I had first thought of it, but now it merely sounded as though, like all other clever witnesses, I was saying too much. I caught a glimpse of Leonie's face, and realised that she thought so too.

Masters stared at me fixedly for what seemed a long time,

and then with a sound which was between a sigh and a grunt turned away.

Uncle Patrick said quietly, "I'm sorry about the sheep, Colonel. I know how damned annoying that sort of thing can be —and how expensive. But honestly I think this idea you've got about Remus must be wrong. He can't get out at night; and after all, if he'd been killing sheep, there would be *some* trace of it on him."

Masters said, "That depends what has happened to him since, doesn't it?" He turned suddenly to Leonie and said quietly, "D'you mind walking down to the end of the orchard with me? I've got something rather pretty to show you." He glanced at me and added, "I'd like you to come too, young man."

Leonie looked at him for a moment in silence, and then rose to her feet and went out without a word. The rest of us followed except Remus, who had lain down again with his nose on his paws. It was the only time I ever knew him let Leonie go out of the house without trying to follow her.

We walked down to the end of the orchard in silence. Masters led us along some distance to the left of where Leonie and I had stood the night before, and then simply pointed. About twenty yards inside the field two of his men were bending over the body of a ewe. Its throat had been torn out and the windpipe was actually bitten in half. The whole front of the animal was a mass of blackish-red blood. In other places great tufts had been torn out of its wool, so that the skin was showing. It was a nasty sight.

Masters said quietly, "There were four like that. Two were out in the middle of the field, one was caught in a thorn bush farther up and the other was in the pond over on the other side." He said it without anger, and indeed almost expressionlessly.

Uncle Patrick said, "It must have been something pretty powerful that did that."

"Yes, mustn't it?" said Masters in the same colourless voice.

"But in fact the dead ones aren't the worst of it. Look over there."

He pointed to where the rest of the flock was huddled, about a hundred yards away. They were not grazing, and some seemed to be lying down. The shepherd was moving around amongst them.

Masters said, "You'll see there are about a dozen lying down, and if you look carefully, you'll see *why* they're lying down."

We stared towards the flock. Even at that distance one could see the ragged tears and the bright scarlet blood against the white wool.

"Will those get over it?" said my uncle.

Masters shrugged. "Some of them may. One or two certainly won't. They're in lamb, of course, so we shan't really know the answer to last night's bit of fun until lambing time. You see, when a thing like this happens a few are killed and some are savaged, but the whole lot are driven to exhaustion and frightened almost to death, poor beasts."

He was staring out towards his flock, and glancing at his sombre face I suddenly realised that it was not just the loss of some valuable sheep that he was worrying about. I looked again at the ghastly body of the dead ewe, and at the brilliant scarlet splodges on the white wool in the distance. I remembered the drumming of the feet and the agonised panting in the darkness, and suddenly, for the first time, I was furiously angry with Remus for making us accessories after the fact of his savagery. A few moments before I had been rejoicing in our victory—in the fact that we had outwitted Masters and beaten him. And now I realised suddenly that all we had done was to act and tell clever lies to shield a dog that didn't deserve to be shielded.

I glanced instinctively at Leonie, to see if her feelings might be like my own. She caught my eye and gave me a quick wink, and I remembered her words of the night before, "When you're having a row, the only point of view to see is your own."

Masters turned to her and said coldly, "I just wanted you to

114

see this, so that you should realise that sheep worrying isn't a joke."

"Did anybody ever say it was?" said Leonie equally coldly.

"Not in so many words perhaps," said Masters, "but I've known plenty of people who thought that it was just their darling dog being playful, bless him. Good morning." He turned abruptly and walked away.

Leonie said, "No apology, you notice. But politeness never was his strong suit."

We went back to the house. Uncle Patrick left us at the door and went off to the wood shed. Remus was still lying exactly where we had left him. As we came in he raised his head and his tail wagged very slightly, but otherwise he did not move. Leonie went across and fell on her knees beside him and threw her arms around his neck.

She said in a fierce whisper, "You old fool—I thought you were going to give the whole show away, looking so guilty. Thank your lucky stars you've got clever Leonie and clever Walter to get you out of scrapes." She hugged him tightly to her and said, "Darling Remus. Darling, darling Remus!"

Suddenly she jumped to her feet and almost ran across to me, and throwing her arms around my neck kissed me on the mouth. There were tears on her cheeks. She whispered in my ear, "Thank you, Walter. Thank you—thank you. You were wonderful. I'll never forget what you did for me as long as I live."

I kissed her in return and hugged her to me. But somehow at the back of my mind there was an unhappy feeling that though we had won the battle, it was not a victory of which to be particularly proud. I hardly spoke to Remus for several days.

Ten

I do not think that Leonie ever knew of my feeling of discomfort about the business of the sheep. Certainly she would not have understood it or shared it. Ethics and social theory were not in her line. To her, all that had happened was that we had saved Remus; and, what was almost as important, defeated Masters. She gave me considerably more credit for my part in the matter than was strictly due, and for some days after I could do no wrong.

Meanwhile, however, poor Uncle Patrick could do no right. I could not see that he had done or said anything unhelpful, particularly as he had not known the facts, and I told her so. But Leonie had got it into her head that he had not backed us up against Masters. She had a bee in her bonnet about Uncle Patrick "not backing her up". Moreover, she believed (probably quite rightly) that had my uncle known that Remus was a sheep worrier, he would have wanted to have him destroyed. For Leonie's immediate purposes, therefore, I must be represented as the understanding and loyal friend and my uncle as the cold-hearted, stuffily conservative enemy.

This completely unreasonable feeling Leonie expressed by unusual warmth and attention to me, and unusual coldness and shortness with my uncle. Sometimes, when we were all together and I did some small thing for her, she would remark to the world in general that it was nice to have a man about the house; or, if we were discussing something she would say, "Of course your uncle doesn't understand how you and I feel about these things."

My own reaction to all this was mixed. On the one hand, it was delightful to be flattered and approved of, and to feel that there were bonds between us which my uncle could not share; on the other, I was fond of my Uncle Patrick and unhappy when Leonie was unfair to him, even if the unfairness worked to my advantage. He never protested or showed any anger about any of these things, at least in front of me; and to his great credit, he never let them destroy his apparent liking for me. But sometimes I would see him glance at Leonie when she had been particularly acid or humiliating, and I knew that she had hurt him. Usually he would then go quietly away by himself and work.

This atmosphere, which was for me at once exhilarating and slightly uncomfortable, continued for some days, and led me to reconsider my whole programme in regard to Leonie. Ever since I had come to Glebe Cottage I had known, of course, that I was in love with her. But even after I had learnt that she was not married and not my aunt, I had thought of it as a hopeless and unrequited love, in the best poetic tradition. My ambition had been that she should accept me as a lover in this sense, and occasionally allow me to kiss her, fondle her, and perhaps, one day, to stroke her knees. This is what had seemed possible in the car coming back from the fair, if only the sherry and the fish and chips had not betrayed me; and it was all I had ever dared to hope for.

Now, however, judging from the way she spoke, Leonie was no longer the aloof, committed, unobtainable mistress who must be the object of a hopeless passion. Rather it seemed that some, at least, of my love and admiration were reciprocated; and, in particular, that she liked me a great deal more than she liked my Uncle Patrick.

This led, in ordinary logic, to some highly exciting possibilities. For if Leonie and I loved one another, and Leonie did not love my Uncle Patrick and was not married to him, why should she not marry me?

I realised, of course, that there were a certain number of difficulties. I should not be able to marry for at least a couple of years, or until I had passed Higher Certificate.[1] Again, Leonie was considerably older than I. But everyone said that I was old for my age; and anyhow, as Leonie herself had sometimes reminded us, she was nearer to my age than to my uncle's.

I was walking along a lane one hot afternoon, thinking deeply about these things, when I heard the unmistakable "plop" of a cricket bat hitting a ball. I paused at a five-barred gate, and looked into what was obviously the village cricket field. Only a square of about forty yards in the centre of the field was mown. Elsewhere the grass was about eighteen inches high, except in one corner where there was a practice net which seemed to be falling down. Here a couple of swathes had been cut to make a wicket. Close to the net there was a shed with a corrugated iron roof. This, presumably, was the Pavilion.

There was only one person in the field—a tall man who had just hit himself a high catch and, dropping his bat, had run to catch it. He did so with considerable neatness and confidence. Then, as he turned to fetch the bat, I realised that it was the Rev. Mr. Hawes. He was wearing grey flannel trousers, tennis shoes and an open-necked white shirt. As I had seen him on a previous occasion, he had his handkerchief bound around his head to act as a sweat rag.

As he picked up the bat he caught sight of me standing at the gate and waved and shouted "Hallo!" cheerfully. It seemed churlish not to raise a hand, so I did so and turned away. I did not like Mr. Hawes, and I was not sure if anyone from Glebe Cottage should be on speaking terms with him. But he suddenly yelled, "Come and have a knock!", at the same time gesturing towards the decrepit-looking net.

I hesitated. Had he invited me to do anything else I should certainly have refused. But I was passionately fond of cricket. I had not touched a bat for nearly two months and knew that, in all probability, I should not touch one again until the following spring. Moreover, the centre patch of grass had been newly mown, and there was that smell in the air of a newly-mown cricket field which is quite unlike any other smell, and, for your true cricket addict, irresistible.

I climbed over the gate. Hawes came to meet me. His eyes were alight with pleasure behind the steel-rimmed spectacles. He said, "Good man! I was longing for someone to trundle[2] to." He handed me the bat and said, "I think there's a pad and a glove in the shed. Better put them on, because it's a bit fiery in the net."

I soon found that this was an understatement. The sunbaked ground was like concrete, and the practice wicket in the net was very bumpy. Hawes would have been an awkward bowler to play, even on a decent wicket. He was, as he had told me, left-handed and quite fast, and from his great height he constantly made the ball swing into you and stand up most uncomfortably. I was, though I say it, a good batsman in the well-taught left-elbow-up-and-nose-over-the-ball tradition, and I did my best; but nevertheless, he hit me once in the chest and once very painfully on the thigh, and finally bowled me with one which pitched on middle-and-leg and hit the top of the off stump, and in my opinion would have bowled anybody.

We paused after that for a rest. I remarked that the ball that had bowled me was a beauty, and he gave a modest giggle and said, "Must have hit a worm cast. That's the joy of playing on village wickets. You don't have to be able to move the ball about. The pitch'll do it for you."

It was less satisfactory when he batted and I bowled. I was an indifferent bowler, and Hawes was no batsman at all. His only stroke was a violent effort to hit the ball out of sight, and I bowled him three times before he at last got hold of one and hit an enormous soaring drive which fell in a tree on the opposite side of the lane. We looked for the ball for nearly half an hour but never found it, and since it was the only one we had, we were obliged to stop.

I had been surprised to find, whilst we were playing, that Hawes's behaviour was entirely normal and pleasant. He was obviously a wild cricket enthusiast, and knew a good deal about the game. But apart from that he was entirely friendly, sensible and modest. It was some time before I realised the reason for this marked change for the better. Hawes was now sober, whereas on the previous occasions that I had seen him or spoken to him he had been more or less drunk.

We put on our jackets and strolled down the lane together, still talking cricket. Then, as we were reaching the outskirts of the village, Hawes stopped outside a small thatched cottage and said, "Come in and have a cup of tea. You must be dry."

Again I hesitated. But by this time I was enjoying our conversation, and I was very thirsty, so I followed him into the cottage. It was a tiny place, rather picturesque from the outside. Inside, on the ground floor at least, it seemed to consist of a single medium-sized room with a bare brick floor.

As we went in Hawes said, "Sorry everything's in such a mess. My Mrs. T. only comes once a week, and to-morrow's her day. The rest of the time I do for myself and sometimes…" he spread out his hands, "Sometimes I *don't* do."

I laughed and said something polite and appropriate. The room was fairly clean, but it certainly was in a remarkable muddle. There were books everywhere, including on the seats of the only two possible chairs. There were no pictures, but a number of cuttings from newspapers were fastened to the walls with drawing-pins. There was a deal kitchen table[3] with remnants of a meal still on it, and a prie-Dieu[4] with a brass crucifix. The place smelt faintly of a mixture of Lifebuoy soap and incense. The general effect was oddly cell-like, but not unpleasant.

Hawes said, "Dump those books on the floor and sit down. Shan't be a moment." He went out into what appeared to be the kitchen, and almost immediately returned with two glasses of beer, one of which he handed to me.

He may have seen that I was a trifle surprised, for he said, "Tea's all right. I'm very fond of tea myself. But after a game of cricket, beer's the only drink. Don't you agree?"

I hated beer, particularly when it had froth on it as this had. But I could hardly say so. Hawes said, "Well, here's how" and took a long gulp of his beer, whilst I nuzzled rather miserably amongst the froth of mine.

Hawes gave a slight giggle and said, "And how is everything at Glebe Cottage? And how is your beautiful lady?"

I suddenly wished profoundly that I had not come in with him. Tea and cricket-talk with Hawes were one thing, but beer and Leonie were quite another. I replied guardedly that things at Glebe Cottage were much as usual, though the apple crop seemed likely to be only moderate, and that Leonie was well. For a moment I wondered whether, when talking to Hawes, I should refer to her as "Aunt Leonie". But I never did so now, even when talking to my uncle, and I knew that if I did so in talking to Hawes he would give me his unpleasant giggle.

To my relief he switched the talk back to cricket, and for perhaps half an hour all went well and pleasantly. Once Hawes went out into the kitchen and fetched himself another glass of beer, but he made no attempt to press another on me. We had been talking, as cricketers have so often talked, about the proper composition of a team to be the greatest of all time, irrespective of period. I had been standing out stoutly for the inclusion of Ranjitsinjhi,[5] whilst Hawes had been pressing to include Victor Trumper,[6] when he suddenly said, "I take it that you're a Christian?"

For a moment I thought the fact that I was a Christian was

some argument for the inclusion of Trumper. Then I realised that there had been a change of subject. I said, "Yes."

Hawes said, "What makes you think that?"

I said, "Well… I suppose a Christian is a person who believes in Christ."

"But surely the devil believes in Christ," said Hawes with a little giggle. "He has plenty of reason to. So presumably he's a Christian."

I was slightly irritated and said coldly, "I really don't know what the devil believes in. What I meant was a person who believes in Christ and tries to follow him."

"And do you do that?" said Hawes, staring at me fixedly through his spectacles.

"Up to a point."

"Up to *what* point?" said Hawes. "The point where it costs you something—where following Him becomes difficult? Or just up to the point where it's convenient?"

He gave a slight wave of the hand and said, "Forgive me for raising this subject, but after all, it's my job." He made a little gesture towards the prie-Dieu and the crucifix, as though they were his credentials. "And if you don't mind my saying so, you must be in a position, at present, which would put a sore strain on any man's faith." He leant forward confidentially and said, "You see, Walter, I'm a young man myself, and I know about a young man's temptations."

I hated to hear my own Christian name coming from his curiously lizard-like mouth, and it was on the tip of my tongue to point out to him that whatever my temptations might be, I didn't get drunk all the time. I did not usually mind piejaw,[7] but piejaw from Hawes seemed to me to be impudence. I said coldly, "I really don't think I follow you, Mr. Hawes."

"Don't you?" he said with a grin. "I think perhaps you do. I only want to help you, you know. As a priest, that's what I'm for. To help you. And I know the sort of temptations you must be going through." He paused and gave a tiny giggle. "After all," he added, "she's very beautiful."

This last sentence threw a new light upon the whole conversation. Until now I had assumed that Hawes was talking about masturbation, simply because, in my experience, anybody who talked to me about God, and about the temptations that beset me, and about how well he understood them, always *had* been talking about masturbation. Now I realised, for the first time, that he was not talking about masturbation but about Leonie; and the discovery rendered me, for the moment, quite speechless with horror and fury.

Hawes was speaking in a half-whisper now, staring at me with wide open eyes, made distorted and enormous by the thick spectacles, and with the lizard's mouth opening and shutting liplessly as though he was tasting something very carefully.

He said, "After all, I've seen you together, you know. I've seen you look at her, and I've known what you were thinking. Women like that are made to tempt us, Walter—to make foul thoughts seem sweet and pretty things—to make us lust for the smell of them, and the touch of them, and the feel of their soft skin under our fingers, and of their lips on ours. We're young men, and our blood is hot. How can we avoid these traps so cunningly laid for us?" His voice rose. "Yet it can be done, Walter. By God's help it *can* be done."

He suddenly rose to his whole lanky height and raised a finger. "You must not reproach yourself," he said with solemn authority. "As a priest I *instruct* you not to reproach yourself. Probably there is very little which you need regret. Perhaps you have looked at her lustfully—undressed her with your eyes, and imagined that soft, white, tempting flesh beneath. Perhaps there have been small matters of sensual contacts—the accidental brushing of bodies against one another—perhaps just a touch of the hand. Perhaps a kiss—seemingly playful…"

He paused expectantly. But I was still speechless. He looked at me for a moment in silence and then said, resuming his half-whisper, "Or then again there may have been more. I tell you, I'm a young man too, and I understand the power of that sort of woman to make the blood race in your veins and make your whole body cry out for her."

He was standing over me now, bending slightly forward. There was a trace of froth at the corners of his mouth, and up near his left eye some small muscle was twitching convulsively.

He said softly, "Whatever it is—whatever you have done with her—however far you have allowed lust to carry you—do not reproach yourself. It is not *you* who are to blame. Find some friend—some priest—some priest who is a friend, and confess it all—*all*—and you will find forgiveness and rest again. For we know, dear Walter, we know, we priests, the power and danger of a lewd and shameless woman, when…"

I suddenly leapt to my feet, and as I did so hit him a violent blow in the chest with my fist. The blow was powerful enough to send him staggering back, so that his heels caught a pile of books, and he sat down heavily. At the same time his spectacles flew off and shot some distance across the bare brick floor.

He sat on the floor for a moment, not looking at me. I think he was rather dazed. I was slightly frightened, for the blow had been a powerful one, and seemed somehow to have struck itself, without any deliberate movement on my part.

I started to say, "I'm sorry, but…" He slowly turned his head towards me and I stopped, mainly because, without his spectacles, his resemblance to a lizard was so very striking.

He smiled rather painfully and said, "Don't reproach yourself, Walter. That's just what I was saying to you. As a priest, I instruct you not to reproach yourself."

He pulled his long legs under him, and getting up, went and picked up his spectacles. He examined them carefully, holding them up to the window.

I said, "Are they broken?"

"No," said Hawes, and put them on again. He smiled at me and said, "You see—there is no harm done at all. As a priest, I have to accept these things as the inevitable result of doing my duty. It was not you who struck me, dear Walter; it was the devil, mad with fear and rage that you should be shown the truth."

It certainly seemed to me that it was some agency outside myself that had punched him in the chest, but I doubted very much if it was the devil. However, realising that he was not hurt, I started for the door.

Hawes said, "Are you going?" He seemed to be slightly surprised.

I said "Yes" curtly.

"I shall pray for you, Walter," he said softly. "I shall pray that you may be sustained…"

I closed the front door of the cottage and started down the lane. As I did so, one of the windows opened and Hawes stuck his head out and called, "Remember—don't reproach yourself. Pray." I made no reply and hurried on.

When I got back to Glebe Cottage, Leonie asked me where I had been, but I merely said that I had been for a walk and had forgotten that it was tea-time. I probably felt that any other explanation would be too complicated.

Eleven

I was shaken and upset by my talk with Hawes. After all, if one excluded the occasion in the graveyard, which hardly counted, he had only ever seen Leonie and me together once, and on that occasion I could have sworn that I did not look at her lustfully or undress her with my eyes. I began to wonder uneasily whether my passion for Leonie might be less well-concealed than I had thought.

Moreover, the encounter had taken place at the wrong moment, just when I had recovered from my first waves of purely animal lust for Leonie, and was beginning to convince myself that what I felt for her was a pure and noble passion; which, with a little luck, might turn into a life-long partnership. If I was to some extent still in trouble with my conscience, it certainly did not help to have my nose rubbed in the fact by somebody with little bits of foam at the corners of his mouth and a twitching left eye. Obviously Hawes had a dirty mind. But much of what he had said was like a picture of my own thoughts seen through a piece of filthy and fly-blown glass.

I was thoroughly confused, and Leonie's behaviour in the next few days did nothing to reduce my confusion. She was still pleasant and flattering, and she continued to use me as a weapon in the sly goading of Uncle Patrick. But at the same time she seemed to be avoiding any close contact with me, and even, for the first time since I came to the cottage, to find reasons for not being alone with me. When she went to Canterbury, she did not take me with her. She refused to read verse with me, saying that she did not feel like it; and in the evenings, after my uncle had gone to bed, instead of settling down for our usual hour's talk she would potter about for a while in the kitchen and then announce that she was tired, and go to bed herself. I found myself at once being praised and flattered, and, it seemed, avoided.

I was puzzled and greatly disturbed. I wondered whether my ludicrous performance on the night of the fair was responsible for the change in Leonie. But if it was, why should she go out of her way to be warm and friendly when my uncle was present?

One day I was sitting in the living-room wondering rather moodily what to do with myself when Leonie came down the stairs. Barely glancing at me, she said shortly, "Come on—let's go for a walk," and made for the door.

I knew from her tone and her appearance that she was in a bad temper, and guessed that she had been quarrelling with my uncle. Naturally I followed at once, delighted at the prospect of being alone with her for the first time in several days.

The sky was heavily overcast and I asked tentatively if we had better not take coats, as I thought it might rain.

"Let it," said Leonie, continuing on her way to the gate. "If I don't get out of this place quickly I shall go out of my mind."

Remus, of course, had fallen in behind us and for some minutes we walked quickly and in silence. Then I plucked up the courage to ask Leonie if anything was the matter.

She laughed bitterly and said, "Anything the matter? Of course not. I'm twenty-seven. I'm stuck in that damned place all the year round. I've got no help. I never go anywhere, or see anybody. I haven't had a new dress for over a year, and the last one came from Marks and Spencer. I haven't been to London or to the theatre for two years. I've no children, I'm living with a sick man who is twenty years older than I am, and I'm not even married to him. Apart from one or two little items like that, everything's fine."

This was almost startlingly like the beginning of a row between my mother and father, but coming from Leonie, it surprised me; for, apart from an occasional grumble when she was in a bad temper, or the occasional dropping of some bitter little phrase, she had never complained to me about her life before, though even to me it had always seemed that it could not be a very exciting or satisfactory one.

Even more surprisingly, she went on, "But your dear uncle can't seem to see it. He seems to think I ought to be having a wonderful time; and if I ever utter a word of complaint, he goes all hurt and cold-faced, and generally tries to make me feel that I'm an ungrateful bitch."

I knew that this was quite untrue and unfair—that in fact, Uncle Patrick worried about her a lot—that this was all just part of the campaign which Leonie was waging against him at the time. But in line with my new policy of trying to detach Leonie from Uncle Patrick I said sympathetically, "I've often wondered how you stick it."

"You haven't wondered it as often as I have," said Leonie, taking a vicious kick at a stone which lay in our path.

I said craftily, "Of course you could always go away, not being married."

"Where exactly?" said Leonie sarcastically.

"Well, you could marry somebody and… go and live with him."

"Of the people I know at present," said Leonie, "the two best bets seem to be Hawes and Edwards. They both like the look of me. Which d'you think it had better be?"

This would perhaps have been a good moment to explain to

her my plan about our joint future; but suddenly a very large drop of rain hit me on the nose, and in a matter of seconds it was raining in torrents. We were right out on the open downs, and the only shelter in sight was a large, decrepit barn some fifty yards away. Leonie yelled "Come on!" and started to run to the barn at full speed.

We reached the barn panting and wet. It was a tumbledown place, which contained a few rusty old farm implements at one end, and a large heap of hay at the other. In places the rain was pouring through the roof almost as heavily as it was outside, but the hay end seemed dry. We flopped down on the hay and beat the loose water off our clothes. Leonie pushed back her wet hair and said, "Damn it—I haven't even got a comb. Take your jacket off and shake it."

I did so. Leonie looked round the barn and said, "This is rather a nice place. Hay and all. Though mind you, Walter, hay's much overestimated. It tickles like hell, and there are things in it that bite you to pieces."

She said it with a broad grin, and I knew that for some reason the run of fifty yards through heavy rain had washed away the black depression that had been on her only two minutes ago, and that it had now been replaced, as it often was, by a sort of giggling recklessness.

I put my jacket on and sat down beside her. She looked at me mischievously and said, "Since this is a sit on the hay, if not a roll in it, I think you ought to kiss me," and then in a lower tone, as though to herself, "Anyhow, if somebody doesn't kiss me soon, I shall burst."

I kissed her and went on kissing her. Her hair and her face were wet and cold to the touch. It was not like the previous time in the car. Then she had let me kiss her, but had not responded. Now she responded fully and frankly, and, it seemed to me, with something like passion.

At last she pulled away from me and said with a grin, "If you're now going to be sick, you'd better go and do it outside."

I said, "I'm not going to be sick," and pushed her gently back, so that she was half-lying in the hay, and put my hand firmly and deliberately on her breast. She lay quite still for a moment, and then with a quick wriggle and a heave pulled herself upright, at the same time pushing my hand away. She muttered something which I did not catch, and started to smooth back her hair without looking at me.

I started to say "Leonie—I love…" but she cut me short and said with a giggle, "What would happen to you at school if you were caught kissing a girl?"

"I've no idea," I said sulkily, irritated by the interruption.

"I'll bet you'd be tanned," said Leonie. "And quite right too. I think I shall tan you now."

She looked round and picked up a hollow dry cow parsley stem and said, "Turn over."

I said, "Don't be silly, Leonie. I…"

"Go *on*, Walter," she said severely. "Take your punishment like a man."

Feeling angry and very foolish I rolled over, and she at once brought the stem down across my bottom, whereupon it naturally broke.

"There!" she said. "And you remember that every time aunty catches you kissing a girl she will whip. See?"

I said, "Then I'll give her another chance now," and tried to take her in my arms again. But she pushed me away firmly and said sharply "I said *enough*, Walter."

"It's not enough. It isn't half enough."

"Then I'm afraid it'll have to be," said Leonie with finality. She got up and started to dust the hay off her skirt.

"But why, Leonie?" I said desperately. "Why?"

"Because I'm behaving like a vulgar bitch and a teaser," she said with sudden savage bitterness. "That's why. At my age rolling in the hay with a fifteen-year-old boy…!"

I don't think she meant the words to be unkind—at least, not unkind to me. The bitter contempt of them was not contempt for me. But at that particular moment I heard them as an unforgivable insult, and I rose and rushed blindly out of the barn. The rain had been only a brief, heavy summer shower and it was now over, but I do not think I should have noticed had there been an earthquake, as I strode away with the newly-soaked turf squelching under my feet.

I think she called after me, and then I heard her running, but I did not turn until she caught me by the arm; and then I stopped and looked down at her angrily, still in a fury of hurt pride and disappointment.

She said, "I'm sorry, Walter."

I said between my teeth, "If you don't like vulgar fifteen-year-olds, why d'you ask them to kiss you?"

"I didn't say you were vulgar. I said I was."

"You mean it's vulgar to kiss somebody you love?"

"No, of course not," said Leonie rather helplessly. "But you must see…"

"What I see," I said with devastating accuracy, "is that you like me to be just the age that fits in with what you want at the moment."

Leonie bit her lip sharply, and I realised with satisfaction that that one had gone home. I pulled my arm away from her and walked on. She did not attempt to stop me again, and I did not look back.

When I reached the house I went straight up to my room, got out my suitcase and started to pack. But half my things were at the wash, and a pair of shoes which Leonie had taken to Canterbury to be mended was missing. I decided at first merely to abandon these things as a sweeping gesture of disdain. But as I collected my remaining clothes and started to put them in the suitcase my resolution began to ebb away. Obviously, I could not ask Leonie to drive me to the station, any more than I could ask her for my missing clothes; and though I knew that there was a bus which stopped at the end of our lane, I had no idea when it went. Moreover, I reminded myself, just to walk out in anger would be rude and ungrateful to Uncle Patrick. I also remembered what Leonie had looked like propped up in the hay, and the firm softness of her breast beneath my hand. I took my clothes out of my suitcase again and put them away.

At tea-time I went downstairs and behaved, I hoped, with quiet dignity, chatting with Uncle Patrick and being entirely polite, if distant, with Leonie. She pretended to be upset, and occasionally shot anxious glances at me which I was obviously intended to see. But I think she knew that she was, or would soon be, forgiven.

We never mentioned the matter again, but that evening she asked meekly if she might read some verse. With what I felt was a rather fine stroke of suggestive irony I made her read "Had we but world enough and time"[1] and when, as usual, she asked me afterwards what it was all about, I explained, with some relish, that Marvell was complaining that his mistress was wasting precious time by being so coy, and that soon their chance to be lovers would be gone.

Leonie nodded and seemed to understand, but I do not know if she saw how clearly the parable applied to us. I saw it only too well. I had now been at Glebe Cottage three weeks, and certainly Time's wingèd chariot[2] was hurrying uncomfortably near. In a week, at the most, I should have to return home; and then before me would lie the vast deserts of the Christmas term. Always before, I had been glad enough to go back to school after the summer holidays, if only to escape from the boredom of my home. Moreover, there had been the bright prospects of Clynes and rugger.[3] But now the thought of a whole term without seeing Leonie seemed a desert indeed.

It was therefore in a sombre mood that I went with Leonie to Canterbury one morning. Although the quarrel in the barn had been patched up, the memory of it still rankled. Worse, it had left me hopelessly unsure about where I stood with Leonie. Just before it happened, I had been planning to ask her to become engaged to me before I went back to school, and had even been rehearsing a painful but necessary interview with my Uncle Patrick, in which we should explain the whole situation to him quietly, sympathetically, but withal firmly. But you can hardly ask a woman to marry you when she has recently said that your whole relationship was vulgar, and referred to you, with seeming contempt, as a fifteen-year-old boy.

We did our shopping in Canterbury and went, as usual, to reward ourselves with a cup of coffee and a bun. We had found a new tea shop, having abandoned the other because of the possibility of meeting Mrs. Simms and Veronica. I think Leonie missed her talks with Mrs. Simms about their dressmakers, but she had fully understood my wish not to meet Veronica, and the change of tea shop had been her own suggestion.

Over coffee Leonie suddenly said, "I suppose you'll be going soon now. I should think you'll be jolly glad."

I said, "I shall hate it."

"Why? It won't be as dull as being here."

I said, "I never enjoyed anything in my life as much as being here with you."

I think she had been fishing for that, but she seemed pleased and touched, as she always did when I said I liked it at Glebe Cottage, and she gave my hand a brief pat and said, "Dear Walter. I simply don't know what I shall do without you."

There could hardly have been a better opportunity to declare myself, and broach the subject of our marriage. But somehow—perhaps as a result of what had happened in the barn—I had learnt a certain amount of caution in dealing with Leonie, and I decided to do a little fishing of my own.

I said casually, "Why? I should think you'd be glad to be rid of me."

"But don't you see—there won't be anybody to talk to in the

evenings, or to go for walks with, or to come and have a coffee." Leonie sighed.

This was all right as far as it went, but it did not go anything like far enough for me. It lacked colour, passion and urgency. I said rather coldly, "You'll have Uncle Patrick to talk to, and Remus to go for walks with, and Mrs. Simms to drink coffee with."

"That's true," said Leonie without enthusiasm. "I suppose it'll be all right. Somehow it always *is* all right." Then, perhaps seeing from my face that she had said the wrong thing, she added with a smile, "But there won't be anybody to make me read poetry."

This was better, though still inadequate. I tried to bring the conversation nearer to the proper emotional level. Gazing down at my half-eaten bun, I said in sombre tones, "At least you'll have somebody. Whilst I shall be… alone."

"Oh nonsense!" said Leonie cheerfully. "You'll have all your friends and… and cricket and…"

"You don't play cricket in the Christmas term," I said distantly.

"Well, whatever game you do play then. Don't you like that bun? Have another instead."

"No, thank you."

"After all, you're not at school for long, you know. I'd make the most of it if I were you."

I had a horrible feeling that she was going to tell me that one's school days are the happiest time of one's life. I leant forward and said tensely, "Leonie—do you realise what life is going to be like for me without you?"

"Without *me?*" She looked at me with what seemed to be genuine surprise, and then smiled and patted my hand again, with that quick gesture which I always loved for its affection, and hated for its patronage. "Why, what on earth good am I to you? I don't even know enough to be able to talk to you about the things that you like. Cheer up, Walter. You'll soon be meeting lots of… of people of your own age who…"

"Like Veronica Simms?" I said bitterly.

Leonie laughed. "No—not like Veronica. Ones you'll *really* like." She sighed. "What wouldn't I give to be seventeen again," she said wistfully. "Though God knows, it seemed pretty nasty at the time."

I was about to say, "And what wouldn't I give to be twenty-seven," and thereby lead the conversation back into the proper channel. But Leonie suddenly looked at her watch and said, "Golly, we're late. We must be getting back. Have we paid?" And that was all.

We went to the car. It was parked in a narrow street not far from the cathedral—quite illegally, I should guess. Just as we were getting into it a voice said, "Ah—good morning. Good morning!"

Leonie said "Oh Christ!" under her breath and got into the car. Hawes was standing beside us, grinning down with his lizard smile.

He turned to me and said, "Well, Walter—when are we going to play some more cricket?"

I had never told Leonie about our cricket, and I hated his use of my Christian name, and the suggestion that there was an intimacy between us. I muttered something about "some day" and also got into the car.

Hawes giggled and said, "One day when the beautiful lady can spare you, eh?"

Leonie had started the engine and was beginning to edge the car forward. Hawes raised his black hat with an elaborate sweeping gesture and stepped backwards into the road. And then suddenly there was a curious sound, which seemed to be a mixture of a shout and a squeal and a clank, and he was flying through the air with his long body curiously bent backwards, like that of an acrobat doing backward somersaults, to hit the flagstones of the street a fraction of a second later with a horrible smashing violence. The milk lorry must have been going very slowly, for the back of it was still beside us when it stopped.

The side of the lorry was so close to us in the narrow street that Leonie could not get out of the driver's side. When we reached Hawes, a dozen people had already gathered round. The driver of the milk lorry, his face a sort of bluish yellow, was saying, "Right under me wheels. Right under me bloody wheels…" I noticed, for some reason, that he had a three days' growth of beard which showed sharply against the yellow pallor of his skin.

Hawes was lying on his back, with one arm doubled under him. He had a long, jagged cut running diagonally across his forehead, and blood was coming from his nose and ears. His eyes were closed, and he was breathing with a loud snorting sound.

Somebody said unnecessarily, "His head's hurt."

Leonie said, "Ambulance, Walter," and dropped on her knees beside Hawes. I was about to dash away when somebody said, "It's coming. They've sent for it."

A man said to Leonie, "Shall we get him on to the pavement, miss?" But Leonie shook her head and said, "No. Don't move him." Somebody had picked up Hawes's black hat and was standing holding it carefully in both hands.

The jagged cut on Hawes's forehead was bleeding freely. Leonie hesitated for a moment, and then whipping off her silk headscarf, folded it rapidly and skilfully to make a bandage. She laid it across the cut and held it there, and for a moment I was ludicrously reminded of the fact that Hawes often wore a sweat rag round his forehead. Somebody said, "Lift his head so that you can tie it." But Leonie said sharply, "No—don't, *don't* move his head. He may have a fracture."

A policeman had arrived and was kneeling on the other side

of Hawes. The driver of the milk lorry was still repeating monotonously, "Right under me bloody wheels."

The ambulance seemed to arrive surprisingly quickly. As they put the stretcher down beside him, Hawes half-opened his eyes. Only the whites of them were showing, and I do not think he can possibly have recognised Leonie. But he said quite clearly, "I think it only fair to tell you… letter to the Ecclesiastical Commissioners." Then they lifted him gently on to the stretcher.

Twelve

Hawes died soon after they got him to hospital. His skull was fractured. My Uncle Patrick came in just at tea-time, looking grave, and told us the news. There was a moment's pause and then Leonie said, "I *thought* that was a fractured skull all right. Well, it's probably all for the best, poor devil. He wasn't doing much good for anybody—particularly himself."

"De mortuis nil nisi bonum,"[1] said my Uncle Patrick gently. Both the gentleness and the threadbareness of the tag were characteristic.

I had been brought up very strictly in the "De mortuis…" tradition myself, and I had been somewhat shocked by Leonie's forthrightness. I said, "He was a jolly good bowler."

When I went to bed that night I remembered suddenly that Hawes had said he would pray for me. I visualised him in that strange, cell-like room, kneeling at the prie-Dieu with the brass crucifix on it, and I wondered with an odd fascination exactly what he had said in his prayer for me. I prayed that his soul might rest in peace. It seemed the least that one could do.

The following morning Time's wingèd chariot hurried even nearer. A letter arrived from my mother, saying that she was returning home in two days' time and suggesting that I should come back at the beginning of the following week so that we might have two or three days to do my packing and to try on various items of school clothes that she had bought me in London. This left me something less than a week at Glebe Cottage, and that morning I went for a long walk and tried to reach some final decision as to what to do about Leonie. The prospect of an immediate engagement, before I went back to school, had faded after our conversation in the bun shop. Undoubtedly Leonie was not always as serious as I might have wished. I had no doubt that, given time, she could be brought to see my point of view; but I doubted whether it was a job that could be done in six days. And yet to go tamely away, with nothing settled, seemed intolerable.

But by the time I returned to the house, something had happened which, for the moment at least, put the matter out of my mind. As I have already said, my uncle was in the habit of taking on jobs about the fruit farm for which he was not really physically fit. On this occasion he had climbed up into one of the big old Bramley apple trees, intending to saw out a diseased branch, and had then become faint and fallen out of the tree. It was not a tremendous fall—only a matter of about twelve feet on to grass. But the ground was very hard, and he must have fallen awkwardly, for he had been found by the silent old man, half-conscious and partially paralysed. When I returned, Leonie and the old man had got him to bed, and the doctor was on his way.

All this Leonie told me, half-crying, while we waited for the doctor. I could not help contrasting her behaviour now with her behaviour the previous day when she had been attending to Hawes. Admittedly, my Uncle Patrick and Hawes were two different propositions from her point of view. But people are usually either surprisingly calm and efficient in emergencies, or else they are not. Yesterday Leonie had been calmness itself in dealing with a man who was obviously badly injured, and with a lot of blood about. Now she seemed almost hysterical with fright. She was half-crying and shaking, and her face was deadly pale. I did my best to comfort her, but I was frightened by her fright, and I had never welcomed anything more than the sound of the doctor's car arriving.

Doctor Walker was reassuring. My uncle, it appeared, was suffering from shock, and he had received a blow at the base of the spine which had caused temporary paralysis of one of his legs. But the paralysis had passed off now. There were no bones broken, and a few days in bed would put him right.

Leonie seemed somewhat comforted, and stopped crying and shaking. But she remained very worried and anxious and insisted on staying all the time beside my uncle's bed, even when he was asleep. I was allowed to see him later in the day, and I must say that for a man who had just fallen out of a tree he seemed to me remarkably normal. He was cheerful, and apart from a bruise on his back and one or two scratches from the branches, he had no injuries or pain. He even suggested that he should get up to supper, but at this Leonie was horrified. Nor would she let me stay with him more than a few minutes, in case it tired him. My private opinion was that talking to me tired him less on this occasion than I had seen it do many times when he was supposed to be well.

I spent the evening alone, Leonie still being upstairs with my uncle, feeling bored and vaguely irritated. I liked Uncle Patrick, and of course I was sorry that he had fallen out of a tree. But nevertheless I could not help feeling that Leonie was making a rather unnecessary fuss. It was not as though he was badly hurt. I contrasted her extreme solicitude towards him now with the unkindness and the obvious desire to hurt him which she had been displaying for over a week.

I was, I think, feeling thoroughly jealous, and rather taken aback. For some while I had ceased to think of my Uncle Patrick as a very serious obstacle to my plans for the future of Leonie and myself. After all, she had made it quite clear that she no longer loved him, and that he compared very unfavourably with me. Yet here he had only to fall out of a tree and get a bruise and a few scratches, and she was acting as though he was the one and only centre of her life—fussing about around his bed as though he was dying, whilst I was left alone downstairs and asked if I would mind getting my own tea. I even remember speculating on what would have happened if Uncle Patrick had been killed by his fall. One would, of course, have been desperately sorry. But the fact remained that Leonie would then… This was going a little far, even for me in that mood, and I hastily trod the thought under foot and began to play with Remus.

Ever since his sheep-worrying expedition Remus had been strangely subdued with me. He had soon recovered his spirits with Leonie, but with me there had remained a trace of guilt and uncertainty. I think he realised that I disapproved of what he had done, whilst Leonie did not. It made him particularly anxious for my approval, and during those days he worked harder and more intelligently than ever at our games. In particular, he would now allow me to bandage his eyes, which he had never let me do before, and would then come and find me, still blindfolded, when I called him. Poor Remus! Whatever his crimes, he was splendid company.

When I came down the following morning Leonie was cooking the breakfast, and looking a great deal more cheerful. She said that Uncle Patrick was much better, and that she thought after all that the doctor might be right, and that he had only bruised his back. Up till then, presumably, she had been sure that he had broken it. She was now nervous about what would happen next, as the accident to Uncle Patrick had happened the day after the death of Hawes, and she was certain that these things always happened in threes.

At the same time she told me that she would have to spend most of her time with my uncle for the next two days, and if I found it too dull and would prefer to go home three or four days early, she would quite understand. I naturally said that I would go if I was in the way, but that I would rather stay if there was anything I could do to help. Leonie was pleased, and said it was very nice of me, and that of course she would prefer me to stay and keep her company.

It was almost the first time in twenty-four hours that she seemed to have noticed that I existed; and during the same time she had hardly said a word to Remus or even looked at him. Even now, having, so to speak, given me a casual pat, she went back upstairs to my uncle, telling Remus not to follow, and I saw him looking at her with a slightly worried and, I thought, hurt expression.

So it came about that Remus and I were left alone again that evening, whilst our mistress—in our joint view quite unnecessarily—remained upstairs. In her slightly over-played part of devoted nurse, Leonie had moved her bed on to the small landing outside the room that she and my uncle usually occupied, so that she might be near him without actually being in the room to disturb him. This brought her perhaps ten seconds nearer the sick bed than she would have been if she had sat with us downstairs in the normal way. But I supposed it must have given her some satisfaction.

Remus and I spent a miserable evening. We were both in a bad temper; and when we tried, rather half-heartedly, to play some of our games, Remus was sulky and unusually stupid. In the end he just walked away and lay down with his nose on his paws, making it quite clear that he wanted to be left alone. I myself was thoroughly bored. There seemed to be nothing to read, and I could not even strum[2] on the piano for fear of waking Uncle Patrick. Yet somehow I could not bring myself to go to bed.

It must have been nearly eleven o'clock when I went and leant out of the window and looked at the orchard. It was a lovely night, and the orchard, with the dark shadows of the trees against the brilliantly starry sky, looked cool and inviting; whilst the house, after a hot day, seemed stuffy and oppressive. I decided that before going to bed I must go for a short walk. For some reason which I have never understood, it did not occur to me that it was silly to take Remus with me. Indeed, I was surprised and flattered when he showed signs of wanting to come. Usually he would have wanted to go upstairs to Leonie. I let myself and Remus out of the house very quietly, so as not to disturb anybody, and went out into the orchard. It was even more delicious than I had expected, and for the first time that year I thought I could smell the coming autumn. Remus kept close to my heels, and it struck me that he was nervous, constantly looking sharply about him, and jumping at every little sound.

I had never been out at night with him before, and I wondered whether, in fact, he was afraid of the dark. I decided to try an experiment. I made him lie down and put my handkerchief between his front paws. I told him that I should go away, and that he must guard my handkerchief until I came back. It was the type of game which we often played in daylight, but as I had rather expected, Remus made something of a fuss about playing it in the dark, and twice when I started to walk away, he simply picked the handkerchief up in his mouth and followed me. I scolded him gently and the third time he let me go.

I walked away about thirty yards amongst the trees, so that I was sure that I was out of his sight, waited for a few moments, and then went back to him. He was still lying where I had left him, with the handkerchief between his paws, but as I patted him and said he was a good dog, I was surprised to find that his whole body was quivering either with fear or excitement. I talked to him quietly and reassuringly, telling him that there was nothing to be frightened of, and then, rather cruelly and extremely stupidly, tried the trick again.

This time I went away and waited for about half a minute before I went back to him. I say "went back to him", but that is exactly what I did not do; for when I reached the place where I had left him, the handkerchief was still there, but Remus was not. Looking around, I clicked my fingers and called him softly, but he did not come.

Even then I was not particularly worried. I thought he had just gone back to the safety of the house, with its lighted window. But I went back to the house and walked all round it, and there was no sign of him; and then suddenly the incredible stupidity of what I had done struck me like a shower of ice-cold water, and I turned and dashed back at top speed to where I had left him, and stood with my heart pounding, looking wildly around. Everything was completely silent. I remembered that utter silence in the orchard on a previous occasion, and I knew in that moment, with sick despair, exactly what had happened.

I ran down the length of the orchard, occasionally stopping and calling him softly, and imitating Leonie's curious undulating whistle. But he did not come, nor did I expect now that he would.

I must have stayed in the orchards for quite half an hour, running, listening, calling, and whistling; but I did so without real hope, and mainly because of the intolerable nature of the alternative—to go back to the house and tell Leonie that I had taken Remus out in the dark and let him get away.

In the end I came back to my log, completely exhausted and despairing, and sat down on it and tried to consider what to do. I decided that I could not possibly tell Leonie the truth—that I must lie. I would tell her that Remus had seemed restless (which was true enough); that the window had been open, and that suddenly he had jumped out of the window and bolted into the darkness. It was not a very brilliant story, but it was the best I could think of in my agitated state.

I hurried back to the house and went upstairs. Leonie was asleep in the bed on the landing, with a night light burning beside her. I shook her gently by the shoulder, and when her eyes opened I whispered, "Leonie—Remus has gone off."

She stared at me blankly and sleepily for a moment and mumbled, "What?"

I said, "Remus… he…"

She understood this time and leapt out of bed, staring at me with wide, terrified eyes. Then she turned and grabbed her trousers, and started to pull them on over her pyjamas. She pulled an old wool jersey over her head, and without a word hurried downstairs with me behind her.

As we went out of the front door she said, "How did he get out?"

I said, "The window was open like it is now. He'd seemed a bit queer all the evening. Then, while I was reading, he suddenly jumped out of the window and bolted. I called him but he just went on."

She said, "This was just now?"

"No. About half an hour ago. I've been looking for him ever since."

"Why didn't you come and tell me at once, Walter?"

I hesitated and then said, "I was afraid I might wake Uncle Patrick."

It was a feeble explanation and I realised it, and thought she might not believe me. But she hardly seemed to hear me. She gave a little groan and said, "It's because I went upstairs and wouldn't let him come. It's always when I leave him that this happens."

Of course we went all over the orchards again, calling and whistling; and of course there was no sign of Remus. Then we went and stood by the wire, as we had done before, and stared out at the expanse of the field beyond.

Leonie said, "There's one good thing—the sheep aren't in that field. Masters has moved them." Then suddenly her body seemed to sag and she said drearily, "But what difference does that make? They must be somewhere about, and he'll find them. I knew something like this was going to happen. It's the third thing."

We were still standing at the wire when there was a distant crack that might have been a gunshot. We both heard it, because we turned and looked at one another, but neither of us spoke. After that there was the silence again, and suddenly Leonie turned abruptly and said, "Let's go back to the house. I can't leave Patrick alone for long."

We went back into the living-room. I said, "Shall we wait for him, like we did the last time?"

Leonie said "Yes" curtly and sank down in a chair and closed her eyes.

After a pause I said, "Had we better get the hot water and things ready?"

Leonie did not reply for a moment. Then she opened her eyes and said dully, "I suppose so" and went slowly out into the kitchen.

I think it was the longest night of my life. It seemed far longer than on the first occasion. Again I dozed from time to time, and each time when I woke, Leonie was opposite me, sitting quite still, with her hands limply in her lap, staring in front of her. We stayed there until dawn, and then Leonie suddenly said "He won't come now" and rose and went out into the kitchen and took the kettle off the gas.

I said, "He still might. It was nearly as late as this before and…"

Leonie just repeated quietly "He won't come now" and closed the front door and led the way to bed.

She was right. Remus did not come. But he did his best. We found him the following morning, in the orchard, only about fifty yards from the house. He was lying in a strange sprawling position, half on his stomach and half on his side, with one leg stretched out behind him. Again there was blood on his mouth, and blood had dried and matted on his chest and ruff; but this time it was his own. He had been shot neatly through the chest, the bullet having gone in one side and out the other. His body was already cold, and there was a long trail of blood stretching back down the orchard towards the wire and we could see it going on into the field beyond. In the field and for most of the way up the orchard the blood was a trail of big round spots, but in the last few yards it was smeared on the ground where he had dragged himself.

It was Leonie who found him. She called me, and when I reached her side, she was standing looking down at Remus with a curious blank expression. Her face was very pale, but she did not cry. I knelt down beside Remus and gently turned him so that I could look at the wound. I found it and looked up at her. She just nodded curtly and comprehendingly. Neither of us spoke. Then she turned and walked back to the house without a word, and I did not see her again for several hours.

Thirteen

The silent man buried Remus for us. Leonie did not want to see him again, or to know where he was buried, so I found a pleasant spot in the orchard near some nut bushes, and told the silent man to bury him there, and went away. In my life I have seen many people buried. They had been human beings, and some of them had been young and intelligent and beautiful. But I have never felt more strongly the grotesque wastefulness of death, than at the thought of all that superb gold-and-black fur, and those velvet ears, and that proud plume of a tail being buried in the ground to rot. This sense of waste was so strong that it drove everything else from my mind—sympathy for Leonie, sense of guilt at my own part in the affair, or anger against whoever had killed him. My anger, as it has sometimes been since, was a pure, blind anger with the fact of death itself.

At about one o'clock Leonie came downstairs and started to cook a meal. She was still pale and rather silent. We said nothing about Remus while we ate. Leonie told me that Uncle Patrick now seemed to be quite well again, and would get up for a while that evening.

We did not eat much, and then Leonie went and sat on the sofa and said, "Now we must decide what to do about Masters." She looked at me calmly and thoughtfully. "I suppose there's no possible doubt that it *was* Masters who killed him?"

I said, "The trail of blood comes right back across that field." I was surprised at Leonie's question. I should have expected her to assume at once that Masters had shot Remus, knowing her feelings about Masters.

"Of course there's no *real* doubt about it at all," said Leonie irritably. "No *sensible* doubt, I mean. But we want to be sure of our ground." She stared at me again in the strange thoughtful way and said, "You've no doubt about it, Walter?"

I hesitated and said, "Well, I can't *prove* it, of course, but it seems fairly obvious. He said he'd shoot Remus if he caught him with the sheep again, and Remus goes off over there and comes back shot."

Leonie said, "Of course it may not have been Masters himself who did the shooting. In fact it's more likely to have been one of his men. I don't suppose Masters sits up all night with his sheep. But anyhow, it would have been done on his orders."

I was still puzzled by this oddly uncharacteristic, almost legalistic approach. I was even more surprised when Leonie said briskly, "I think the best way would be just to go and see Masters and ask him point blank about it." She got up and said, "Would you like to come with me?"

I said, "You're going to see him now?"

Leonie said, "We might as well. I should like to get it settled. Don't come if you don't want to. There's no reason why you should be mixed up in it."

I said, "Of course I'll come" and followed her out to the car, still slightly mystified. As we got into the car I said, "I don't quite see what good it will do to go and see him, Leonie. Supposing he just says he doesn't know anything about it?"

"Then he'll be a liar," said Leonie simply. "But he won't do that anyhow."

"Why not? It's the obvious thing for him to do."

"You'll see," said Leonie briefly.

We drove to Colonel Masters's house comparatively slowly and safely—certainly a great deal more carefully than we had driven on the night of the cocktail party. I noticed again the curious, slightly unnatural calm that had come over Leonie since that morning. She seemed to be speaking and moving with a strange, deliberate slowness and quietness which was quite unlike her normal manner, and which I found faintly disturbing.

Colonel Masters, in an old tweed suit and a sun hat, was stooping over one of the flower beds in front of his house, with a trowel in his hand. From the rear he looked like the back of an elephant. He straightened up and turned as we stopped at the gate, and then, as we went in, came slowly towards us. As we approached one another he said quietly, "Ah—hallo, Leonie. I thought perhaps I should be seeing you soon." He did not smile as he said it.

"Why?" said Leonie.

Masters slowly tucked his neckerchief farther into his shirt. His thick throat was almost black from the sun. He said, "Is it about the dog?"

"Did you shoot Remus?" said Leonie simply.

"Of course not," said Masters with a bland little smile.

"Or tell somebody else to?"

"My dear girl," said the Colonel gently, "I told you the last time we discussed this that my people had instructions to shoot any dog that came and attacked my sheep. Last night, they tell me, a big Alsatian came and started to run the sheep, and one of the men shot at it. That's all I can tell you. He doesn't even know if he hit it."

I heard Leonie draw her breath in sharply. There was a moment's pause, and then she said, "Then why did you tell me a moment ago that you didn't shoot him?"

"You asked me," said Masters carefully, "whether I had shot Remus. Obviously this dog can't have been yours, because it was on my land worrying my sheep; and you've told me repeatedly that your dog never worries sheep, and is always in the house all night. That's so, isn't it?" He was looking at her now with the odd, half-sneering smile that I had noticed before when he spoke to her.

There was a moment's pause, and then suddenly the smile vanished, and he said curtly, "Did the dog get home?"

Leonie said in a low voice, "Yes. He got home. Or nearly."

"Is he badly hurt?"

Leonie swallowed, and I saw that she could not say the words, so I said, "He's dead, Colonel Masters."

The Colonel turned his long-distance stare on me for a moment and then turned back to Leonie. He said, "Well, I'm sorry this should have happened, Leonie. But I did warn you."

Leonie said, "We warned one another, didn't we?"

"I know you were fond of your dog. I have dogs that I am fond of myself. But I don't mind telling you that I've done you a good turn."

"Yes?" said Leonie bitterly.

"Do you realise what it would have been likely to cost you if I had turned this over to the police? The Magistrates here are very hot on sheep worrying. And rightly. You'd probably have been fined a hundred pounds for a start, and the dog would have been ordered to be destroyed. Then you would have been made to pay for the damage—and I don't mind telling you that that would have come to something that you—or rather Parrish—would have found it uncommonly difficult to afford."

Leonie said "I'm deeply grateful to you" and then suddenly the calm bitterness broke for a moment and she said fiercely, "Why did you have to shoot him? Why couldn't you… drive him away or something…?" Her voice broke, and for the first time since we had found Remus's body I thought she was going to cry.

"Don't be silly, my dear," said Masters, impatiently but not unkindly. "You must know that when a dog is on a rampage like that you can't get anywhere near him." There was no reply to that. We knew it only too bitterly well.

Suddenly Masters turned to me and said, "There's just one thing I'd like to ask you, young man. I want to be sure that the trouble I've been having has all been from the same dog. Yours is dead now, and he was caught at it, so you needn't mind telling me the truth. But he was out after them the other night, wasn't he—the night when you said he was in your room? And you'd washed him after he'd come in? That was it, wasn't it?"

I hesitated for a moment, and as I did so Leonie said quietly, "Yes."

"I thought so," said Masters with a grim little nod of satisfaction. He turned to me again and said bitingly, "You're a pretty cool liar for your age."

Leonie said, "Walter only said that because I asked him to."

"Chivalry," said Masters. "I expect they teach you that at school. Do they teach you lying too?"

Leonie took me quickly by the arm and turned me towards the gate. As we walked towards it, Masters said to our backs, "I'm sorry, Leonie, but you've had a long run on this, and now you've no one to thank but yourself."

As we were driving away Leonie said, "Forgive me, Walter."
"What for?"
"That I let… that he could say that to you."

"Why should I care what *he* says?" I said contemptuously. But I did care, all the same, in one sense. For up to that point, even after I had seen Remus dead, I had had my old sneaking feeling that Masters was in the right and we were in the wrong about the whole matter. Even a few minutes before, when he was telling us bluntly and straightforwardly what had happened, the feeling had remained. But the sneer—the obvious pleasure in a blow that hurt—was unforgivable.

"Never mind," said Leonie with a little shrug. "He won't talk to people like that much longer. The thing now is to decide how to do it."

"How to do what?"

"Kill him, of course," said Leonie calmly. She turned to me with a broad smile and added, "Don't you remember I told him that I would kill him if he killed Remus?"

I looked at her, startled; but she was still smiling a broad and happy smile. She said, "Come on, Walter, you've got brains. How do we set about killing Masters?"

The smile reassured me. I said with mock solemnity, "Well now—let me see… there are various things that we could do. We could put poison in his whisky, or we could cut a tree down and lay it across the road in the dark, so that his car…"

"Oh no," said Leonie with decision. "He's got to be shot. That's what I said I'd do to him if he shot Remus."

"We haven't got a gun. I might make a catapult, but I don't think a catapult would do for him. He's too big. Perhaps we'd better use a blowpipe and poison darts. That's how the natives kill elephants, and he's very like an elephant."

"Go on," said Leonie happily.

"Or how about a bow and arrow?" I said, warming to the game. "Then we could say it was an accident, like they did when Sir Walter Tyrrel shot William Rufus.[1] We could say we were shooting at a deer and the arrow glanced off a tree and killed Masters. And then we could send his body home on a charcoal burner's wain.[2] Except that there aren't really very many charcoal burners' wains about."

Leonie laughed. I was delighted, not only because she was enjoying my nonsense, but because for a moment she seemed to have forgotten her grief over Remus.

As we reached home Leonie said, "Don't say anything to your uncle, of course. The fewer people that know about this, the better chance there is of getting away with it."

"Not a word," I said in a conspiratorial whisper.

I had never known any human being whose moods could change more quickly than Leonie's. When we were in the car and I was joking about how to kill Masters she had seemed surprisingly cheerful. But no sooner had we reached the house than the black cloud descended again. Perhaps it was that there was no Remus to come bounding out to meet her which finally brought home to her that he was gone forever. That evening she was very silent and depressed, and immediately after supper she said she had a headache and went to bed.

Rather to my surprise, Uncle Patrick did not go to bed too, but stayed up with me. He seemed fully recovered now, and he had been sleeping for most of the last two days, so he probably did not feel tired. Also, I think he was being polite to me, feeling perhaps that I had been having a dull time.

He played to me for a while, though not for long, as his back was still hurting him slightly. I suggested that he should go to bed, but he replied that he was quite all right as long as he could rest his back against something, and then settled down and said, "Well—I suppose you'll be leaving us soon now."

I said that I was going early on Tuesday morning: Uncle Patrick nodded and said, "It's been a great pleasure to have you here, Walter. We shall miss you badly. You've been splendid company for Leonie, and she's very fond of you. She gets very lonely, you know."

I said, "I'm afraid she's going to miss Remus."

"Yes," he said sombrely. "She hadn't much before, and now she has even less, poor girl."

He glanced at me for a moment, and then looked away and said, "You see, Walter, I'm not young enough or… active enough, to be much fun for her." He glanced at me quickly again, as though he was hoping that I would say something— perhaps that I should pretend to disagree. He had always been very courteous to me, and I should have liked to be courteous in return, and to tell him that I was sure that Leonie was perfectly happy and contented with him. But feeling as I did about the whole matter I could not do it, and just said nothing.

"I want her to be free," said my uncle, more it seemed to himself than to me. "People ought to be free when they're young."

"And when they're old," I said, trying to make an intelligent-sounding contribution.

"Perhaps," said my uncle. "But particularly when they're young." He hesitated for a long moment and then said, "There's something I think you should know, Walter. You're old enough to understand these things now. Leonie and I are not married."

"I know," I said. "Leonie told me."

My uncle nodded. He did not seem at all surprised. He said, "Well—that's *why* we're not married. I want her to be free, you see."

Something in the way that he said it irritated me—perhaps a hint of self-righteousness. It was on the tip of my tongue to say that if he was so anxious for Leonie to be free, he ought not to keep her around at Glebe Cottage cooking the meals and washing the dishes and being bored, but to let her go away and marry someone younger, like myself. But I looked at his pale thin face—the face of a chronically sick man—and I could not put it so brutally. Instead I said, "How would you feel if she went away and married someone else?"

My uncle smiled his crooked little smile. He said, "That's an awkward question, Walter. In some ways it would be… the end of my life. But if she wanted to, I would never try to stop her. I've always told her so. But…" He made a little gesture. "Leonie is a very loyal person."

He was staring straight in front of him thoughtfully, but now he turned and gave me the wry smile and added, "If she were in love, of course, I should have no say in it. Always remember, Walter, that most women are completely loyal to the man they're with, until they fall in love. And then…" He gave a little shrug.

"Then they just start being completely loyal to somebody else. I realise that that could happen to Leonie."

He was looking at me with an odd wistful smile, as though he wanted me to understand something more than he was saying. A great light suddenly dawned on me—a light which sent a shudder of excitement through my whole body. I had been puzzled as to why my Uncle Patrick, who was usually so reticent should have been talking to me in this intimate way. But now at last I understood. Obviously, he had realised that Leonie and I were in love; and he was trying in his polite way to convey to me that he knew he could not keep her from me—that it was inevitable that I should take her from him.

Yet, mixed with the feeling of exultation at his admission of my triumph, I felt much compassion for my uncle. After all, it was not his fault that he was so old.

I said kindly, "All the same, Leonie's terribly fond of you, you know. She was awfully cut up when you fell out of the tree. In fact," I added, with a victor's magnanimity, "she hardly took any notice of me at all when you were in bed."

"Yes," said my uncle. "I'm sorry about that. It must have made things very dull for you. Never mind—you must come again soon, and we'll try to make it more amusing. When d'you go back to school?"

I said, "In ten days' time," almost automatically. My thoughts were far away.

I sat on my bed for a long while that night, formulating my plans. The conversation with Uncle Patrick had been a tremendous step forward, representing as it did his resignation to the inevitable. I had long ago ceased to feel that to take Leonie away from him would be in any way treacherous or disloyal. It would merely be the fortune of war—something which life itself had arranged, which happened to be fortunate for me and unfortunate for him, but for which neither of us could really be held responsible. Nevertheless, it was a relief to know that he realised this.

In the last few days in particular, since the tree episode, I had been a little worried lest Leonie's characteristic loyalty, even to somebody whom she did not love, might have been a thing that my uncle would exploit. But he had now made it perfectly clear to me that, knowing she was in love with me, he would not expect this loyalty to continue.

This was all splendid as far as it went; but there remained the problem of how to bring matters to a head with Leonie and get the matter settled once and for all. The time now was desperately short. Looking back, it seemed that since I had first made up my mind to suggest marriage to Leonie, life had been one series of time-wasting frustrations. Firstly, that admirable opportunity in the barn had been wasted through Leonie's sudden and unaccountable change of front. Then there had been my uncle's fall, so that I had hardly seen her for three days. And now there was the death of Remus, which had made her glum and unapproachable.

I thought back over all the times we had spent together, and it seemed to me that apart from the first few minutes in the barn, the moment when I had seemed closest to Leonie and had been most sure of my ability to make her do anything that I wished had been the night when we went for a walk in the wind and had hopped down the hill together, and had gone to the churchyard—the night when, but for the sudden appearance of Hawes, she had said that she would have danced naked round the tombstones for me. It was that which had to be re-created. Not, perhaps, that situation, but that atmosphere. I was still trying to work out how to re-create it when I went to sleep.

Fourteen

Soon after breakfast the following morning Leonie went off in the car. She did not say where she was going, nor ask me to go with her, at which I was hurt. When she returned about two hours later my Uncle Patrick and I were sitting outside in the sun, talking in a desultory way. By unspoken agreement neither of us had mentioned our conversation of the night before. There was, after all, no need, as the situation was obviously quite clear to both of us.

Leonie said "Hallo" briefly and went past into the house. As she did so she caught my eye and gave a quick jerk of the head to indicate that I should follow her.

We went into the kitchen and Leonie closed the door. She turned to me and said with a kind of quiet excitement, "I've found out something. Something that can be very useful. He goes for a walk, early every morning."

"Who does?"

"Masters, of course. Every morning he walks round the farm before breakfast. Well—to get from one half of the farm to the other he must go through Poachers' Wood." She paused and looked at me suggestively.

I said, "What about it?"

Leonie lowered her voice and said, "Don't you see that that might be a marvellous place to get him? There are always people banging about somewhere in that wood, so that nobody'd take any notice of a shot. And anyhow, I know he's had a lot of trouble with poachers, and if he was found there, everyone would think that it was a poacher who'd done it."

In the press of more important matters, I had forgotten about the "let's murder Masters" game, and anyhow I was tired of it.

I said, "We must get some rubber for that catapult. D'you think they've got any in Canterbury?" But I said it without enthusiasm and purely to amuse her.

"We don't need a catapult," said Leonie quietly.

"No—I told you. You need an elephant gun. Have you got one?"

There was a moment's pause. Leonie said, "You don't seem very keen. I think it's a marvellous idea."

"It's brilliant. You should have been a master criminal."

"All right," said Leonie rather crossly. "You don't have to be in it unless you want to. I can manage perfectly well by myself."

I saw that she was disappointed, and I remembered that when we had played this game the previous day it had lifted her out of her depression and made her seem almost happy for a while. I put my arm round her and said, "Of course I want to be in it. It isn't every day that you get a chance to murder somebody. Anyhow, the poacher idea isn't at all bad. Particularly if we had an alibi for ourselves."

Leonie said, "What *is* an alibi, exactly? I've never been quite sure."

"Well, it's… something to prove that you couldn't possibly have done it—whatever's been done, I mean. You arrange beforehand to be able to prove that when it happened you were somewhere else."

"I see," said Leonie, with the exact expression and tone that she always used when I was trying to explain some particularly complicated piece of verse to her. I was about to say "That was an alibi when we told Masters that Remus had slept in my room." But I did not want to remind her of Remus, so I said, "Look—supposing we kill Masters at seven o'clock in the morning, in Poachers' Wood…"

"Yes?"

"Well, if we can prove that at seven o'clock in the morning we were somewhere else quite different, then it couldn't possibly have been us, could it?"

"But if we were somewhere else, how could we kill Masters?" said Leonie with a puzzled frown.

"We *weren't* somewhere else," I said patiently. "We just seem to be able to *prove* that we were."

"How?"

"I don't know at the moment," I said, patting her on the shoulder. "I haven't thought about it yet. I'll think it out and tell you later."

"All right," said Leonie with relief. "It sounds the sort of thing that you do better than I do."

"Probably. And in the meantime, you'll get the elephant rifle?"

"I'll see to that," said Leonie with quiet confidence. She looked round the kitchen vaguely and said, "Now what on earth are we going to eat?"

∾

I had decided that whatever else might be left to chance, about my crucial talk with Leonie, it must take place at night, and out of doors. Ideally there should be a high wind as well. I realised that this might be too much to expect, but that it should take place at night was essential. Night has always had a strong emotional significance for me. During the day I am, on the whole, a rather earth-bound person, with a tendency to think in practical, realistic terms, and to see the difficulties in any enterprise almost too readily. But in the dark it is different. Difficulties become mere indistinguishable trees in the wood whose shape, though dimly seen, is magnificent. Night not only gives me courage, but a sense of power. It is then that I, like Hamlet, could drink the hot blood and do the bitter business. I should, perhaps, have been a night watchman.

I had accordingly decided that after supper that evening, when my uncle would probably have gone to bed, I would ask Leonie to come for a night walk with me and during it to explain to her, quietly but passionately, how necessary and inevitable it was that she should leave my uncle and marry me. I was not proposing to insist on actual marriage before I left Glebe Cottage. There was too little time. But I wanted to be sure that we should at least regard ourselves as engaged.

In the afternoon, therefore, I went out into the orchard to my favourite log and sat down with the intention of working out in detail exactly how I should put my proposal to Leonie. Most irritatingly, however, I found it difficult to concentrate. From my log I could see the place, only about twenty yards away, near the nut bushes, where Remus was buried. The thought of Remus started off a whole series of other thoughts, none of which concerned my immediate problem.

In particular, however hard I tried to concentrate on the vital question of Leonie and myself, I always came back, quite absurdly, to the question of how we should set up an alibi if we were *really* going to murder Colonel Masters in Poachers' Wood.

I thought perhaps that it was the nearness of Remus's grave which kept bringing this to my mind, and went farther into the orchard to another spot from which I could not see it. But it made no difference. Every time I started to compose the opening phrases of my address to Leonie—phrases which were purely introductory, and only intended to set the conversation at the proper level of high seriousness—my mind would wander off to some wild scheme for tying a piece of string to the trigger of a gun and stretching the string across a path in the wood so that the Colonel would be shot when he tripped over it. In the end I gave up and, drowsy in the heat of the afternoon, let my mind have its own way and started to design the perfect crime.

I had read very few detective stories, and, indeed, very little about crime at all. But I remembered that someone had written somewhere that the perfect murder would be one carried out by a single person operating without accomplices; and that it would be the completely motiveless murder of a total stranger. This was not encouraging, since Leonie and I were certainly accomplices, knew Masters, and had a motive—even if one which would hardly seem strong enough to most people to lead us to murder. The *really* perfect crime was obviously out of the question. What was needed, as I had told Leonie, was an alibi…

It was a very hot afternoon, and even when my brain was allowed to think about the alibi, it did not do so very brilliantly. But by tea-time I had thought of something which, though not particularly original, seemed to me to be along the right lines. We had discovered that my train for home left Canterbury at about half past seven in the morning, which was presumably about the time when Masters would be on his early morning walk. The previous night, when Uncle Patrick was asleep, Leonie and I would put his watch on half an hour. In the morning we would go to see Uncle Patrick, who would still be in bed, at about half past six. We would tell him that it was seven o'clock, and that I must go now to catch my train. As something of a master stroke, we would ensure that he actually *looked* at his watch, which would, of course, say seven o'clock.

We would then take the car towards Poachers' Wood, leave it concealed, go into the wood, murder Colonel Masters, return to the car and still have comfortable time to catch the train, arriving at the station at, say, twenty past seven.

Our alibi would then be complete. Uncle Patrick would be able to swear that we left at seven, and the ticket collector that we were at Canterbury station at seven-twenty. Even with Leonie driving, it was a good twenty minutes to the station, and certainly there would have been no time in that twenty minutes to have gone into Poachers' Wood and committed a murder.

I was not altogether satisfied with the plan. It assumed that Colonel Masters would conveniently come through Poachers' Wood at the right moment; and it occurred to me that it would be necessary for Leonie to get hold of Uncle Patrick's watch again when she got home and put it back to the right time—which, since it was a wrist watch, might be a little difficult. But by now I was tired of the whole thing, and it was tea-time. I decided that my alibi would be good enough to amuse and impress Leonie if she ever asked about it; whilst if she showed any signs of being too critical, I could always switch us on to the more difficult, and in some ways more amusing, problem of begging, borrowing or stealing an elephant rifle. At least I had got the silly business out of my mind for the moment, and now found that I could concentrate much more easily on what I was going to say to her that evening.

I ate practically no supper. I was waiting tensely for the meal to be over. There were still things that might go wrong. Leonie might decide to go off to bed, Uncle Patrick might decide to sit up again and play the piano, and I could hardly take Leonie out for a walk and leave him alone. Or then again, Leonie might decide to stay up, but refuse to come for a walk, when I knew I should lose at least half of my courage and effectiveness.

Happily, none of these things happened. Leonie seemed to be in one of her cheerful moods; Uncle Patrick went off obligingly to bed, and by nine o'clock I was able to suggest to Leonie, with careful casualness, that we should go for a walk. She said, "Yes, let's" at once, and went off to get her jacket. Whilst she was gone, I took out my handkerchief and carefully wiped the palms of my hands, which were damp with perspiration.

I received a setback as soon as we left the house. Leonie said, "I tell you what—let's go to Poachers' Wood. I haven't been there for ages, and we ought to spy out the ground."

I said, "You can't do much spying out in the dark. Let's walk up to the barn."

"No," said Leonie firmly. "We can go there afterwards. I want to go into Poachers' Wood for a minute or two."

This was annoying. I particularly wanted to make my statement sitting on the hay in the barn, and all my rehearsals had assumed it as a setting. Moreover, I was in no mood to waste time on any of Leonie's nonsense about Masters. But I realised that there was nothing to be done about it, and went with her rather sulkily towards Poachers' Wood.

On the way she asked me whether I had thought any more about the alibi. I thought of saying that I hadn't and didn't propose to, but I knew that this would only annoy her, which was the last thing I wanted to do at that moment. I therefore told her briefly what I had thought of—the business about the time and Uncle Patrick's watch, and so on. She seemed impressed and delighted, and squeezed my arm and said I was very clever.

Poachers' Wood was quite large. There must have been nearly a hundred acres of it, and, as Leonie had said, it lay across the middle of Masters's estate. To get to it we had to climb a high gate with barbed wire on the top of it, and Leonie tore her trousers slightly, which annoyed her. She said, "Masters *would* have everything plastered with barbed wire, wouldn't he? He's a barbed-wire sort of man."

The wood was one of those frequently found in Kent and Sussex which are used for growing chestnut poles. The poles are cut down every seven or eight years, and new ones grow from the roots. This one must have been nearly ready for cutting, for it was very dense. Outside it was not very dark, though there were clouds over the moon; but in the wood itself the darkness was profound, and it was very silent, except once when something, probably a rabbit, startled us by rushing away with a sudden rustle and crackle from right under our feet. Leonie gave a little gasp and grabbed my arm hard. I knew she was frightened, and was glad of it. Darkness being my element, I was not particularly frightened myself. But it was pointless to be blundering about in a dark wood where we could hardly see the path before us, and I felt that the more frightened Leonie was the sooner she would be prepared to come back and go to the barn, and we should be able to get on with the real business of the evening. But for the moment she went on, saying to me in a whisper, "I think he must come along this path. There isn't another that goes right through the middle."

Suddenly, and very startlingly in the silence and blackness, there was a momentary flicker of bright light amongst the trees only about thirty yards ahead of us. We both saw it and stopped. A moment later there was another brief flicker, and a low whistle. Leonie put her mouth close to my ear and whispered, "Poachers."

I nodded silently. Again the light shone, but this time it remained steady for a moment, and in that moment we had time to glimpse the figures of two men amongst the trees not far from the path. They were crouching on their haunches working at something on the ground. They had probably been netting rabbits. As we watched they rose to their feet and moved towards the track. Then the light was switched off.

It had looked as though they might be moving towards us, and I grabbed Leonie by the arm and pulled her to one side off the track amongst the trees. The rustle of our feet on the fallen leaves seemed very loud. We took cover behind one of the thick chestnut plants and waited. Almost certainly we had as much right in the wood as the men, if not more. But neither of us wanted to walk into a gang of poachers in those circumstances.

There was a faint crackling of twigs as they made their way out on to the path, and for a moment a very low mutter of voices. After that there was silence again. We must have waited at least a minute, but they did not pass our hiding place, and I decided that they must have gone the other way.

I was just about to tell Leonie so when I felt her fingers tighten on my arm. I turned my head quickly, and at first sensed rather than saw or heard someone coming along the path by the way we had come. A moment later the figure of a man, seemingly huge from our crouching position, appeared out of the darkness. He was walking quickly, but remarkably silently. He passed within half a dozen yards of us, and as he did so I saw he was carrying a shotgun. Even in the darkness there was no mistaking that massive figure. Colonel Masters was out after the poachers.

We waited again—longer this time; and then I took Leonie by the arm and led her out on to the path. We hurried as quickly and silently as we could back along it by the way we had come.

We said nothing until we were over the gate with the open country before us again, and then Leonie gave a little groan of disappointment and said, "Oh God, what a pity! With poachers about and all. We could have done it, if only we'd had the gun. And nobody could possibly have known we'd been there. Oh hell!"

I had been somewhat shaken by the way in which Masters had materialised so silently out of the darkness, and what she said irritated me. I said crossly, "We should have looked pretty silly if we'd walked into him, shouldn't we? Come on—let's go to the barn."

Leonie hesitated and then said, "All right" but without much enthusiasm.

Our barn lay in the opposite direction from Poachers' Wood, and to get to it we had to go past Glebe Cottage. As we neared the house Leonie suddenly said, "Look—I just want to pop indoors for a moment. Walk on slowly, and I'll catch you up."

She turned in at the garden gate and ran down the path. I

strolled slowly on, feeling tense and not very happy. The moment was upon me, and it had to *be* the moment, for there might not be another opportunity. But the business in Poachers' Wood had done nothing to create the atmosphere I wanted. I wished profoundly that there had been a high wind. Leonie caught me up within a hundred yards and I saw that she had put on an overcoat. I was surprised, for it was a warm night. I took her arm and we walked on towards the barn in silence for a few moments. Then Leonie suddenly said, "Walter dear—I want to say something… I'm telling you now so that you won't be disappointed and say I cheated. But if we *do* go to the barn—no kissing to-night. I don't feel like it."

I said, "I don't want to kiss you. At least, I do, but that's another thing. I want to talk to you."

"Fine!" said Leonie. I thought she said it with some relief. After a pause she said, "What d'you want to talk to me about?"

I said, "I'll tell you when we get there," and after that we walked on in silence until we reached the barn.

It was dark in the barn, but not as dark as it had been in the wood, and I could see the outline of Leonie's face, glimmering with a sort of pearly whiteness. A lot of the hay was gone, but there was still plenty left. We sat down together side by side, and I took a deep breath and started.

It went very well on the whole, and the longer I went on the easier it became. I told her that I loved her—that within a day of being at Glebe Cottage I had been in love with her, and that my love had gone on growing stronger and stronger ever since. I told her that she was the most beautiful woman I had ever seen, and by far the nicest. I had not meant to tell her about the business of having watched her in the bath; but somehow it was necessary that she should know about it, and so I blurted it all out, and explained how it had made me want to look after her and protect her.

During all this Leonie sat with her shadowy face turned to me. She sat quite still, and said nothing, except that she occasionally murmured softly "Dear Walter" or "Darling" and squeezed my hand. When I came to the bath episode she gave a little snort which was half a giggle. But I did not mind. I knew that snort, and it did not mean that Leonie was laughing at me. It meant rather that she was flattered and slightly confused.

At the end of what I had thought of as Section I of my speech—the account of my feelings for her—I asked her if she had known that I loved her.

She hesitated for a moment and then said, "Well—yes, Walter dear. I suppose I did know. In a way. I didn't know it was as bad as this, but I knew that you wanted to… kiss me and so on."

This did not strike me as very well put. "As bad as this" sounded as though I had been telling her that I had a cold; and I did not much like "kiss me and so on". But I let it pass and asked her point blank if she loved me?

She hesitated for much longer this time, and for one awful moment I thought she was going to deny it. But then she said, "Of course I love you, Walter. I love you a lot. You're quite one of the nicest people I've ever known, and you've been terribly kind to me over lots of things. Remus, and Masters, and at that cocktail party, and making me read, and… all sorts of things." She squeezed my hand again and said, "You don't know how much I shall miss you."

This led me neatly to Section II of my statement—our future. I explained to her that when two people felt as we did about one another, then the obvious thing was for them to get married. I realised, I said, that there was some difference in our ages but it was more apparent than real. Mentally we were very much the same age. Anyhow, I pointed out, people often married whose ages were much more different than ours.

I had expected that the idea of marriage, instead of merely continuing as lovers, might be a new thought to her, and I paused, waiting for a reaction. But Leonie sat, still and silent for a long time, just looking at me, with her warm hand in mine.

Then she said in a low voice, "You're rather young to be thinking about getting married, aren't you, darling?"

I had, of course, expected this, and I explained to her what I had in mind—that we should merely become engaged for the moment, but with an understanding that we would get married as soon as I had passed Higher Certificate and could leave school and get a job. I told her frankly that I had not got a ring to offer her, because I was down to the last five shillings of my thirty-two-and-sixpence. But she said quickly, "Oh, that doesn't matter, Walter. Lots of people don't have engagement rings. And anyhow, I couldn't wear it if I had, because we should have to keep this a secret from everybody, shouldn't we? I mean from… from your Uncle Patrick and people."

Nothing could have been more perfect, for this led straight into my third section, and what I regarded, to some extent, as being my trump card—the whole question of Uncle Patrick. I told Leonie about my conversation with him—of how he knew of our love for one another, realised that it was inevitable that he should lose her, had accepted the fact with characteristic unselfishness, and certainly would not stand in her way.

This time I think she was really surprised. She said "*What?*" in a low voice several times, and asked me a number of questions about exactly what Uncle Patrick had said.

I answered all her questions, and then said, "So there you are, darling. You see, there's absolutely no reason why we shouldn't be engaged, and then get married in… in about two years' time. It's just a question of… whether you will."

For the first time now she turned her head away, and sat looking straight in front of her for a long while—so long that I could not bear it and said, "Well?"

She turned and stared at me for a moment, still in silence, and then she suddenly put out her hand and took mine again and said very gently, "All right, Walter dear. I'll be engaged to you—so long as it's just a secret between ourselves. And… and some day I'll marry you, if you haven't found somebody else you like better by then. But…"

I felt hot tears filling my eyes. I put out my arms to her and said huskily, "Leonie—I…" But she pulled back a little and said, "Wait a moment. There's something I want you to do for me first."

I said, "I would do anything in the world for you. *Anything.*"

"Right," said Leonie. "Then help me over Masters."

It was a moment of devastating bitterness. She had listened so carefully, she had not laughed at anything I said, which I had half-feared she might, and she had seemed to be absolutely serious. And now suddenly she was talking again about a childish and silly game which had long since ceased to be any fun.

I said with sulky anger, "I don't want to spin kids' stories, I want to talk about life."

She said, "But you said you'd help me, Walter. You said you'd do anything for me." She sounded hurt and disappointed.

"But there isn't any more to make up," I said wearily. "I told you about the alibi this evening. What else do you want?"

Leonie said, "I want you to teach me how to use this."

She took something out of her pocket and held it out to me. It was cold and heavy. I peered at it in the semi-darkness and saw that it was an automatic pistol. I was startled and said, "Where did you get this?"

"It's Patrick's. He brought it back from the war. It's a German one."

"Does he know you've got it?"

"Of course not. I doubt if he even remembers that he's got it himself. It's been about for years. I want you to show me how it works."

The sensible thing of course would have been to say that I had never seen an automatic before and knew nothing about them. But it happened that a few months before there had been a lecture to the school rifle club on safety in handling firearms, and I had seen an automatic pistol, and heard it explained, though I had never previously had one in my hand. I could not resist playing my favourite role with Leonie of the man who knows everything. Moreover, as I ran my fingers over the pistol, I found that the magazine in the butt was missing, and this reassured me. For a moment I had been taken aback when Leonie produced the pistol, but now I realised that this was all an elaborate part of our fantasy.

Leonie said, "Go on—show me how it works."

I said, "I can't show you in the dark, silly."

"I've got a torch."

She fished a small electric torch out of her pocket, and shone it on the pistol. It was an ugly and efficient-looking affair, not long-barrelled like a Luger, but squat and compact. I should judge that its calibre was eight or nine millimetres. For something that had been "lying about for years", it seemed in excellent condition.

Remembering the lecture, I looked to make sure that there was not a round in the breech. There was not. It took me a moment or two to find the safety catch, which was in a different place from the one which we had been shown.

Leonie said, "What are you doing?"

"I was looking for the safety catch. Here it is, you see. As long as you have that on, you can't fire. There's another safety thing too. You can't pull the trigger unless you squeeze the back of the butt as well. That's in case somebody grabs the gun and tries to pull it away from you. Unless you're squeezing the butt as well as pulling the trigger, it won't fire, so you can't shoot them by accident."

"I'm not interested in not shooting people by accident," said Leonie impatiently. "What I want to know is how you shoot somebody on purpose. Fire a shot, and show me how you do it."

"I can't. There's no magazine," I said with some relief.

Messing about with the safety catch was one thing, but actually firing the pistol was quite another.

"What's a magazine?"

"The thing that holds the cartridges. You see that goes in here at the bottom of the butt."

"And it's no good without that?" said Leonie, disappointed.

"Of course not. You can't fire a gun without ammunition."

"Oh hell!" said Leonie. She considered for a moment, and then said, "You say it goes in that hole at the bottom?"

"Yes."

"There was a thing in the drawer that looked as though it might go in there. But I thought it was something else. Do you think that might have been the magazine?"

"It might. People do take them out sometimes, when they want to be sure that the gun's quite safe."

"Good," said Leonie. "I'll get it to-morrow, and we'll try."

I hesitated and then said, "Look, Leonie—I don't think you ought to mess about with this thing. Automatics are nasty brutes, and if you're not careful, you might *really* shoot somebody."

"Yes," said Leonie. "Masters." She said it quietly and simply, but there was something about her tone that made me uneasy.

I said feebly, "You know we agreed to use an elephant gun for him."

"This will be better. Not so clumsy. It *will* kill him, I suppose, Walter? I mean, it's big enough?"

"That would kill anybody if you hit them in the right place."

She nodded and put the automatic back in her pocket. Then she turned to me and smiled, and held out her hand, saying, "Thank you very much, darling. That was very kind of you. I'll get the magazine to-morrow, and then you can show me more. You're sweet and very clever, and once I've killed Masters, we'll be engaged, just like you say."

I took her hand in mine. Leonie said, "And since we're practically engaged, I think you could kiss me just once. That is —if you want to."

I kissed her. I was delighted that she had stopped the silly game, and come back to more serious matters. But by unspoken consent it was not a very long or passionate kiss. Leonie, as she had warned me, "did not feel like it"; and for my own part I was suddenly feeling desperately tired after the excitement and tension of our talk.

There was something else too. Handling the automatic had made me strangely uneasy. There was something heavy, cold, grim, and purposeful about it which was out of tune with sitting on the hay with Leonie. I did not even like to think of it in the pocket of her coat. We went home rather silently, and I was reminded two or three times of its presence by its bumping gently but solidly against my thigh as we walked with linked arms.

When we were back at the house I said to Leonie, "What are you going to do with that thing? Put it back?"

"Of course not," said Leonie. "Not until I've finished with it. I tell you—we'll get the magazine to-morrow. In the meantime I shall put it up in the pickle cupboard. That has a lock. And Patrick would never go there anyhow."

She took the pistol out of her pocket and went into the kitchen, and I heard her closing and locking the door of the pickle cupboard. When she came back I said, "Leonie darling— I think you ought to put the gun back, and not mess about with it any more. I don't like your having it. Anyhow I'm awfully tired of this joke about Masters."

She looked at me in surprise and said, "What joke about Masters?"

"About shooting him."

Leonie smiled at me strangely and said gently, "But I *am* going to shoot him, Walter dear. Hadn't you realised that?"

"Don't be ridiculous," I said uneasily.

"But of course," said Leonie calmly. "I told him that if he shot Remus, I would shoot him, and he *did* shoot Remus. So…"

"But you're crazy, Leonie. You can't kill him for that."

"Why not?"

"Well… it would be murder."

"He murdered Remus."

"But that's an entirely different thing. You know it is. Remus was wonderful, but after all he was a dog; and Masters may be pretty terrible, but he's a man."

"So you think Masters is a more important person than Remus?" said Leonie dangerously.

I said bluntly, "Of course I do—in a way. Anyhow, Leonie, let's face it—we saw what Remus had been doing to those sheep. You could hardly expect Masters to go on putting up with that. After all he did warn you…"

"I see," said Leonie icily. Her eyes were very narrow, and her mouth very small. "So Remus was just a dog, and because he ran after sheep, Masters was quite right to shoot him, and in Masters's place you would have done the same thing yourself, eh?"

"I didn't say that," I said uncomfortably. "I said…"

"If you didn't say exactly that, it's what you meant. If that's how you feel, the only pity is that you didn't say so before. Still, at least now I know where I am."

She turned and almost ran out of the room. I hurried after her and called "Leonie!" as she ran up the stairs. But she did not stop or turn her head, and I heard the door shut behind her as she went into the bedroom.

Fifteen

I spent a most wretched night. Once again disaster had come in the very moment of victory. Here was Leonie prepared to agree to everything—to our being engaged and later to our being married. I had never even hoped that she would agree so easily, or with so little argument. And then, as the sole condition, she had to produce this crazy business about my helping her to kill Masters. The utter unreasonableness and unfairness of it almost moved me to tears of self-pity. I knew I would have done anything in the world to win Leonie, short of murder; and murder was the one thing she chose to ask of me.

I was also ready to kick myself for having been startled into such blunt tactlessness about Remus. The last thing in the world, as I now realised bitterly, which would cause Leonie to think calmly and sensibly was anything which sounded like a criticism of Remus.

But over and above all—even surmounting my fear that I might have lost Leonie forever—was something very like panic at the realisation that Leonie was in deadly earnest about killing Masters; and that what I had thought of as a rather silly and boring fantasy game was, in fact, the cold-blooded planning of a murder. It was no comfort to go on repeating words like "ridiculous", "absurd" and "nonsense". There was the chilling thought that people *did* sometimes murder other people—often for what seemed quite inadequate reasons. I knew from experience that Leonie was a notable hater, and that Remus had been, in some ways at least, the thing she valued most in her life. That she should kill Masters might be a crazy idea, but I realised only too well that it was not an inconceivable one. Somehow the coldness and weight of the pistol as she handed it to me, and the silent deadliness of the thing as I had looked at it in the torchlight, had about them a chilling reality, even more frightening than anything Leonie had said. I considered going downstairs and breaking open the pickle cupboard and taking it. But the pickle cupboard was a remarkably solid old piece, and I had nothing to break it open with. The only tools in the place were kept in my Uncle Patrick's shed, and that was locked too. The gun, for the moment, was out of reach.

Clearly, somebody ought to be warned about the whole business. In theory, of course, if one knew a murder was going to be committed, one went to the police. But the police in the immediate neighbourhood consisted of one fat, stupid-looking constable, and I had no idea where he lived. Besides, if I reported to the police that Leonie was proposing to shoot Colonel Masters, the result could only be that Leonie would be in serious trouble, which I desperately wanted to avoid, and her utter loss to me, which I wanted to avoid even more. I was at an age when reporting things to the proper authorities is not really a possible answer to anything.

I could, of course, tell Uncle Patrick, but again Leonie would be bound to find out that I had sneaked on her and would never forgive me, thereby making the whole of the rest of my life completely pointless. To warn Masters himself would be a treacherous desertion to the enemy. I did consider, at one moment, writing him an anonymous letter, on the general lines of "if you value your life, keep away from Poachers' Wood. Signed: A friend." But I remembered that huge figure padding silently through the wood in the darkness with his shotgun, and from what little I had seen of the Colonel I doubted if he was a man who could be easily frightened off his own property by an anonymous letter. It would merely put him on his guard, and then Leonie might easily be trapped and caught red-handed.

By about two o'clock I had still found no adequate answer to the problem, but I was completely worn out, and undressed and crawled into bed. As soon as I did so, and began to go to sleep, my panic disappeared. In the warm safety of bed a sense of the absurd improbability of the whole thing returned to me, and my last waking thought was that, in the morning, it would be obvious that Leonie had really been joking, and that she would greet me with the equivalent of cries of "April fool!"

Although I had gone to sleep so late I was downstairs before eight o'clock. Leonie was pottering about in the kitchen preparing breakfast. She did not greet me with a cry of "April fool!" but when I kissed her good morning she looked at me with a half-shy, half-wistful smile, which seemed to me to have a trace of guilt in it. I was immensely relieved, for I knew that as long as Leonie was looking small and wistful I could arrange anything. It was only when her eyes were narrowed and her mouth was small that I found it difficult to dominate her.

I said at once, "Leonie darling—what we talked about last night… you know it's nonsense."

"You mean about our getting married?" said Leonie innocently, with a quick sideways glance at me.

"No—about Masters."

Leonie filled the kettle and put it on the gas in silence. Then she said sulkily, "Why is it nonsense?"

"You don't want to be hanged or go to gaol for life, do you?"

"But if we did the alibi thing, like you said, nobody would ever know that we were anything to do with it," she said. But she said it rather in the manner of a child who has been told that it cannot play in the garden because it is pouring with rain—resigned, but unable to resist one more argument.

I said, "Don't be silly. They'd find the bullet, and they'd know what sort of gun it came from. Uncle Patrick would remember that he had a gun like that somewhere, and then where would you be?"

Leonie gave a sulky little shrug of the shoulders but said nothing. "Besides," I said, "the alibi won't work unless I was in on the whole thing. And I just shouldn't let you do it."

Leonie turned and looked at me. "You mean you wouldn't help me, Walter?" she said dispiritedly. She looked so hurt and disappointed that I was deeply touched. I had to swallow hard before I said firmly, "No darling, I *won't* help you. I will in absolutely anything else, but not in this."

She turned away slowly in silence. I added desperately, "After all, even if you didn't get caught, think what it would do to *us*. Fancy having to live our whole lives together knowing that… that *that* had happened. We should be like the people in 'Crime and Punishment'."[1]

Leonie said sombrely, "I don't know what happened to them. But I can see that it might be a bit nerve-racking.' She took the knives and forks out of the drawer, and then sighed and said, "All right."

"You mean you won't do it?"

"I suppose not. I suppose you're right, and it just isn't worth it."

I felt a sudden wave of lightness and relief. I kissed the top of her head and said, "Of course it isn't, my silly darling."

"You're very sensible sometimes, Walter."

"That's what I'm here for," I said gently. "To look after you, and see that you don't get into trouble or hurt yourself." I said it quietly and in a matter of fact way, but internally I was immensely pleased and excited by the turn things had taken. It was a great relief that Leonie had agreed not to kill Masters. But it was also a source of great pride to me that she had accepted my advice meekly, submissively, and admiringly, as coming from someone more clever, more sensible, and more knowledgeable than she.

I said firmly, "And of course we'll stick to the arrangements that we made about being engaged and married." It was not a question but a statement.

Leonie said, "Of course", and gave my hand a quick pat and went and poured some milk into a jug. My eye fell on the pickle cupboard, and I said authoritatively, "You'd better put that gun back to-day."

Leonie nodded in silence. Then she suddenly looked up at me and said, "Anyhow, I don't really particularly want him to be dead."

"Masters?"

"Yes. After all, what good would it do me?"

"None at all," I said heartily.

"It wouldn't bring Remus back to life, would it?"

"Of course not."

"So why should I care whether Masters is dead or alive? In fact, I think perhaps I would like him to be alive, and have earache all the time, or rheumatism, or something like that."

I was a trifle shocked by the wistful, almost longing way in which she said it. But I reminded myself that Leonie was always a good hater, and that Christian charity towards one's enemies did not enter into her scheme of things. Anyhow it did not matter if she hated Masters, now that I knew that she would not murder him and thereby cause a lot of trouble.

I said humorously, "What you mean is that you would like him to have rheumatism and St. Vitus' Dance[2] at the same time."

"Yes. That would do beautifully," said Leonie, staring down at the frying-pan with a little smile, as though she could see the Colonel's agonised jerkings.

She was silent for a few moments and then said, "But there's something else I'd like even better. You see… earache and rheumatism and things like that wouldn't be anything to do with *me*."

"I'm not quite sure what you mean."

"Well, I'd like something to happen to him, but I'd like it to be something that *I* had done—and that he knew I had done." She was still staring thoughtfully at the frying-pan, with the same strange, wistful little smile. She said slowly and almost dreamily, "I thought about it all last night after I went upstairs. I knew that you were right about killing him, and that I didn't even want to very much. But I wanted to do something to him to pay him out. Not only for killing Remus, but for being a brute, and a bully… and… such a big… *cad*." She paused, and with a sudden vicious jab, impaled a piece of bacon on a fork. She said, "You don't know about all of it, Walter. But he *is* a brute and a bully and a cad. Really he is."

I thought of the cocktail party, and of the deliberate rudeness, and the half-sneering smile with which he had looked at her, and the business of pushing the drink into her hand when she said she didn't want it; and, indeed, of every time that I had ever seen them together. I said, "I can well believe it."

"Yes," said Leonie, in the same dreamy way. "I'd like to pay him back for that. I'd like to *frighten* him—to make him go down on his knees to me, and beg me not to… to do something to him. He wouldn't look so big then, would he, down on his knees? I'd like to make him beg my pardon for killing Remus, and for… a lot of other things. And then when I'd made him grovel enough, I'd like to slap him across the face, and go away and leave him." She gave a sort of shuddering little sigh and added gently, "I think I should like that better than—almost anything in the world."

There was something about the quiet way in which she said it, and that shuddering sigh of longing, that was both frightening and embarrassing. I said gruffly, "Well, never mind about him, darling. You're burning the bacon."

This happened on Monday. The following day I was to go home. There were but two possible trains—the one at half past seven in the morning which had been the foundation of my alibi for Leonie, and another at about midday. It had been agreed that I should go on the midday train, which, though even slower than the morning one, would give time for a last orgy of coffee and buns in Canterbury.

The remainder of Monday was an anticlimax. Leonie was preoccupied with collecting my clothes and ironing those which needed ironing. Of the few hours that remained before the heartbreak of our parting she spent at least three ironing, sewing on a casual button and taking spots off my suit with petrol.

I had had far too little sleep and too much excitement in the last twenty-four hours. My head ached dully, and once my relief and satisfaction at the solution of the Masters problem had worn off, I was depressed almost to tears. I went for a walk, and tried to recapture the pleasure that I felt in some of the well-known places—the barn, where Leonie had agreed to be my wife; the hill we had hopped down hand in hand; the graveyard where we had been startled by Hawes, and so on. But all any of it served to do was to remind me of the agonising fact that the following day I should be going, and that I should not see Leonie for over three months.

Indeed, there was not even any certainty that I should see her then. It was unlikely that my parents would agree to my coming to Glebe Cottage again in the mere three weeks of the Christmas holidays. If they did not, it would be Easter—*Easter*—before I saw Leonie again.

I looked at the trees and reflected, sadly if not very originally, that the leaves would have to yellow and fall, and the trees stand bare through the winter, and then bud again and be in leaf, before the sight of Leonie could quicken my life again also. It struck me that this reflection might well form the basis of one of my autumn poems, and I began to try to think of a suitable opening. But my head was still aching, so I went into the little Saxon church instead, and thanked God for all he had done for me during my visit. These things included meeting Leonie, and I was genuinely and profoundly thankful for them. But it is difficult to be fervently thankful for anything when you have a headache and are miserably depressed.

My headache went away in the afternoon, but the day remained dull, heavy and depressing. Leonie's spirits seemed to have been affected by mine, for she was silent and abstracted, as though she, too, felt the cloud of my departure hanging over us. The only person who seemed in good spirits was Uncle Patrick, who made a number of jokes about the pleasures of returning to school, and gave me a message to my father which I barely heard, and certainly never delivered. I remember glancing at my watch at about six o'clock and wishing profoundly that it had been the same time the next day, when I should have been at home, with the parting over and the cold future to face as best I could.

I had hoped at least for a couple of hours alone with Leonie before going to bed that night, but even that was denied me. As it was my last evening, Uncle Patrick insisted on sitting up with us after supper and playing me various things which he knew I liked. To cap all, at about ten o'clock Leonie put away her knitting and announced that she was going to bed, and so even our last good night kiss had to be a formal affair which took place in front of my uncle.

I do not know what we talked about after Leonie had gone, or how long we stayed up. I do not think it can have been long, but all I can remember clearly was that when at last, to my profound relief, we rose to go to bed, my uncle took out his wallet and saying, "By the way—just in case I forget in the morning… a little more profit for the tuck shop," held out a pound note[3] to me with his crooked smile. I took it and mumbled some words of thanks. He meant it very kindly, and it was money that he certainly could not afford. But just at that moment, and in all the circumstances, to be given a pound note by my Uncle Patrick set the crown on a heart-breaking day.

I awoke at just after six the following morning, with that finality which meant that there was no chance of going to sleep again. Leonie had packed my bag on the previous evening, and it stood there now, only needing to be closed and fastened, a grim reminder of what was before me. I lay in bed for a few minutes, and thought at one point that I heard Leonie moving about downstairs. She always woke early, and it was her habit to get up and do most of her housework before breakfast.

We had arranged to leave about ten, so as to give Leonie time to shop in Canterbury, and then to have coffee with me before taking me to the train. But I knew the things that I wanted to say to her could not be said in twenty minutes in a crowded bun shop, with the ever-present menace of Mrs. Simms and Veronica. I decided to get up and to go downstairs, hoping for a last hour or so alone with her.

I put on my carefully de-spotted suit, which still smelt faintly of petrol. I had worn it very little at Glebe Cottage, and had forgotten how abominably short the legs of the trousers and the sleeves of the jacket now were. I reflected dully that I must ask Leonie if she knew where my cap was.

I looked out of the window as I was dressing. It had rained the night before, and now mist was rising steamily from the warm ground, so that every hollow was full of it, and the barns on a slight rise in the distance seemed to float on it as though on an opalescent sea. It was very beautiful, and I stood and looked at it for some moments. But then I reminded myself that I was too heartbroken to enjoy it, and went downstairs.

I went out into the kitchen, and to my surprise Leonie was not there, and the dirty plates and dishes from the previous evening, which were the things she always did first, were still untouched. I decided that I could not have heard her after all, but I knew that she would certainly be down within a quarter of an hour, and I was just turning to go back to the living-room to wait for her, when I saw that the key was in the lock of the pickle cupboard. It had certainly not been there the night before. I opened the cupboard quickly. It contained a number of jars of pickles, but what I was looking for was not there.

I think I knew in that moment what had happened, but for some reason my mind would not at first accept it. I told myself that Leonie must have taken the automatic to put it back wherever she had found it amongst Uncle Patrick's things—that she was almost certainly still in bed.

This at least was something which could be checked. I went upstairs and, tip-toeing across to the door of the bedroom that she shared with Uncle Patrick, very quietly opened it a crack so that I could see into the room. The room had twin beds. In one my uncle was asleep. He was snoring very slightly. The clothes of the other bed were thrown back and it was empty. I went downstairs in four jumps. The front door was unlocked. I set off at top speed in the direction of Poachers' Wood.

As I hurried through the thin mist, sometimes running and sometimes walking, I saw all too clearly what had happened. Finding me unwilling to help her, Leonie had simply decided to drop me as an accomplice, but she had never dropped her crazy plan. I understood now the reason for her sudden apparent change of front—for the meek and submissive agreement with my views which had surprised and delighted me at the time. I remembered too the quiet, almost dreamy hatred with which she had spoken of Masters, and broke again into a run.

It had not seemed very far to Poachers' Wood when I had walked there hand in hand with Leonie in the dark, but it seemed much farther now. Long before I reached the gate with the barbed wire over which one entered the wood I was panting. My feet and the legs of my trousers were soaked by the heavy dew. In places the mist was so thick that I could only see a few feet in front of me; and then again I would come out from a bank of it, and there would be the wood, visible in the distance, but still tantalisingly far away. I glanced at my watch. It was six-twenty. I told myself that it was certainly too early for Masters to be on his walk—that it was perfectly possible that he did not come through Poachers' Wood anyhow—that Leonie might have gone out for some completely different reason, and that I might be on a wild-goose chase. But none of these things really comforted me, and as I climbed the wired gate, I was straining my ears for the distant crack of a shot which might mean that I was too late.

The mist was dense amongst the chestnut poles, and water was dripping from the leaves in a steady patter. I could hardly see the track in front of me. I paused once or twice and listened. The wood was not silent now as it had been at night. It was alive, and loud with the dawn chorus of the birds and the rustle of the falling water drops on the dried leaves. But I could hear nothing else, and hurried on.

For some reason I had been sure that Leonie would be near the place where we had seen the poachers—where we had hidden and seen Masters pass; but when I reached the place there was nothing. I had been so sure about it that I searched among the trees at the side of the path, and even found what I thought was the one that we had hidden behind. But there was no sign of Leonie. Under the trees it was like being out in a heavy rainstorm, and when I came out on to the path again I was very wet. Pausing for a moment, baffled, I felt most vividly again the sense of helplessness which I had experienced when looking for Remus during one of his sheep-chasing expeditions. Here again was someone who must be near at hand, and who must be found, and found quickly, if tragedy was to be averted.

Here again one dared not call. Here again one was waiting with tingling nerves for a gunshot.

I was standing there staring round me rather helplessly, wet, and breathing heavily, when an idea came to me. The chestnuts of which the wood was mainly composed were not very high. But scattered amongst them at intervals were considerably larger and older trees, including some fine oaks. Some of them were forty or fifty feet high, and their tops stood well above the level of the low-lying ground mist. It struck me that if I could find one that was climbable, and get up into its upper branches, I should be able to see over both the chestnuts and the mist, and even perhaps to get some general view of the wood over quite a large area. That at least would be better than blundering about on the path, where I could not see more than about five yards in any direction.

I selected a large oak and pushed my way through the chestnuts to it. It was a fine old tree with a bole nearly four feet wide, which was quite unscalable without climbing irons. But some of its branches drooped nearly to the ground, and by taking a run and a jump, I managed to get my hands around one of them and haul myself up by my arms until I could lie across it. The rest, to a respectably skilful tree climber in full practice, was comparatively easy, and soon I was sitting astride a crotch of the tree, quite forty feet from the ground.

The view from the tree was not as good as I had hoped. I could only see down between the chestnuts within a comparatively small circle, and immediately below me the layer of mist still hid the path from view. But about thirty yards farther on I now saw that another path crossed mine at right angles. Where the paths crossed there was a small clearing, and here the mist was much thinner, so that I could see both paths distinctly for a short distance, before they were swallowed up again in denser blankets of mist.

One of my wrists was bleeding where I had scraped the skin off it, and the whole of the front of my suit was covered in green smears from my climb. There was still no sign of Leonie.

I decided that the climb had been a waste of desperately valuable time, and was just about to start down the tree again when a brown English setter trotted out of the mist on the cross-path and paused in the clearing where the paths met. Close behind him came his master.

Colonel Masters looked the perfect gentleman farmer. He was wearing gum-boots, into which his trousers were tucked, an old Harris tweed jacket, a dark red pullover and a silk muffler. His check cap was set at a slight angle, and he carried a riding switch,[4] with which he occasionally slashed idly at the longer grass that grew beside the path. He was walking with the same surprisingly light tread that I had noticed before, and as he walked, his big shoulders moved with a slight proud swing—almost a swagger.

For some reason it had never entered my head that I might meet Masters without first having found Leonie, and for a moment I was thrown into a complete panic as to what to do—whether to shout a warning from my position in the tree, to keep quiet, or to climb down and follow him. But after pausing for a moment in the clearing Masters turned down to his right, taking the path along which I had come, which would lead him to the gate. I knew that wherever Leonie was, she was not on that path. She must have missed him somewhere in the wood; and now, in five minutes, Masters would be over the gate and out of Poachers' Wood in safety, and the danger would be over. Then, as I was relaxing with a sigh of relief, the bushes on the far side of the clearing parted and Leonie appeared some ten or twelve yards behind Masters.

She was holding the automatic in both hands at hip level, as a man might hold a sub-machine gun, and it was pointed at Masters's back. She was wearing her old blue trousers and a man's open-necked cotton shirt. The shirt was wet through from the water which had dripped on it as she hid amongst the chestnuts, and it clung clammily to her shoulders and breasts. Her wet hair was sticking to her forehead, and there was a smear of mud on one of her cheeks.

I think she may have said something in a low voice, or perhaps Masters may have heard some movement behind him, for he whipped round sharply. I could see the startled look on his big red face as he stared at her for a moment in silence. Then he said, "What the devil are you up to, Leonie?" He spoke quite quietly, but his high, penetrating voice carried clearly to me in my tree top.

She said something, but I could not hear what it was. I could see the strained tension of her arms as she gripped the pistol. Masters said "Don't be so damned silly!" and took a step towards her. But she jerked the automatic threateningly, and spoke again in a sharp low voice, and he paused. There was a moment's silence and then Leonie started to speak rapidly and jerkily. I still could not catch, at that distance, exactly what she was saying, but I could see her narrowed eyes as she almost spat the words at him. Once I fancied that I caught the word "Remus", and I guessed that she was telling Masters that she was going to kill him, and why. Masters stood staring at her with the same half-startled, half-angry expression, running the end of the riding switch through his fingers.

Meanwhile I was sitting perched in my tree, completely helpless. I had visualised some sort of scene as this, and had resolved that the thing to do would be to throw myself dramatically between them. But you cannot throw yourself dramatically between people who are on the ground when you are forty feet up in an oak tree and thirty yards away. I was afraid to shout to Leonie for fear that I might startle her into pulling the trigger of the automatic by accident. I remember the wild hope flashing through my mind that she might have forgotten the safety catch.

Leonie had stopped speaking now, and there was a moment's dead pause. Then Masters's big red face broke into a broad smile. It was not his usual sneer, but a broad grin of what seemed to be genuine amusement. He gave a sort of chuckle and said, "You crazy little bitch!"

Leonie spoke sharply and angrily, and seemed to point with the automatic towards the ground. The Colonel chuckled again and, saying something that I did not catch, started to walk slowly towards her. Leonie brought the automatic up to cover him again, and jerked it angrily and threateningly, but this time he did not stop. He just went on walking towards her very slowly, putting one foot carefully in front of the other, and meanwhile staring at her with his head slightly thrust forward, as though he was stalking something.

I saw Leonie instinctively take a step backwards, and slowly raise the automatic until it was pointing at his chest. Masters was within five yards of her now, and I waited in helpless agony for the tearing crack of the shot. But it did not come, and he was still coming slowly and relentlessly on, and suddenly I no longer had any fear for Masters, but only for her, as the huge bulk of a man bore down on her, with the big head thrust forward and that curious, silent, stalking tread.

He came on until he was standing close in front of her, with the automatic almost touching his chest. Then he stopped, as though deliberately inviting her to fire, and said something in a low voice. He was no longer smiling now. Slowly and almost casually he put out a huge hand and closed it over her two small ones as they held the pistol and turned it away from himself. Then with a sudden quick wrench he tore it out of her hands, glanced at it for a moment and tossed it contemptuously aside into the grass. Leonie half-turned as though to run, but he grabbed her arm and half-spun her round, and slashed her twice with the riding switch with all his strength. She gave a little cry of pain, half-moan, half-sob, and straightened up with her head thrown back, clutching at her buttocks where the switch had cut her. As she did so, Masters seized the collar of the wet cotton shirt and with a single wrench, tore it down so that her shoulders and breasts were left bare.

I tried to shout, but my throat was dry, and the only sound I could make was a gasping croak. And then, as I slithered desperately out of my awkward position in the crotch of the tree, Leonie gave the same strange moaning cry, and her eyes closed and her arms came up and round Masters's thick neck. His arms went round her, and he pulled her to him so that her feet were lifted clear off the ground. Her bare breasts were crushed against his chest, and Leonie was pressing her lips passionately to his.

I watched for perhaps five seconds in a sort of paralysed daze. And then the whole meaning of it came to me, and I started to scramble recklessly down, sliding and scraping, and finally dropping the last twelve feet to the ground, so that I fell forward on my hands and knees. As my feet hit the ground I felt a sharp burning pain in my ankle, but I hardly noticed it, and jumping up, ran and struggled through the wood with my breath coming in great panting sobs, towards the gate, and away from what I had seen.

I have no clear recollection of getting back to Glebe Cottage, except that I know that once I was clear of the wood I realised that my right ankle was hurting abominably, and that I could not run. But my next clear recollection is of being back in my room, and of being horrified at the terrible mess my clothes were in. I tried desperately to brush off the green smears which covered them, but the green stuff was damp and would not move, and in the end I tore off the suit and stuffed it into my suitcase, and hurriedly put on the old flannel trousers and sports jacket that I had usually worn at Glebe Cottage. Then I shut and fastened the suitcase and hurried downstairs. There was not a moment to lose, for if I did not hurry there was the possibility—the insufferable possibility—that Leonie would come back to Glebe Cottage before I could be gone.

As I left my room I glanced at my watch. It was still only a quarter to seven and with ordinary luck Uncle Patrick would still have been in bed. But this was no day for ordinary luck, and as I went out of the front door he emerged from the wood shed. He looked at my suitcase in surprise and said, "Why hallo—off already?"

I half-pulled myself together and babbled something about having decided to get the early train after all. My uncle said "Where's Leonie?" and I gestured vaguely towards the road and said, "She's waiting."

My uncle said no more. I have often wondered what he made of my hurried departure then, or indeed later. But he was not an inquisitive man. We shook hands and I think I said, "Thank you for having me", and he said, "You must come again soon"; and then, blessedly, I was out of the gate and hobbling down the lane away from Glebe Cottage, as fast as my painful ankle would carry me.

I had had, up till then, no plan. Since I had seen Leonie with her arms round Masters's neck, and her lips pressed to his, there had been nothing but the blind desire to get away. But now I realised that, if by some stroke of luck there should be a bus for Canterbury from the end of the lane within the next ten minutes or so, I might catch the seven-thirty train. Seven-thirty had been part of the alibi.

My ankle was hurting badly, and I suddenly found that my eyes were full of tears. They had the curious effect of making the ground seem much nearer, and so I hobbled on down the lane, clutching my suitcase, and seeing the world as though I was three feet high.

I waited for five minutes at the bus stop, and again there was the dread that Leonie might come along the road, or go back to Glebe Cottage and hear that I had gone, and come to look for me. I hid behind some bushes. But then I heard a distant and characteristic honking of a horn, and knew that for once that morning my luck was in.

I caught the train with two minutes to spare. The cross-country journey took, as usual, five and a half hours and involved three changes. I have no recollection of it, save of an utter confusion and bewilderment, in which I seemed to be thinking of everything at once; and, above all, of a sense of most bitter hollowness and loss.

There was, of course, no one to meet me, and I had to take a taxi out to the house. The fact that I had arrived nearly five hours earlier than had been expected did not seem to cause any particular surprise, though my father grumbled a little at the cost of the taxi. My mother was in good spirits and seemed glad to see me, and was impatient to show and try the things that she had bought for me in London. Nobody seemed very interested in what had been happening to me at Glebe Cottage, which was a great relief, as I had been dreading a fire of questions. My father asked after Uncle Patrick, and seemed mildly, but not very, concerned when I said that he had fallen out of a tree. He remarked that things like that were always happening to Patrick.

My mother said, "How did you get on with your Aunt Leonie?"

"Quite well, up to a point," I said, with more exactitude than I had intended.

My mother said, "She can be great fun at times."

"Yes."

My father reflected and then said, "Very fond of dogs." These seemed to be my parents' standard comments on Leonie.

I said, "Her dog died while I was there."

"Really?" said my father. "She won't have liked that."

"She didn't."

I remembered Remus with his head on his paws, and Leonie

kneeling beside him with her arm around his neck, whispering into his ear. I said, "He was a very beautiful dog, too."

My father rose to go back to his study. My mother said, "Come upstairs, Walter. I want to see if any of these things need to be altered."

I stood patiently whilst my mother gave little tugs to various garments she had bought me, and occasionally put in pins where buttons needed altering. The clothes were quite all right. My mother had gone to the official school tailor, so that everything she had bought was respectable, if uninteresting. For myself, I do not think I should have noticed, or cared, if she had produced a knickerbocker suit in large red and white checks.

My mother was duly horrified at the condition of my suit, and managed to convey, without actually saying so, that it was disgraceful that Leonie should have allowed me to bring it home in that state.

"But then Aunt Leonie doesn't take much trouble about clothes, does she?" she said with a confidential smile. I agreed that she did not. "She often wears the oddest things herself," said my mother. "What did she wear while you were there?"

I swallowed and said, "She usually wore trousers."

"*Trousers?*" said my mother. "She would." She shot a quick glance at me and added, "But she can be great fun in a way.'

"Yes."

I realised that my mother had expected me to be more enthusiastic about Leonie, and that she was pleased to find that I was not. As she went through the pockets of my suit, preparatory to sending it to the cleaners, my mother came on Uncle Patrick's pound note, which I had slipped carelessly into my breastpocket and forgotten.

She said, "So you didn't use all your money?"

"No."

"Well I suppose you ought really to give it back to your father. But if I were you I should just keep it and say nothing." She handed me the note with a wink, and went out with my suit.

The note was one of the old brown ones of that period. I stared at it with hatred, for somehow, quite illogically, it seemed to be the price at which my heart had been valued, fit to be given for some Potter's Field,[5] to bury strangers in, or hurled dramatically away. But I knew of no Potter's Field for sale, and plenty of desirable things that were, and after all it was not Leonie who had given me the note, so I folded it up carefully and put it inside my prayer book for safety.

Florence, 1961

Notes

Epigraph

1. As this poem is not attributed to anyone else it would appear to have been written by Balchin himself. He is known to have written poetry at various points in his life but, to the best of my knowledge, this is the only example of a *published* Balchin poem.

One

1. *D.S.O.* Instituted in 1886, the Distinguished Service Order, or DSO, is a decoration awarded to members of the British armed forces in recognition of distinguished service during wartime.
2. *Bar.* A bar is a metal strip below the clasp of a medal awarded as an additional distinction.
3. *M.C.* Introduced in 1914, the Military Cross, or MC, is a decoration awarded to members of the British armed forces for distinguished active service on land.
4. *Lord Birkenhead.* Frederick Edwin Smith, first earl of Birkenhead (1872–1930), was an English lawyer and Conservative politician who was also a great personal and political friend of Winston Churchill. A former lord chancellor, he served as Secretary of State for India in Stanley Baldwin's administration between 1924 and 1928.
5. *George Robey.* Sir George Edward Wade (1869–1954), known professionally as George Robey, was an English music hall comedian, singer and actor who revelled in the sobriquet 'The Prime Minister of Mirth'. He was also a very successful pantomime dame in performances that toured to the English provinces.
6. *'Yes We Have No Bananas'.* This novelty song, written by Frank Silver and Irving Cohn, enjoyed great popularity in the 1920s, topping the American song charts for five weeks upon its first release in 1923.
7. *the General Strike.* This industrial action took place in the UK between 4 and 12 May 1926 and was called by the Trades Union Congress in an attempt to prevent wage reductions and improve working conditions for coal miners. About 1.7 million workers came out on strike, mainly in the transport industry and in heavy industries. The strike was unsuccessful as the government enlisted volunteers to maintain essential services.
8. *Lawrence.* David Herbert 'D. H.' Lawrence (1885–1930) was an English novelist and poet. His best-known novel, *Lady Chatterley's Lover*, was first published in 1928.

9. *W. B. Yeats.* William Butler 'WB.' Yeats (1865–1939) was an Irish poet, dramatist and prose writer who wrote some of his best poetry in the 1920s, as exemplified by collections such as *The Tower* (1928). He won the Nobel Prize for Literature in 1923 and was active in Irish politics as a member of the senate of the new Irish Free State during the time that Balchin is writing about.

10. *the later nineteen twenties.* In this paragraph, Balchin may well be thinking of some of the events and personalities that had made an impact on him in the second half of the 1920s, when he was firstly in his final years at Dauntsey's School and then an undergraduate at Cambridge.

11. *"Labor et Puritas".* This Latin motto, probably invented by Balchin, translates into English as "Work and Purity".

12. *School Certificate.* Introduced in 1918, the School Certificate was a UK educational qualification which survived until 1951, when it was replaced by the O-Level and, subsequently, by today's equivalent, the General Certificate of Secondary Education (GCSE). Walter is clearly educationally advanced because the School Certificate was usually taken at the age of sixteen.

13. *"Go, lovely rose".* This is the opening line of the poem 'Go, Lovely Rose' by the English poet and politician Edmund Waller (1606–1687).

Two

1. *Wykehamists.* Pupils of Winchester College, a public school in the city of Winchester in the south of England. The name Wykehamist commemorates the fact that the school was founded by William of Wykeham, Bishop of Winchester.

2. *Sidney's feelings about Stella.* Sir Philip Sidney (1554–1586) was an English poet whose sonnet sequence *Astrophil and Stella* was published posthumously in 1591. Some critics have suggested that Sidney identified himself with Astrophil and that the love of Astrophil for Stella described in the sonnets represents Sidney's for Lady Penelope Rich (née Devereux), a married English noblewoman and maid of honour to Queen Elizabeth the First.

3. *Alfred Austin.* Alfred Austin (1835–1913) was an English poet who, in 1896, succeeded Alfred Lord Tennyson as Poet Laureate.

4. *Lever.* Charles James Lever (1806–1872) was an Irish novelist.

5. *Teale and Widgeon.* Balchin has invented two obscure Victorian writers. Amusingly, each of the names differs by just one letter from that of a duck native to Britain.

6. *about three hundred pounds a year.* Equivalent to a purchasing power of about £18,500 today.

7. *thin cat-ice.* The expression is tautologous because cat-ice means thin ice according to the *Oxford English Dictionary*.

8. *picador.* In bullfighting, a picador is a person mounted on horseback who goads the bull with a lance.

Three

1. *between Paddington and Charing Cross.* In 1928, Walter could have taken a Great Western Railway service from the station closest to his home in Wiltshire to the GWR's London terminus, Paddington. He could then have travelled on the Bakerloo Line of the London Underground railway from Paddington to Charing Cross and changed trains for a Southern Railways service to Canterbury.
2. *thirty-two-and-sixpence.* In decimal coinage, this is equivalent to one pound sixty-two and a half pence. In terms of its modern-day value, it equates to about £100.
3. *bull-nosed Morris.* The Morris Oxford 'bullnose' was a motorcar made by William Morris of Oxford between 1913 and 1926. Its nickname was derived from its round-topped radiator, which was originally known as a 'bullet nose'.
4. *two stations.* In 1928 (as is still the case today), Canterbury had two railway stations, Canterbury West and Canterbury East, situated about half a mile apart.
5. *five pounds a week.* Equivalent to a purchasing power of about £300 a week today.
6. *Saladin riding around the Crusader in* The Talisman. Published in 1825, *The Talisman* is the second of two *Tales of the Crusaders* novels by the Scottish poet, playwright and novelist Sir Walter Scott (1771–1832) and concerns the Third Crusade of 1189–1192. The opening chapter of the novel describes the first meeting between a Scottish crusader known as Sir Kenneth and a Saracen emir later revealed to be Saladin. During this encounter, the Saracen circles the crusader on horseback several times, searching for a weak point at which to attack him. The passage in Scott's narrative that Balchin would seem to be referring to reads as follows: 'the Saracen cavalier, when he had approached towards the Christian within twice the length of his lance, wheeled his steed to the left with inimitable dexterity, and rode twice around his antagonist, who, turning without quitting his ground, and presenting his front constantly to his enemy, frustrated his attempts to attack him on an unguarded point…'
7. *rag.* A dated word meaning a prank or practical joke.

Four

1. *Remus was no transmogrified Auden and Isherwood character.* Balchin is thinking of *The Dog Beneath the Skin*, a 1935 play written by the English poet Wystan Hugh 'W. H.' Auden (1907–1973) in collaboration with the English novelist and playwright Christopher William Bradshaw Isherwood (1904–1986). It concerns a quest undertaken by Alan Norman in search of Sir Francis Crewe. Norman is accompanied on his journey through Europe by a large dog, who turns out to be Sir Francis in disguise. Balchin's 1947 play-cum-novel *Lord, I was Afraid* was said by book reviewers to have been influenced by *The Dog Beneath the Skin*.

Notes

2. *the Table of Kindred and Affinity.* Found in *The Book of Common Prayer*, the Table of Kindred and Affinity is a list showing which relations are forbidden by the Church of England to marry one another.
3. *dog collar.* An informal term for a clerical collar.
4. *stock.* A piece of black material worn underneath a clerical collar.
5. *stipend.* A clergyman's salary.
6. *Pusey/Newman/Keble.* Edward Bouverie Pusey (1800–1882) was an English theologian who, in 1833, founded the Oxford Movement (a religious movement that revived the Catholic influence in the Church of England), together with his fellow clerics John Keble (1792–1866) and John Henry Newman (1801–1890).
7. *Glebe Cottage.* Historically, a glebe was a piece of land that supplied income for a clergyman as one of the benefits of performing his clerical duties.
8. *"They flee from me that sometime did me seek,".* This is the first line of 'They Flee From Me', a poem by the English ambassador and poet Sir Thomas Wyatt (ca. 1503–1542).
9. *Coleridge.* Samuel Taylor Coleridge (1772–1834) was an English poet and theologian. He is probably best known today as the author of the poem 'The Rime of the Ancient Mariner'.
10. *T. S. Eliot.* Thomas Stearns Eliot (1888–1965) was a US-born British poet and playwright, famous for works such as 'The Waste Land', *Four Quartets* and *The Cocktail Party*.
11. *"bare ruined choirs".* The line comes from Shakespeare's Sonnet LXXIII:
    > That time of year thou may'st in me behold
    > When yellow leaves, or none, or few, do hang
    > Bare ruin'd choirs, where late the sweet birds sang.
    It is generally accepted by literary critics that Shakespeare is comparing the bare branches of trees in autumn to the abbeys that were left derelict following the dissolution of the monasteries by Henry VIII. Here, 'choirs' refers to the part of an abbey in which the service was sung, and not the people (monks) who sang it.
12. *the Forty-eight Preludes and Fugues.* A collection of the music of Johann Sebastian Bach.

Five

1. *I knew plenty about people being cut.* Used in this context, the word 'cut' means to completely ignore someone.

Six

1. *the penitent Magdalen.* Following a sermon delivered by Pope Gregory I in 591, in which he conflated Mary Magdalene, the follower of Jesus, with two sinful women mentioned in Luke's gospel, it was popularly believed from medieval times onward that Mary had formerly been a prostitute. What Balchin is saying, therefore, is that Walter was hoping that Leonie

would behave more like a woman formerly of low morals who had subsequently repented her sins.

2. *gum-boots.* A dated expression for a pair of wellington boots.
3. *witches' sabbat.* A sabbat (or sabbath) is a supposed midnight meeting of witches.

Seven

1. *a sort of Potiphar's wife business.* In the Bible (*Genesis 39*), Potiphar was an Egyptian officer who served as captain of the Pharoah's guard. His wife tried to seduce Joseph but, when he rebuffed her advances, she falsely accused him of trying to rape her, which led to his imprisonment.
2. *hairy.* Balchin could mean either that Veronica was being awkward or difficult or that she was angry or ill-tempered.
3. *"Hell hath no fury like a woman scorned,".* This is a paraphrase of a line in the play *The Mourning Bride* by the English playwright and poet William Congreve (1670–1729).
4. *Peeping Tom.* A furtive voyeur who derives sexual pleasure from watching other people undress or have sex. The expression originates from the name of the person (Thomas) who watched Lady Godiva ride naked through Coventry.
5. *Sir Galahad.* One of the knights of King Arthur's Round Table, Sir Galahad was renowned for his gallantry and purity, and for being the most perfect of all knights.

Eight

1. *Peterham.* Balchin might be thinking of Petham, a village situated about five miles south of Canterbury, although it is not known to have had a notable fair. Balchin lived in Stelling Minnis, a village about eight miles south of Canterbury, for several years after World War Two.
2. *"And to conclude, I know myself a man, Which is a proud and yet a wretched thing,".* These are the final lines of 'Of Human Knowledge', a poem by the English lawyer and poet Sir John Davies (1569–1626).
3. *Coney Island.* Part of the borough of Brooklyn, Coney Island is an entertainment area situated on the south shore of Long Island in New York. In the late 1920s, the period during which *Seen Dimly Before Dawn* is set, Coney Island was the largest amusement park in the USA.
4. *a spiral slide.* A helter-skelter.
5. *I felt as Melas must have felt after Marengo.* The Battle of Marengo was fought on 14 June 1800 between the French and the Austrians in Piedmont, Italy. Following a surprise attack by the Austrians, under the command of General Michael Friedrich von Melas, the French forces, commanded by Napoleon Bonaparte, routed the Austrians and drove them out of Italy.

Notes

Ten

1. *Higher Certificate.* Balchin means the Higher School Certificate, a UK educational qualification which was usually taken at the age of eighteen and which was replaced, in 1951, by today's A-Level.
2. *trundle.* A cricketing term meaning to bowl at gentle medium pace. Hawes is being modest because he has previously stated that he bowls "Left arm quickies" and Walter discovers that his bowling is "quite fast" during the net session that follows.
3. *deal kitchen table.* A table made from planks of fir or pine wood.
4. *prie-Dieu.* A piece of furniture used for the act of praying. It consists of a kneeler and a narrow upright front section topped with a ledge on which one can place books, one's elbows or, in this case, a crucifix.
5. *Ranjitsinjhi.* Regarded as one of the finest batsmen of all time, Ranjitsinhji Vibhaji, Kumar Shri, Maharaja Jam Sahib of Nawanagar (1872–1933), better known as Ranji or Ranjitsinhji (note that Balchin has the spelling slightly wrong), was an Indian prince who played fifteen Test matches for England between 1896 and 1902.
6. *Victor Trumper.* Another of cricket's all-time greats, the Australian batsman Victor Thomas Trumper (1877–1915) played forty-eight Test matches between 1899 and 1912.
7. *piejaw.* Pi-jaw (Balchin has the spelling wrong) is a moralizing speech or lecture, especially that delivered by an adult to a child.

Eleven

1. *"Had we but world enough and time".* This is the opening line of the poem 'To His Coy Mistress' by the English politician and poet Andrew Marvell (1621–1678).
2. *Time's wingèd chariot.* This expression also originates from Marvell's poem 'To His Coy Mistress', the line in question being "But at my back I always hear, Time's wingèd chariot hurrying near."
3. *rugger.* An informal term for rugby football. If one assumes that Walter's public school is in the south of England, which seems a fair assumption to make given that his home is in Wiltshire, then he would almost certainly have played rugby union, not league.

Twelve

1. *De mortuis nil nisi bonum.* A literal translation of this Latin phrase would be something like 'Of the dead, [say] nothing but good' although, in common parlance, one would instead say 'Do not speak ill of the dead.'
2. *strum.* An odd choice of word because one strums a guitar or other stringed musical instrument, but not a piano.

Thirteen

1. *when Sir Walter Tyrrel shot William Rufus.* King William the Second of England (ca. 1060–1100) was also known by the name William Rufus. On 2 August 1100 he went hunting in the New Forest in southern England with his friend Walter Tirel. The hunting party spread out in the forest. In the legend that Balchin is alluding to, Tirel shot wildly at a passing stag and his arrow pierced the chest of Rufus, killing him. However, the exact cause of the king's death has never been definitively proven.

2. *charcoal burner's wain.* Charcoal burning is an ancient occupation consisting of the burning of wood in a kiln for a week or more to remove water and other volatile constituents. The charcoal thus produced is then burnt to achieve the high temperatures necessary for processes such as glassmaking and iron smelting. Naturally enough, charcoal burning tended to take place in large forests, such as the New Forest. In some versions of the story of the death of William Rufus described in the previous note, the body of the dead king is said to have been discovered by a charcoal burner, who transported it to the city of Winchester (the seat of the government at the time) on his wain, which was a wagon or cart.

Fifteen

1. *like the people in 'Crime and Punishment'.* Crime and Punishment is a novel of 1866 by the Russian writer Fyodor Dostoevsky (1821–1881) in which a penurious man hatches a plot to kill an unscrupulous pawnbroker for her money. After committing the crime, he is racked with guilt and disgust.

2. *St. Vitus' Dance* or, more properly, St Vitus's dance is an archaic name for Sydenham's chorea, a neurological condition that mainly affects children and adolescents and is characterized by involuntary, jerky movements, especially of the face, shoulders and hips.

3. *a pound note.* Equivalent in value to about £60 today.

4. *riding switch.* A slender, tapering whip used by horse riders.

5. *some Potter's Field.* Historically, a potter's field is a burial place for paupers and strangers.

Nigel Balchin: A Condensed Biography

Nigel Balchin

Titles of novels printed in bold font identify those scheduled for republication as part of the Nigel Balchin Collection.

Nigel Balchin was, inter alia, a playwright, an author of non-fiction books, a Hollywood scriptwriter, a television dramatist, an advertising and marketing expert, an industrial psychologist and an authority on Oriental rugs and carpets. More pertinently in the current context, he was also one of the foremost popular novelists of the middle decades of the twentieth century. Balchin's fiction has long been revered by his peers: during his lifetime, his novels were praised by eminent fellow writers such as Anthony Burgess, John Betjeman, L. P. Hartley and Elizabeth Bowen; since his death, Balchin's admirers have included Clive James, Philippa Gregory, Julian Fellowes and Ruth Rendell.

For the purposes of this biographical sketch, I wish to focus primarily on the fourteen novels that Balchin wrote, and to show how the material for those novels was partly extracted from his own life experiences.

Balchin was born in Potterne, Wiltshire in 1908. His father was a small shopkeeper and his mother was the daughter of a railway guard. On his father's side of the family, Balchin was descended from a line of well-to-do gentleman farmers who tilled the soil in the Godalming area of Surrey but, by the time of Balchin's birth, the money had largely gone and his father was forced to work long hours in order to support his wife and children. Balchin's third novel, *Lightbody on Liberty* (1936), is concerned with the fortunes of a small shopkeeper and aspects of the story were influenced by the experiences of William Balchin, Nigel's father.

Towards the end of the First World War, Balchin's parents moved from Potterne to another part of Wiltshire so that their youngest son could begin his secondary schooling at the Dauntsey Agricultural School, a minor public school in the village of West Lavington. In his teenage years, Balchin enjoyed a conventionally happy rural childhood on the edge of Salisbury Plain. When not occupied by his schooling, he played a full part in the social life of his village by indulging in amateur dramatics, singing in church concerts, attending village fetes and playing sport (as a schoolboy, he was adept at rugby, soccer, hockey, fives and cricket). He also undertook many long walks on the sparsely inhabited expanses of the Wiltshire Downs. This love of the countryside that he had found on his doorstep as a child informed Balchin's second novel, 1935's **Simple Life**.

In 1927, aided by a scholarship, Balchin took up an offer to read Natural Sciences at Cambridge. His college was Peterhouse and one of his fellow Petreans was the future film star James Mason, who remained a close friend for the rest of Balchin's life.

By the end of Balchin's second year at Peterhouse his interest in Natural Sciences was wearing thin. This was predominantly because the Ministry of Agriculture, who were funding Balchin's education, wanted him to specialize in the study of agriculture, with a view to obtaining a job as an agriculturist once he had graduated. Having no intention of following such a career, Balchin challenged the Ministry's diktat, got his own way and was able to study psychology instead of agriculture in his final term at university. This was a momentous decision, and one that would direct the course of Balchin's working life for at least the next fifteen years.

With the assistance of a charismatic psychology professor called Frederic Bartlett, Balchin secured a position with the National Institute of Industrial Psychology when he left Cambridge in 1930. The NIIP was a pioneering organization that attempted to use psychological techniques to solve practical problems encountered in British industry. As an industrial investigator, Balchin's job consisted of visiting factories and other places of work, where he sought to improve working conditions for the staff, primarily by making them more comfortable and removing handicaps that hindered them in their work. This portion of Balchin's life strongly influenced his debut novel *No Sky*, which was published in 1934 and described the work and home lives of a time-and-motion man in an engineering factory.

The highpoint of Balchin's five-year stay with the NIIP came when he was intimately involved in a large market research project that culminated in the launch of Black Magic chocolates in January 1933. But as Balchin's star rose, he became an asset that the NIIP could no longer afford to hold onto. Early in 1935, Balchin left the NIIP to join Rowntree's, the manufacturers of Black Magic. He remained with them until the outbreak of

World War Two, specializing in the consumer testing of different brands of confectionery.

Balchin's work for the NIIP enabled him to launch a parallel career as a writer. During the 1930s, he wrote a large number of articles for scientific journals and also for magazines such as *Punch*. Two collections of Balchin's *Punch* articles were spun off from the magazine and published in the form of his first two non-fiction books. These volumes—*How to Run a Bassoon Factory* (1934) and *Business for Pleasure* (1935)—saw Balchin in playful mood, satirizing the work he had accomplished for the NIIP.

Balchin married Elisabeth Walshe, a graduate of Newnham College, Cambridge, in 1934. They had met during Balchin's final year at university. Over the course of the following ten years the marriage produced three daughters, one of whom grew up to become the renowned child psychologist Penelope Leach.

Balchin began World War Two as a linkman between Rowntree's and the Ministry of Food before, in 1940, he transferred to the Ministry itself, where he took charge of the allocation of raw materials such as sugar and cocoa to food manufacturers. Balchin's horror at both the suffocating bureaucracy that impeded efficiency at the Ministry and the venal self-interest of some of the businessmen he had to deal with found the perfect outlet with the publication, in 1942, of *Darkness Falls from the Air*. Artistically speaking, this was Balchin's first really successful novel, and it would have sold much better had the prospect of substantial sales not been scuppered by the paper shortages extant at the time.

In the summer of 1941, Balchin left the Ministry of Food and enrolled in the army. He experienced a meteoric rise through the ranks of the military: appointed a captain in August 1941, he had risen as far as brigadier by May 1945. As well as advising on the practicality of new pieces of weaponry, Balchin also overhauled the army's personnel selection procedure, at the same time introducing the service to the concept of rudimentary computerization in the form of Hollerith punched cards, which he had first used in connection with the Black Magic market research project.

Balchin's military career provided him with many of his best ideas for *The Small Back Room*, his 1943 smash-hit novel. Later successfully filmed by Powell and Pressburger, *The Small Back Room* was the story of a research scientist grappling with power struggles at work by day and his own personal problems— alcoholism and a fragile relationship with his girlfriend—by night. It made Balchin's name as a novelist.

Buoyed by the success of *The Small Back Room*, Balchin chose to become a full-time writer upon his release from military duties at the end of 1945. Published just a few months before his demobilization, ***Mine Own Executioner***, Balchin's first post-war novel, was about a psycho-therapist who tries to help a Spitfire pilot who has made several attempts to murder his wife in the wake of brutal treatment at the hands of the Japanese. Its realism enhanced by information Balchin had gleaned from psychiatrists he had worked with during the war, ***Mine Own Executioner*** sold in vast quantities and was lavishly praised by the critics. It was also made into a respectable film, for which Balchin himself wrote the screenplay.

Accused by book reviewers of adhering to a formula when writing novels—the juxtaposition of work and domestic problems in the lives of middle-class professional men, set against the backdrop of the Second World War—Balchin decisively broke away from that formula as the end of the 1940s approached. First, in 1947, came *Lord, I Was Afraid*, a series of fantastical (and often satirical) dramatic scenarios presented in the form of a play. Despite being admired by Anthony Burgess and J. G. Ballard, the book sank without trace. It was followed a year later by *The Borgia Testament*, an account of the life of the Renaissance tyrant Cesare Borgia written from his perspective and in a very modern idiom. It is the only Balchin novel not to have been based at least to some extent on events from the writer's own life.

To the relief of his regular readers, Balchin then retreated to more familiar territory in 1949 with *A Sort of Traitors*, a novel about two scientists tempted to commit treason in order to get some important research about the suppression of epidemics into the public domain. Predictably, Balchin's sales figures rebounded after the dips suffered by his two previous pieces of fiction.

Balchin's marriage to Elisabeth Walshe, despite surviving for almost twenty years, was never an especially stable one. At the beginning of World War Two it was damaged when Elisabeth had a brief fling with Christian Darnton, a composer of avant-garde classical music. Balchin's reaction was to savagely lampoon Darnton via the medium of Stephen, a self-pitying poet, in *Darkness Falls from the Air*. Then, in the late 1940s, Elisabeth began an affair with the painter and sculptor Michael Ayrton. Balchin permitted the liaison to drag on for several years, hoping that Elisabeth would eventually see sense and return to him, before bowing to the inevitable at the end of 1950, when he initiated divorce proceedings. Once more, Balchin used the creation of fiction as a pressure valve to release the frustration that had built up inside him as a result of Elisabeth's unfaithfulness. In *A Way Through the Wood*, published in 1951, he poked fun at Ayrton in the form of Bill Bule, an irresponsible aristocrat who steals the wife of the book's Balchin-like narrator. Raw and searingly honest, *A Way Through the Wood* is Balchin's most heartfelt novel.

In 1949, Balchin embarked on a new relationship with Yovanka Tomich, a Yugoslav émigré twenty-two years his junior who was initially employed to type his manuscripts. Energized by this upturn in the fortunes of his romantic affairs, Balchin's writing acquired a new vigour and this led to the creation of two of his finest novels. 1953's *Sundry Creditors* anatomized the workings of a Midlands engineering company with skill and precision and, like *No Sky* before it, was informed by the author's previous career as an industrial psychologist. But it also achieved contemporary relevance because it contained portraits—some affectionate, others much less so—of members of the Rowntree's top brass whom Balchin had dealt with over the previous few years, when he had served as a consultant on advertising and marketing matters.

The Fall of the Sparrow (1955) was completely different to its predecessor and saw Balchin once more boldly striding out into new territory. The book consisted of the life story, over a span of about thirty years, of Jason Pellew, a likeable but aimless drifter who suffers all manner of mishaps as a result of psychological flaws. To write this haunting and very believable novel, Balchin called upon his memories of Dauntsey's, Cambridge and his wartime research work for the army. During this very fertile period for Balchin's fiction, he also released a short-story compendium entitled *Last Recollections of My Uncle Charles* (1954).

During the second half of the 1950s, Balchin's working life was dominated by film scriptwriting. He won the 1957 BAFTA award for Best British Screenplay for the wartime espionage movie *The Man Who Never Was*, which led to a lucrative offer from Hollywood. Balchin toiled away in Tinseltown for three years in the employ of Twentieth Century Fox but he found the work uncreative and soul-destroying, and pined for Yovanka and the couple's young son Charles. The films he scripted in Hollywood were largely forgettable. The best-known movie he worked on was the infamous Richard Burton–Elizabeth Taylor remake of *Cleopatra* but his script had been mothballed long before filming began.

When his Fox contract expired in 1959, Balchin returned to Europe but, for tax reasons, he chose to live outside the country of his birth. After a brief spell in Paris, he settled in Italy. Here, he continued to write film scripts, but with no more success than previously. For a writer who relied primarily on his ability to convert events from his own life into sellable fiction, the film industry does not seem to have provided him with much inspiration: only the opening chapter of *In the Absence of Mrs Petersen* (1966) is concerned with the mechanics of movie making. But that novel focused more on Balchin's volatile on–off relationship with Yovanka (he had married his former secretary in 1953) and one of its main plot threads was inspired by stories about her Yugoslav relatives that she had told him.

Balchin returned to England in 1962, and settled there permanently. Written during his time in Italy, *Seen Dimly Before Dawn* was published the same year. Like *The Fall of the Sparrow*, the new novel saw Balchin once more in nostalgic mood, as he summoned memories of his childhood to write an addictively readable story about a precocious fifteen-year-old schoolboy who falls in love, over the course of a summer holiday, with his uncle's tantalizing mistress. Balchin located the action in the Kent countryside, a part of the world he knew well as he had lived near Canterbury for several years immediately after the Second World War.

As the 1960s wore on, Balchin became increasingly troubled by alcoholism although, in truth, he had been a heavy drinker ever since his first marriage had begun to fall apart. His drinking badly affected the quality of his writing in the last few years of his life.

After *In the Absence of Mrs Petersen*, an above-par thriller, albeit one that failed to emulate past glories, there was to be just one more Balchin novel. *Kings of Infinite Space*, a science-fiction story about a deep-space mission, was published in the autumn of 1967, when interest in the space race was approaching its zenith. Balchin had spent the summer of 1966 in America, meeting astronauts and visiting NASA locations. Although *Kings of Infinite Space* is true to life, and possesses some historical interest for those of an astronautical bent, it must be rated a failure at the ordinary narrative level and it supplied a disappointing full stop to Balchin's intermittently illustrious career as a novelist.

The final few years of Balchin's life saw a series of moves to successively smaller residential premises as he and Yovanka downsized in an attempt to preserve what little money was still dribbling into the novelist's coffers. Ideas for good novels continued to elude Balchin and the BBC rejected a number of projects he pitched to them. With a hint of desperation, he accepted a lucrative offer from the US-based Famous Writers School to work on a British version of a correspondence course in creative writing. He fell ill on returning from a meeting with the FWS in America and died three days later, on 17 May 1970. He was sixty-one. Balchin left behind a widow and five children from his two marriages. He was laid to rest in Hampstead Cemetery in north-west London. Glowing obituaries appeared in newspapers on both sides of the Atlantic.

Derek Collett

August 2021

Nigel Balchin Bibliography

Novels

No Sky (Hamish Hamilton, 1934)
Simple Life (Hamish Hamilton, 1935)
Lightbody on Liberty (Collins, 1936)
Darkness Falls from the Air (Collins, 1942)
The Small Back Room (Collins, 1943)
Mine Own Executioner (Collins, 1945)
The Borgia Testament (Collins, 1948)
A Sort of Traitors (Collins, 1949)
A Way Through the Wood (Collins, 1951)
Sundry Creditors (Collins, 1953)
The Fall of the Sparrow (Collins, 1955)
Seen Dimly Before Dawn (Collins, 1962)
In the Absence of Mrs Petersen (Collins, 1966)
Kings of Infinite Space (Collins, 1967)

Non-fiction books

How to Run a Bassoon Factory; or Business Explained (as Mark Spade; Hamish Hamilton, 1934)
Business for Pleasure (as Mark Spade; Hamish Hamilton, 1935)
Fun and Games: How to Win at Almost Anything (as Mark Spade; Hamish Hamilton, 1936)
Income and Outcome. A Study of Personal Finance (Hamish Hamilton, 1936)
The Anatomy of Villainy (Collins, 1950)
How to Run a Bassoon Factory; or Business Explained and *Business for Pleasure* (as Mark Spade, combined volume with an introduction by Balchin; Hamish Hamilton, 1950)

Other books

Lord, I Was Afraid (play; Collins, 1947)
Last Recollections of My Uncle Charles (short stories; Collins, 1954)

About the Nigel Balchin Collection

The novels reissued as the Nigel Balchin Collection have been specially chosen to comprise a comprehensive and representative sample of the finest and most interesting novels written by Balchin. At least one novel has been selected from each of the four decades during which he was active as a novelist. When complete, the Nigel Balchin Collection will constitute the widest selection of Balchin's fiction to be simultaneously in print since the 1960s.

Every novel has been freshly typeset and then carefully proofread against the first hardback edition to ensure fidelity to Balchin's original text. Each edition also includes a biographical essay about Balchin, an introduction to the novel in question and helpful explanatory notes compiled by Balchin's biographer, Derek Collett.

For the very latest information about the Nigel Balchin Collection, including likely publication dates, visit the Nigel Balchin Website: www.nigelmarlinbalchin.co.uk

Enjoyed reading this novel? Like to know more about the man who wrote it? Then why not consider purchasing *His Own Executioner: The Life of Nigel Balchin*? The only biography of the author of *Seen Dimly Before Dawn*, this book tells the story of Balchin's life in a clear, engaging and authoritative fashion. Visit the Nigel Balchin Website at www.nigelmarlinbalchin.co.uk for details of how to buy this acclaimed biography.

Praise for *His Own Executioner: The Life of Nigel Balchin*:

'First-rate biography' – *The Literary Review*

'Collett paints a convincing picture' – D. J. Taylor, *The Times Literary Supplement*

'A riveting and revealing biography' – Cathi Unsworth, author of *That Old Black Magic*

Coming Soon in the Nigel Balchin Collection

Simple Life: An intriguing novel about a young advertising executive who leaves the London rat race behind in search of a simpler, more physical existence in the country, and gets far more than he bargained for. Very funny in places, *Simple Life* is also a superb evocation of the Wiltshire countryside of Balchin's boyhood.

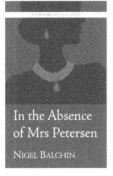

In the Absence of Mrs Petersen: Thrills and spills on the Continent, as Jim Petersen tries to smuggle jewellery out of Yugoslavia in company with the captivating Katherina, a virtual facsimile of his recently deceased wife. As well as being an exciting thriller, *In the Absence of Mrs Petersen* is also a wry dispatch from the trenches about the everlasting battle of the sexes.

Lightning Source UK Ltd.
Milton Keynes UK
UKHW042306061221
395183UK00002B/25